A
SPY
IN
SAIGON

A SPY IN SAIGON

A Kat Lawson Mystery

Nancy Cole Silverman

To Bruce, with all my love.

"Do not dwell in the past; do not dream of the future, concentrate the mind on the present moment."

— BUDDHA

Praise for A Spy in Saigon

"*A Spy in Saigon* is the perfect blend of high-stakes international suspense and yearning for what might have been. Deviously plotted and deliciously scribed, Silverman delivers a pulse-pounding thriller that reminds us, be careful of what you ask—you might not get the answer you expect. Kat Lawson's search for long-unanswered questions put her in the crosshairs."—James L'Etoile, award-winning author of River of Lies and the Detective Nathan Parker series

"*A Spy in Saigon* is a superbly crafted blend of espionage, history, and scars left over from the war in Vietnam. Set in 2000 in Vietnam, Silverman weaves a web of characters and hidden motivations that create a captivating narrative of mystery and suspense, while exposing unanswered questions about one of America's most tumultuous eras."—Adam Sikes, U.S. Marine Corps Veteran, CIA paramilitary officer, and author of *Landslide.*

I

Part One

Chapter One

Ho Chi Minh City

August 2000

The only connection I had to Vietnam was the gold four-seasons bracelet my husband had given me. During the war, all of Eric's pilot buddies brought home jewelry for their wives—sapphire earrings, ruby rings, and pearl necklaces. It was December 1972. I was toasting champagne at a holiday party with a group of Air Force wives, the gold bracelet on my slender wrist, as we cheered for what we hoped would be their homecoming. But what did we know? We were young, in love, and eager to move on with our lives. The bracelet was the last gift Eric would ever give me. It arrived Christmas week. One week before he was shot down. Six months before my college graduation.

My name is Kat Lawson. I'm a travel reporter, or at least that's what my resume says. In truth, I'm a spy. I work undercover for the FBI while on assignment with *Journey International,* a popular travel publication. My job is that of a legitimate reporter, and my assignments, for the most part, are routine, except when they're not, and things don't go as planned. I'm not an agent. I'm a contractor, a freelancer. Someone the agency uses when they need to do something off the books. If that sounds unusual—and it did to me until I came to understand that during the Cold War, the FBI and the CIA used civilians with legitimate resumes, like flight attendants, public relations people, or traveling salespeople, to deliver messages to agents and contacts overseas when they didn't want to expose their assets.

It was my publisher and FBI handler, Sophie Brill, who asked me to go to Vietnam to write a travel feature. She was familiar with Vietnam. She had been to Vietnam in 1995, when Bill Clinton had established the American Embassy in Ho Chi Minh City. Sophie had hoped to put together a traveling art show on the effects of war and art, but that never happened. And now, with tourism opening, Sophie wanted an in-depth feature and thought I would be the perfect fit. I had no problem accepting Sophie's offer. It had been almost thirty years since Eric had been shot down, and that part of life I had quietly tucked away and seldom mentioned to anyone. It was a lifetime ago, and while I had a vague idea of the country from letters Eric had sent home, I was more concerned about visiting a communist country than uncovering any deep-seated memories from my past. Interest in Vietnam and Ho Chi Minh City, once known as the Paris of the Orient, was on the rise. Glitzy new hotels with sky bars and rooftop swimming pools were replacing the cracked facades of old French residences and government buildings. Sophie sought a feature article that would showcase Vietnam's growth and provide readers with new travel experiences. For this, I would be paid $10,000. Five thousand up front, the other five upon the completion of the story, and the discreet delivery of a legal-sized manila envelope with five forged American passports and fifty thousand dollars to a Mr. Nguyen, at a local jewelry store in Ho Chi Minh City.

My instructions were simple. I was to fly to Los Angeles from my home in Phoenix, where I had worked as an investigative reporter for the local newspaper. Or did, at least until I was dismissed due to an inappropriate workplace relationship, and my career was derailed—*but that's a whole other story*. Once in L.A., I would pick up a direct flight to Hong Kong, then change flights to Ho Chi Minh City—or, as the South Vietnamese like to call it when their communist minders weren't around—Saigon. Twenty-four hours later, I would land at Tan Son Nhut Air Base and, after clearing passport control, take a taxi to the Hotel Majestic, a five-star, colonial-style hotel with a view of the Saigon River, located close to the Opera House and Ho Chi Minh City

Hall. After checking into the hotel, I was free to spend a restful night, taking advantage of the best in Asian hospitality. I was looking forward to a spa treatment, a glass of wine at the bar, and a nice meal, while I adjusted to the fourteen-hour time zone difference.

The following day, I planned to visit Mr. Nguyen's small jewelry store on Trai Street, one of the busiest shopping districts in Saigon. There, I would drop off the envelope as instructed and wait to pick up a smaller envelope in return. It was all very straightforward. Once I had completed the delivery, I was free to take pictures and make notes on tourist sites for the magazine while I waited for my cell phone to ring. At such times, an anonymous agent—*they're always anonymous*—would tell me when and where I was to go to drop off the envelope I had picked up.

As a courier, I would never come into contact with of the undercover agents working in the field. However, as a foreigner, I could expect my Vietnamese hosts to monitor my every move, and I'd need to be aware of my surroundings at all times. That said, my job was simply to make a delivery. Nothing more. Nothing less. It's cleaner that way, Sophie said, and less problematic should I ever be caught.

Caught. That's not a word I like to think about. I've had some close calls, but nothing I couldn't handle. After my first couple of undercover assignments, I enrolled in a self-defense class. I'm no black belt, but I'm athletic and confident in my skills. What I hadn't counted on was my addiction to the adrenaline rush of a tight situation. The sweaty palms, the rapid heartbeat. The excitement of the unexpected. As a journalist, I was always driven by the pursuit of a good story, but add in the excitement of working undercover, and sometimes I just can't help myself.

* * *

I hadn't thought about the gold four-seasons bracelet Eric had given me since the day I had locked it away with all his letters in my dresser drawer. But when I saw it, or one very much like it, beneath the glass counter where I had gone to deliver the envelope Sophie had given me, my mind clouded with memories of Eric and the black velvet box he sent home before Christmas. I took my hat off and placed it on the counter.

"You like?" From behind the counter, a man approached. Short. Boyishly small with a friendly smile and a heavy Vietnamese accent.

"I'm here to see Mr. Nguyen." Despite practicing the jeweler's name, my American accent was terrible.

The man corrected my pronunciation. "Uh-yen," he said. "He is busy. Perhaps I help? My name is Ahn."

Ahn reached beneath the glass counter, picked up the gold bracelet, and placed it in my hand. It looked so much like the bracelet Eric had given me. Holding it, I ran the tips of my fingers lightly across the intricately carved chinoiserie design of each season. Summer. Winter. Fall. Spring. Each one-inch square was delicately etched and set between smaller gold squares with rose accents. I put it down. Eric said pilots carried the bracelets hidden in their flight suits for good luck. If they were shot down and lucky enough to get picked up by friendlies, meaning South Vietnamese troops and not the Viet Cong, the pilots would break the gold links apart and reward their rescuers for their efforts. And, if all their missions went well and they weren't shot down, the pilots would bring home an 18-karat gold bracelet to commemorate their survival and give it to their wives. But Eric wasn't lucky. He thought he had flown his last mission, packed my bracelet away, and sent it on ahead so I would have it in time for the holiday celebrations. He planned to be home in time for New Year's. But a buddy had asked Eric to take a flight for him. His wife had flown to Thailand to meet her husband for R&R, and she had mixed up the international timeline and arrived a day early. Could Eric take his mission?

I had no idea Eric had flown that fatal mission. I was putting the finishing touches on his welcome home cake, convinced he was winging his way back to me on some Air Force transport. I joyfully imagined that in less than twenty-four hours, we'd be celebrating, smearing frosting on each other's faces. Laughing. Kissing. Making love. But when the base Commander's black Oldsmobile pulled into my drive, I knew something terrible had happened. My stomach sank. Eric wasn't coming home.

I put the bracelet down and pushed the tray away.

"Perhaps I show you something else. Something you like better." Ahn put his finger to his lips, then reached beneath the counter, pulled out a blue heart-shaped diamond necklace, and placed the pendant's centerpiece in the palm of my hand. "Is from Saudi Royal Family."

I held the heart-shaped blue diamond stone up to the light. It was as big as a walnut and surrounded by a rope of white diamonds. "The House of Saud?"

Ahn's eyes glanced behind him, as though to check we were alone. "I have more. You want to see?"

The words were no sooner out of Ahn's mouth when a man appeared in an open doorway from behind the glass counter. I recognized him immediately from the photos Sophie had shared with me.

"Mr. Nguyen?"

Nguyen stopped abruptly. His eyes were wide. A look of terror on his face. A gunshot whizzed past my ear. I looked over my shoulder. A man stood in the doorway, aimed a gun at the jeweler, and fired off a second shot. I screamed and ducked. Nguyen turned and ran back through the door to the back of the shop. The intruder pushed me aside. I crouched down below the counter, too frightened to move. The man fired off a third shot, hitting Nguyen in the back as he tried to escape. Then, jumping over the counter, the intruder raced toward Nguyen's crumpled body and, standing over him like an executioner, fired one last shot into his target's chest. Then, stuffing his gun behind his back, he fled through the office and out the back door.

I stood back from the counter and clutched the necklace to my chest. My hands were shaking. Above me, the shop's yellow-white security lights began to oscillate. A siren blared. Ahn took one quick look in my direction, then raced for the front door. Whatever had happened, whatever I had witnessed, I was too shocked to realize what I was doing. Without thinking, I slipped the necklace inside my backpack and followed Ahn, as quickly as I could, out the door.

Ahn disappeared into the crowd ahead of me. Panicked, I stumbled over a shoeshine stand and into a fruit cart, spilling pomelos and lychees into the street. The merchant yelled, and I ran. Anxious to get as far away from Nguyen's store as possible, I pushed my way through a crowd of shoppers, men in business suits clutching cellphones to their ears, women with babies on their backs, and others in tight silk dresses. I got as far as the end of the street and stopped. Ahead of me, a traffic circle with bicycles and motorcycles, of every shape and size, darted in and out between each other, like a swarm of angry bees, going in every direction. Next to me, pedestrians stepped fearlessly into the street, oblivious to the risk.

The concierge at the hotel had warned me that morning that Westerners found walking in the city challenging. I would need to forget everything I had ever learned about crossing the street and just step out into traffic. But I couldn't do it. It went against every instinct I had. I glanced back up the street to Nguyen's store. The police had arrived. Blue and red lights had now joined the white security light swirling in front of Nguyen's door. I looked back at the traffic circle and weighed my chances. A family of five on one bike zipped by, a dad on a cell phone, a kid between him and his mama-san with a baby in arms, and another on her back. I had never seen anything like it. I waited for a small break in the traffic, hugged my backpack to my chest, and stepped out into the street. Like the game of Frogger, I paused, waited for an opening, took a step forward, back, forward again, then froze as a horde of motorcycles whizzed by me so close the hair on my arms stood up.

"Hey, Lady, you need help?" A bicycle rickshaw pulled up behind me. The driver hollered. "Get in. I take you anywhere you want to go."

Like a life raft, I grabbed for the rickshaw's armrest, folded my body into the open seat, and willed my heart to slow down. Convinced I was safe, I rested my backpack on my lap, then turned to look at the driver behind me. He was a small, slim man, wearing an open cotton shirt that exposed his brown chest and a bucket hat low on his brow. He had a broad smile and crooked, tobacco-stained teeth. I figured him to be about my age. Maybe forty to forty-five years old.

"You are American?" he asked.

I nodded.

"What's your name?"

"Kat Lawson."

"If you like, I can drive you and show you city. Very reasonable rate. Is okay?"

At that moment, I would have paid my rescuer whatever money he asked for. As far as I was concerned, he had saved me from the traffic circle of death, and I was more than grateful.

"It's more than okay," I said, mimicking his broken English.

"My name is Tomy. If you like, I sing. You like Beach Boys?" Tomy began to peddle the rickshaw, and traffic parted around us seamlessly. "I know American music. I learn from GIs. They say I sing like Brian Wilson."

I knew better than to think my driver's name was Tomy. Most Vietnamese, at least those who had worked with Americans, had given themselves Western names. Vietnamese is a very tonal language, difficult for Americans to grasp, and given that this man had just rescued me, and liked to think he could sing like Brian Wilson, who was I to argue?

Tomy didn't wait for my answer before launching into one of my favorite melodies. "Wouldn't it be nice if—"

My eyes started to tear the minute I heard the first notes. It was the song Eric used to sing to me. Eric was never much of a singer. He could hardly carry a tune. But he had a way of convincing me he could do anything and that together, we were unstoppable. He persuaded me, even though I was barely through my senior year in college, that we should get married. I think he worried I wouldn't stick around until he came back if we didn't do something to make our relationship permanent, and he wasn't taking any chances. He said he wanted to make sure I didn't walk away with some other guy. Not that I would have. Eric was my first love, my college sweetheart, and I was his girl. We had met at a college fraternity party on campus the day before my first classes. Eric was a senior, and I was a freshman. Things got serious between us fast. When Eric graduated, he was commissioned as a second lieutenant in the Air Force, and, fortunately, he was stationed at the air base near the university, which allowed our relationship to continue. When Eric's orders came through for Vietnam, we didn't even think about it. Getting married just felt like the right thing to do.

I wiped my eyes with the back of my hand. I hadn't expected the memories to come flooding back. But since touching down at Tan Son Nhut Air Base, thoughts of Eric were closer than they had been in years, and with them emotions I thought I had put behind me a lifetime ago.

"You okay?" Tomy leaned over the handlebars of the rickshaw. "If you like, I sing different song."

"No. I'm fine." I waved my hand in front of my face like it was no big deal.

"You like I take you somewhere special?"

"I could use a coffee. Is there somewhere quiet you could take me?" At that moment, two motorcycles roared by, and I pulled my backpack to my chest. "Somewhere not so noisy. I need to make a phone call."

What I wanted and what I needed was to call Sophie. My stomach was in knots, and Sophie needed to know that Mr. Nguyen was dead and that I still had the envelope she had given me.

"I know a good place. Very quiet. You can talk there. No one will bother you."

I reached into my backpack, grabbed my camera, and took several shots of the sidewalks jammed with shoppers in their straw conical-shaped hats and fruit stands loaded with all kinds of colorful fruits. A government car with red flags attached to its side mirrors sped by us. I snapped a quick shot and then stuffed my camera back into my bag. It was unusual to see a car. The streets were crowded with every kind of motorized cart and bike I could imagine, but there were few cars on the road. The price of an automobile was well beyond the means of the average South Vietnamese, and the presence and flashing lights made me nervous.

Tomy peddled through a traffic circle and then took a quick right onto a narrow street, followed by another with sidewalks stacked with new and used small appliances, housewares, pots and pans, and electric cords. The area looked like a swap meet for kitchen aids and spare parts. Another turn, another street, and more of the same with crowded storefronts and sidewalks, this time crammed with power tools, neon lights, and all kinds of lighting. It was as though all of Ho Chi Minh City was one big box store with aisle after aisle—street after street—of like-market items for sale.

Tomy peddled the rickshaw into an alleyway, then stopped and got off his bike. "Here. Come with me. You sit and make call. Very quiet."

As I got out of the rickshaw, I glanced behind me to see if we had been followed. Satisfied no one was behind us, I tailed Tomy down the alley, a hardscrabble back entrance for a mixed-use neighborhood of storefronts and aging apartment buildings. Bicycles lined the sides of paint-peeled buildings with unmarked wooden doors that scraped against their alley entrance, offering little security. Ahead of us, a man sat on a pink, plastic child-sized chair in front of an equally small table. He was sipping tea and nodded as Tomy approached.

Tomy said something to the man in Vietnamese, then pointed at the table for me to sit down.

"Kat, this is my friend, Sam. He will make us tea. Much better than coffee. You like. I promise."

Sam got up and disappeared behind an open doorway draped with red and gold glass beads, while Tomy pulled a small chair out for me to sit down, then followed his friend inside.

Despite my long legs, I'm five feet ten, I managed to settle myself on a chair designed for a four-year-old, then pulled my cell phone from my bag. Ever since the Y2K scare, when the world worried computers would crash and airplanes fall from the sky, the FBI had updated their phones, and Sophie had secured a small but powerful flip phone for me, which, despite sketchy service outside the city, would allow me to bypass international operators and link directly to her office. I punched in a series of secret codes, and while waiting for the call to go through, reached into my backpack for my pen and notepad. Instead, my fingers were entangled in a loose chain. I pulled the chain from inside my bag and stared at the heart-shaped blue diamond in my hand. Property of the Saudi Prince. My troubles had just gone from bad to worse.

Chapter Two

"Kat? Why are you calling? You're only to use this number in case of an emergency. What's up?" Sophie answered the phone just as Tomy and Sam returned with a pot of tea and three tall glasses filled with ice.

"I'll call you later." I slipped the blue diamond necklace back into my backpack and hung up.

Tomy placed a tray on the table in front of me. "You okay? You look worried?"

I smiled and raised my shoulder. "I shouldn't be. It's just all those bikes and the traffic. I guess the Vietnamese don't believe in stoplights. Or crosswalks, for that matter?"

"We have one. Don't need more. Nobody would pay attention anyway. This is not like West." Tomy poured a serving of green tea over the ice and offered me a glass. "You here in Saigon alone?"

I noticed Tomy's use of the name Saigon, not Ho Chi Minh City, and wondered if it was a deliberate mistake. It would have been considered risky to call Ho Chi Minh City by anything but its proper name if he thought there were communist minders around.

"I'm a journalist. I'm here to write a story about tourism."

Tomy looked at Sam, said something in Vietnamese, and then looked back at me. "We think maybe you need guide. Sam and me, we work with Americans as guides during the war. Maybe we help you now?"

I picked up my glass and took a sip of the sweet tea. It was cool and refreshing, and while the location where Tomy had brought me was not in any way commercial, it was, as he promised, quiet. I felt a sense of comfort knowing that Tomy and Sam had worked with Americans. A lot of the South Vietnamese had been very useful to the Americans during the war, and the fact that Tomy was willing to show me a side of Saigon that tourists might not ordinarily see made me think he could be helpful. He knew the city, and after this morning, it was obvious that getting around wasn't going to be easy.

"All right. I could use a guide. There's a lot I'd need to see in a relatively short time. I'm only here for the week, and—"

"No problem. We start now. I give you a highlight tour of the city and show you important places. You pay me cash every day. Fifteen US dollars. Is good?"

"Fifteen dollars? For a rickshaw ride?" I winced. Not so much because of the price, but a rickshaw? "I think I'm going to need more than a rickshaw to get around. This is a big city."

"No. Not rickshaw. We have a truck and motorbike. Motorbike is best for city."

"You have a truck? *And* a motorbike?"

If Tomy and Sam had a motorbike and a truck, they were more than just rickshaw drivers. The expense of a truck alone in a city like Ho Chi Minh was beyond the means of the average citizen. Ownership of both made me think they were not only members of the communist party—which every citizen in Vietnam was expected to be—but members in good standing. This meant they were either spies or extremely skilled entrepreneurs who managed to conceal their good fortune from their communist comrades.

I choked back a cough. "You want me to ride on the back of a motorcycle?"

The idea of darting in and out of traffic on the back of a small motorbike with a man half my size frightened me. But, even more than my concern about balancing on the back of a bike that didn't look big enough to hold two people, was the thought that Tomy might be a spy. Sophie had warned me to be alert, and I wondered if our *accidental meeting* in the middle of the traffic circle hadn't been so accidental after all. Had my communist minders assigned Tomy and Sam to follow me?

"Not motorcycle. Moped. You like. I promise."

"I don't know."

"Why? You want to drive?"

"No. Not at all." I shook my head while I considered my options. If Tomy and Sam had been assigned to follow me, perhaps I should call a cab and return to the hotel. Or, I smiled as the thought took shape. What better way for me to convince my watchers that I was nothing more than a journalist on assignment than to hire them as my guides?

"But, if you don't mind, I'd like to go back to the hotel first. I'm staying at the Majestic. It's hotter than I had expected, and I'd like to take a quick shower." With my fingers, I felt for the shoulder seams of my t-shirt, lifted it slightly, and exhaled. It felt like it had melted into my body. "I need to freshen up."

What I needed was to call Sophie, but this time from behind closed doors. I wanted Sophie to hear from me before she heard from anyone else that Nguyen had been shot and that I had no idea what I was supposed to do next.

"Good. We go now." Tomy stood up and reached for my backpack.

I grabbed his wrist. I wasn't about to risk anyone making off with my backpack. Not with the Saudi Diamond inside. "You don't need to do that. Force of habit. I always carry my stuff. But thanks."

Tomy shrugged and said something to Sam, who then disappeared back through the beaded doorway.

"We wait here. Sam goes to get bike." Tomy took a pack of cigarettes from his pocket. "You like smoke?"

I shook my head. "No, thanks."

"It's a bad habit. But I think, if war didn't kill me, cigarettes won't. So I smoke. Everybody smokes."

* * *

I was surprised how quickly I began to feel comfortable on the back of the bike. Despite the congestion, the blare of horns, bicycle bells, and the sudden stop-and-go while we paused for traffic or sped up to avoid being hit, it was exhilarating. A high that I began to recognize as the life-pounding pulse of the city.

"You like?" Tomy spoke with the butt of his cigarette in his mouth as we merged into a traffic circle. "City is beautiful, yes?" He pointed to the Continental Palace. "One hundred and twenty years old. She looks same now as she did during the war. Good bar on top. Maybe we go later."

Two blocks more, and a few more unsettling twists and turns in and out of traffic, and Tomy pulled his bike up onto the sidewalk in front of the Majestic Hotel.

"You go in. I wait at the bar in the lobby. No rush."

I left Tomy downstairs and crossed the lobby's marble floor to the elevator. The Majestic's entrance was like a palace with highly polished floors, huge stained-glass windows, and crystal chandeliers. The perfect setting for idle travelers to sit at any of the small bunching tables and enjoy sipping tea.

I got as far as the elevator when the bellman called me.

"Ms. Lawson?"

I stopped, the tip of my finger on the call button.

"You have a message. An invitation." The bellman handed me a red envelope, nodded curtly, and left me standing in front of the elevator door. Other than my name scrawled handsomely on the outside of the envelope, there was no return address or indication of who had sent it.

I scanned the lobby to see if anyone was watching and saw no one. Anxiously, I pushed the elevator button and waited for the car to arrive. When it did, I stepped inside, happy to see I was its only occupant, and hit the button for the fourth floor. When the doors closed, I tore open the envelope.

The Red Poets' Society
Invites you to an evening of
Cocktails and Conversation.
The Rooftop Garden Bar
The Rex Hotel

9 p.m.

Red Poets' Society? I had no idea who the Red Poets' Society was or how they got my name. I did, however, know something about the Rex Hotel. In prepping for my assignment, I had researched the Rex; with its central location and views of the wharf, Bach Dang Quay, and the Saigon River, the hotel had been a popular hangout for senior-level military and war correspondents. I tapped the card against my hand. This was no casual invitation. Whoever had sent it wanted to get a good look at me, and I planned to nurse that for all it was worth and get a good look in return. I stuffed the card inside my backpack and waited for the elevator doors to open.

My cell phone vibrated from inside my backpack as I got out of the elevator, and the doors closed behind me. My nerves, already on edge, responded with small electric shocks. I reached into my bag, grabbed both my phone and room key, and stepped quickly to the door.

Sophie had warned me before I left for Vietnam that I might not only be followed but that my room would likely be bugged. As a guest of the Majestic, I could expect everything luxury could afford, plush bath towels, silky sheets, and fresh flowers in my room. Everything that is, but privacy. I was advised to check the room for bugs. Cameras could be hidden anywhere, including in air vents and inside mirrors. For modesty's sake, Sophie suggested I close the bathroom air vent and, when in doubt, throw a towel over the bathroom mirror. As for communication, the cell phone Sophie had given me was designed to scuttle the voices of any incoming callers, thus assuring their anonymity and the context of their call. From my end, however, it would be more difficult. I would need to create enough background noise to cover the sound of my voice, and whenever possible, I was instructed to speak in code.

I closed the door behind me and, following Sophie's explicit instructions, went directly to the bathroom, dropped my backpack on the floor, and started the shower. When I was convinced the sound of the water was enough to cover my voice, and the room had steamed up and the mirror clouded over, making it next to impossible to see across the room, I dialed

Sophie's number.

Sophie picked up on the first ring.

"Talk to me, Kat. What's going on?" Sophie's words ran together like machine gun fire.

I cupped my hand over the mouthpiece of my phone and whispered. "We have a problem."

"I heard—"

"How do you know?"

As an extra precaution, I stepped into the shower, clothes and all, and pulled the curtain shut.

Sophie explained that right after I had tried to call her, she had received a call from the Special Agent in charge of the operation, telling her there had been a shooting inside the jewelry store. An informant within the police department had called him to report the incident.

"What happened, Kat?"

"Nguyen's dead. Someone shot him right in front of me." I leaned back against the shower wall. "What's going on, Sophie? You said this was going to be a routine drop-off. Nothing to worry about. What's happening?"

Sophie ignored my question. "Did anyone see you?"

"I don't know. Yes. No. Maybe?" Everything I had seen blurred in my head.

"Kat, get hold of yourself. Which is it? Yes, or no? Did you see anyone? Did the shooter see you?"

I closed my eyes, steadied my breathing, and replayed the scene in my head.

"It all happened so fast. I went to Nguyen's jewelry store, just as we had planned. The clerk said Nguyen was in the back and he'd be out in a minute. I didn't think anything of it, and then the clerk started showing me some things. A couple of minutes later, Nguyen came in, but he stopped just short of the counter. He had this weird look of surprise on his face, like he wasn't expecting me. And then I got it. He wasn't looking at me, but at a man standing behind me. He must have entered as Nguyen was coming into the room. I heard a gunshot. Then I glanced over my shoulder. I didn't know what to do. It was awful. Nguyen fell to the floor, and then this man jumped over the counter—over me—and fired point blank into Nguyen's chest."

"Kat, listen to me. Did you get a look at him? Could you recognize him if you saw him again?"

"I don't know. It all happened so fast. He was wearing sunglasses and a hat. I think he had dark hair. To be honest, I'm not even sure if he was Asian.

"What about the clerk?"

"He ran. But I got his name. He said it was Ahn. And right before the shooter came in, he was showing me a diamond necklace. He said it had belonged to a Saudi Prince."

"Kat, I'm not concerned about some necklace. What about the manila envelope I gave you? Do you still have it?"

I looked down at my backpack on the bathroom floor. I had never had the chance to take the envelope out of the lining of my bag. "Yeah, I've got it."

"Keep it hidden. You may need it later."

"Later? What do you mean, later? Didn't you hear me? Nguyen's dead."

"I heard just fine, Kat."

"What's all this about, Sophie?" What's the money for? Why the passports?"

"Like I've told you before, you don't need to know. You're better off not knowing."

"Yeah, well, that was before I saw a man get shot this morning. Executed. Right in front of me. With what I've been through, I think I deserve to know what's going on. If you can't tell me that, at least tell me, am I in some kind of danger?"

"To be honest, I don't know. This was unexpected. I'll have to nose around. Until then, keep the envelope in a safe place."

"Wait. Don't hang up. There's something else I need to tell you. When I got back to the hotel, the bellman handed me an invitation to a cocktail party tonight. It's from some group called the Red Poets' Society. Do you have any idea who they are?"

Sophie paused.

"Sophie?" I knew from her silence that she knew something, and I sensed she wasn't surprised. "What is it? Who are they?"

I'm not sure. But my hunch is that they're a nest of spies. A diverse group of former military personnel, intellectuals, writers, and journalists from all sides.

"You've seen this before?"

"They wouldn't be the first. The East German secret police, the Stasi, established a group with a similar name in East Berlin before the wall fell. It was called the Red Poetry Society. It was a sort of book club. Have you ever heard of them?"

"Never."

"I'm not surprised. Most Americans are unaware of them. During the war, the Nazis had burnt so many books that the reading levels of the East German people, particularly those under the Stasi command, had fallen below that of the Western world. So, the Stasis chose classic novels and encouraged the writing of poetry. They believed poetry would be a good way to get inside the heads of their countrymen and their young officers so they could learn what they were thinking. But it backfired. Their poetry inspired a powerful freedom of thought movement, and as tensions between the East and West rose, so did tensions within the Stasis' ranks. It was that freedom of thought that helped to bring about the fall of the Berlin Wall."

"So, this Red Poets' Society, you think it's a watchdog of some kind?"

"What I think is that you're in a country where everyone is watching everyone, and you've received an invitation to a cocktail party so they can get a closer look at you."

"Who's they, Sophie?"

"That depends. It could be Vietnam's Communist Party. The Russians have been there since before the war. Or the Chinese. Take your pick. They're all close, and they all spy on each other. They've got eyes and ears on everyone. The better question is, have they figured out who you are? Did anyone see you leave Nguyen's shop this morning?"

"I don't think so. I was gone before the police came."

"That's good news. And it confirms the report I got from our undercover there."

"Who?"

"You know I can't tell you that. However, I will tell you that he called me to say the police don't have a record of anyone being in the shop. So, tonight's party? I wouldn't worry about it. It's likely a preplanned event, pure protocol. Nothing more than an invitation to a party so our communist minders can get a look at you. They do that a lot. But if you suspect anyone is on to you, we're going to have to pull you out and abort the mission. I don't want to do that. We've invested too much."

Now would have been a good time to share my suspicions about Tomy and Sam with Sophie. But I wasn't sure if they were spies or just good guys who liked Americans and were helping me out. Either way, I wasn't going to risk Sophie pulling me off the mission and losing half my guarantee. I needed the money, and this was one of those decisions I needed to make for myself.

"So, assuming they, the Russian, the Chinese, or the Vietnamese, don't know who I am, what is it I'm supposed to do now?"

"Exactly what you've been hired to do. Write a story about tourism in Vietnam. Make anyone watching you believe you're nothing but what it says on your passport. A single American female on a business trip to Vietnam. A reporter."

"And what about the necklace?"

"What necklace?"

"The Saudi diamond necklace. The one Ahn was showing me."

"Please, tell me you didn't take it."

"I didn't *take* it. I stuffed it in my backpack. By mistake. It was an accident."

Sophie exhaled. "Of course it was."

I could have done without sarcasm, but I wasn't surprised. Sophie is twenty-five years my senior, and while she's my handler, we don't always agree on how things should be done in the field. She thinks I take unnecessary risks—but, hey, I'm the one with the boots on the ground. As for me, I think Sophie's too conservative. But together we make a good team. I'm her eyes and ears on the ground, and one way or another, she manages to always bring me home.

"So, what do I do with it?"

"Hide it. But not in your room. It's not secure there. Nothing is. You can assume there are cameras in the room, and the staff at your hotel will snoop through everything you have. Find a place to store it where it won't be discovered. Preferably on you."

"That's it? That's all the advice you've got for me?"

"For now, yes." Sophie sounded impatient. "But, if I were you, I'd hope whoever assassinated Nguyen can't recognize you and that Ahn doesn't think you stole the diamond. It could be trouble if he did."

Chapter Three

"I told you I didn't steal the Saudi diamond!" When Sophie didn't answer, I realized I was talking to myself.

Sophie had hung up, and I was left standing fully clothed in the middle of the shower, soaking wet, and staring at my phone. I don't know what I expected from Sophie. She couldn't protect me. She was more than eight thousand miles away. Other than to tell me that her idea of good news was that her source—an unidentified Special Agent, whose name and face I didn't know and would probably never meet—had called to tell her that the police had no record of any witnesses to the shooting, I didn't share her optimism. I had just seen a man murdered, and I was nervous about lying low and doing what I could to maintain my cover. If the shooter had seen my face or Ahn thought I had stolen the diamond, I had likely become an unintended target and needed to protect myself.

My last couple of assignments with *Journey International* taught me the importance of learning how to blend in and hide contraband. In addition to the high-tech cell phone I carried, Sophie had given me a backpack with secret compartments where I had hidden the manila envelope I was to give Nguyen, plus several uniquely designed weapons that had been devised for my protection. The first was a simple tube of lipstick, lip gloss on one end, and a small hidden penlight on the other. The second was a lightweight, silver titanium barrette, an innocent-looking hair clip I wore to keep my hair out of my eyes, that concealed a three-inch stiletto blade, enough to do serious damage when opened. The third was a handsomely knotted macramé belt, a fashion accessory made from jute and secured with a slip knot. With one quick flick of the wrist, the knot and the belt would unravel into twenty feet of rope. Fourth were my platform wedges, which had been hollowed out to conceal items, like the blue diamond pendant I now needed to hide.

I stripped out of my wet clothes and hung them over the shower rod to dry, then grabbed a towel, wrapped it around myself, and headed to the bedroom, where I took a fresh cotton blouse and a pair of green khakis from the closet. With my wedge sandals in one hand and my clothes in the other, I returned to the bathroom. With the vent closed and the mirror still clouded with steam, I felt it was safe enough to transfer the diamond from my backpack to the hidden compartment in my shoe. Satisfied I had made the transfer without notice, I dressed, then took a towel to the mirror and wiped it clean.

* * *

Thirty minutes later, I was back downstairs. I found Tomy at the bar, a fancy, brass-gilded, marble counter surrounded by a dozen barstools next to the hotel's entry. Tomy was drinking a beer and chatting with a big man who looked like he needed a shave and could have been a former NFL linebacker.

"Kat!" Tomy stood up and waved for me to join them. "Come. I want you to meet a friend."

As I approached the bar, Tomy's friend put his drink down, wiped his mouth with the back of his hand, and stood up. He was at least six-five, heavy set, and scanned me like he might have a piece of meat.

"Kat, this is Davy Crockett."

"Really? Davy Crockett?" *Was he joking?*

Crockett took my hand and grinned approvingly.

"Don't let the name throw you, ma'am. I'm as legit as they come, but Tomy here's the only one who gets away with calling me Davy. Most people just call me Crockett. But do me a favor, don't put a Mister in front of it. Mister was my daddy, and he's long since gone, so Crockett's fine with me. Less, of course, you wanna call me Puddin Face, like my mama did." Crockett had a slow southern drawl.

I tried to pull my hand away, but Crockett had a grip like a gorilla and wouldn't let go.

"Tomy here tells me you're a travel writer. Anything you need to know, you can ask me. I was a platoon leader here during the war—4th Infantry, and proud of it." Crockett dropped my hand and rolled his sleeve up to reveal a tattoo. A pair of crossed rifles on the inside of his forearm. "We saw a lot of action."

I smiled politely, pulled my hand from his, and massaged my fingers. They felt like they had been in a vice.

"These days, I make my living selling insurance or assurances of sorts if that's what you need. Came back to Nam in eight-six. Couldn't stay away. Country gets under your skin. The food. The women. This place is exciting. A lot of Americans here doin' business. Maybe I can be of help to you, too, if you like. Buy you a drink if you want."

Crockett pulled his sleeve down, and as he did, I noticed he was wearing a metal band around his wrist. He caught my eye and stopped.

"You know what this is?" He pointed to the bracelet. "It's an MIA bracelet."

I didn't say anything. I was more than familiar with the band he wore on his wrist. I had worn a similar band with Eric's name on it for seven years while I struggled with his death before I finally put it in the drawer with my memories.

"It's got the name of one of my men on it. A few of the lucky ones came home. Some never got to make that choice. Others? Hell, I don't know, they may have stayed. Deserted. Who knows? No one's askin' these days."

I didn't like people who thought some MIAs *chose* not to come home. I lived with the wives and families of those who were missing. None of them wanted to think that some might choose not to come home.

Crockett signaled the bartender to bring three beers.

"Thanks, but I've got a busy day planned." I wasn't about to get stuck listening to Crockett's war stories and his crap about MIAs who chose not to come home. "Tomy was going to—"

"Show you around? Nonsense. You and I should get to know one another." Crockett grabbed my forearm. "I could tell you a thing or two about tourism you wouldn't find in any guidebook."

"I'm sure you could, but—"

"Let me tell ya something about the South Vietnamese. They're ambitious people, particularly now that the Viet Cong are gone. You know who the VCs are today?"

Crockett paused. I shook my head.

"Venture capitalist. Back in the early nineties, money was rollin' in. Investors were crawling all over the country. China, Taiwan, Korea, Japan, Singapore. They came in droves. And in '94, when the US got rid of its embargo, a lot of us came back. But the fellas up north, those little commies, they didn't much like that. Thought too much foreign influence wasn't good for the country. Put a lot of dumb ass rules and regulations on business, and some of the big shots looking to make a fortune left. But not me. We joke about it." Crockett picked up his drink. "Know what the Vietnamese government's done that France and the US couldn't?"

Tomy interrupted. "Defeat the Vietnamese people."

Crockett clicked his beer glass to Tomy's. "You got it."

The bartender placed a glass of beer on the counter, and Crockett picked it up. "You sure I can't convince you to stay and have a drink? Shame to let this one go to waste."

"I'm sure it won't. But I need to go. Tomy promised to show me around this afternoon. I've got a lot I need to see."

"My loss. But maybe we can catch up later? The bar here gets busy around sunset. Come on back, I'll buy you a drink."

Chapter Four

"You okay?" Tomy patted my leg as I straddled the back of the bike. "Something wrong?"

"No. I'm fine." But I wasn't fine. My hands shook as I reversed the sunhat I had brought with me and stuffed my hair beneath the brim. Sophie told me she didn't think I had been seen leaving Nguyen's shop. But how could she be certain? And what about Ahn? What if he was looking for me?

"You like my friend?"

No. Not at all. But I wasn't about to tell Tomy that I thought Crockett was a drunk, an egotistical, self-absorbed ex-GI who liked to throw his weight around, and I didn't want to sit around the bar and listen to him brag about his past experiences.

"Interesting guy," I said. "Does he always hang out at the bar in the middle of the day like that?"

"It's his office. He meets his American clients there. Cheaper than renting office space, he says."

"What's he do?"

"He's an insurance broker."

"Here?"

"There's a lot of American and International business here these days. People need insurance. It's a job."

I wondered about that.

"Tell me something. You think he's right about MIAs?"

"That some deserted, didn't go home, and chose to stay?"

Tomy shrugged. "I don't know. You hear rumors. Every war has some, but—"

"Have you ever seen any?"

"How would anyone know? There are many Americans here now. Maybe some never went home or returned after the war. It's impossible to know."

Tomy gunned the Honda's engine, and we zipped out from beneath Majestic's tall, rounded porticos. With one hand on my head to hold my hat and the other on Tomy's shoulder, we sped a short distance until we came to the Opera House, a surprisingly ornate structure designed by a French architect to resemble the Petit Palais in Paris. I snapped several pictures from the back of the bike as we cut through traffic toward the Reunification Palace, where on April 30, 1975, a North Vietnamese tank smashed its way onto the palace lawn. Posted on top of the palace and along the boulevard were Vietnam's red flags with a bright gold star in the center. A reminder to all who visited of Vietnam's unity and resilience in the face of outside influence. From the palace, we motored on to Saigon's Notre Dame Cathedral and the Central Post Office. Everywhere there were signs of construction. Modern high-rises crowded out old, dilapidated structures, pockmarked from rounds of rocket mortar. By the time we arrived at the War Remnants Museum, I could feel my phone vibrating from within my backpack. I knew it would be Sophie. I tapped Tomy on the shoulder and pantomimed my hand to my ear, that I had a call I needed to take.

Tomy found a place to park, and I got off the bike and searched in my backpack for my phone. I barely had time to say hello before Sophie started talking.

"Kat, listen to me. Are you alone?"

"No." I put the phone to my ear and moved away from Tomy so that he couldn't hear.

"Be careful what you say. My voice is scrambled on this line, but if anyone close to you is listening, it wouldn't be good. You got that?"

I looked around as I answered. "Yeah, I got it. What's up?"

"You need to go back to Nguyen's jewelry store. Find Ahn. Talk to him. Tell him you think the old jeweler put something aside for you. That you were there to pick it up."

"You want me to go back and—"

"And get more pictures. You got that?" Sophie wasn't taking any chances that I might misspeak and say something that might blow my cover. "Go back to the jewelry store, Kat. Talk to Ahn. See what he knows."

I paused. The last thing I wanted to do was go back to Nguyen's jewelry store. "You're sure? I'm not much of a photographer. Maybe there's someone else?"

"There is no one, Kat. It's why you're here. We needed someone no one knows or might recognize."

I didn't like where this conversation was going. Sophie had assured me before I left the States that, although this assignment was slightly more complicated than my previous ones, due to Vietnam being a communist country, the Agency didn't expect any heroic acts from me. Physical confrontations were reserved for agents in the field. This assignment was pedestrian, a simple drop-off. Nothing to worry about. I'd be fine.

"I'm sorry, Kat. Things have escalated, and time is running out. We didn't expect Nguyen to be shot, and now that he's dead, we need to revise our plan. You can leave if you like, but right now, you're our best hope. If we don't get the package Nguyen prepared for us, some very bad things will happen."

"Like what?"

"I can't tell you that. However, I can assure you that lives depend on our obtaining that information. And quickly. We don't have a lot of time."

I weighed my response. I needed the money. Sophie had advanced me half in good faith, and if I returned home before I had a chance to write the story, I would be out the additional five thousand dollars she promised me. An amount my anemic bank account could ill afford to go without. Jobs that paid this well were scarce. Plus, I had a Saudi diamond worth thousands, if not a cool million, hidden in my shoe and the sense that I was on to a good story. I was hooked and maybe a little overconfident. *If nobody had seen me, what did I have to worry about?* There's nothing to compare to the adrenaline rush I feel when chasing a story. I considered my response and chose my words cautiously. This conversation had to sound like I was talking to my publisher, and not my handler.

"All right, but I may need a little more time."

"We don't have time, Kat. Do you still have the Saudi diamond?"

"Yes."

"Good. Tell Ahn if he wants you to return the diamond, he needs to find the envelope Nguyen was going to give you. Trust me, Kat. Ahn knows something. Tell him that if he refuses, you'll go to the Saudi embassy, give them the diamond, and tell them where you got it."

"You're sure about this?"

"I did a little research after we got off the phone. The diamond was stolen from the home of a Saudi prince back in 1989 by a Thai janitor named Kriangkrai Techamong. He made off with twenty million dollars' worth of jewelry that belonged to the family, and the Saudi family understandably wants the jewelry back. The Thai government arrested Mr. Techamong when they learned of the theft and returned the jewels. But there's no honor among thieves. Turns out, the jewels the Thai government returned to the Saudis were fake. They were copies. So, the Saudis sent a couple of their people over to find the jewels and ended up assassinating several Thai officials. To this day, there's been a feud between the two countries."

I gripped the phone and looked up at the sky. How difficult could it be to go back to the store and meet with Ahn? I didn't imagine I would have any difficulty negotiating a trade for a million-dollar diamond in exchange for an envelope. If Ahn had gone back to the store after the shooting and realized I had the Saudi Diamond, he would probably welcome me. If I could exchange the diamond for the envelope, it would be one less worry I'd have that anyone with knowledge of the Saudi Diamond might be following me. It seemed like a simple enough solution.

"Okay. I'll go back and get more pictures. Anything else?"

"No. Call me when the job's done."

I hung up the phone and wondered if the assassin who had shot Nguyen had been a Saudi assigned to track down whoever had the Saudi Blue Diamond. However, it didn't make sense to me that if the assassin had come in search of the diamond that he hadn't threatened Nguyen or torn the shop apart in his search for it. Instead, the shooter hadn't said anything and chose to shoot Nguyen point-blank. And from the look on Nguyen's face when he saw him, he knew what was coming. Ahn's sudden escape made me wonder if the assassin wanted to send Ahn a message. And from the way Ahn bolted from the store, he had gotten that message loud and clear. All the more reason Ahn would be anxious to have the diamond returned.

I went back to Tomy. He was sitting sidesaddle on the bike, smoking a cigarette. "Are we anywhere near where you picked me up this morning?"

"Not far. Why?"

"I think I left a credit card at one of the stores. I need to go back. You don't have to wait for me. I can take a cab back to the hotel."

"No problem. We go now. I know a shortcut."

Tomy's shortcut was an e-ticket ride through parts of the city tourists would never see. We darted into oncoming traffic, down alleyways, past three and four-story walkups, their balconies crammed with rusted air coolers, laundry, and the occasional birdcage, then out onto a main thoroughfare and back to the traffic circle where Tomy had rescued me that morning.

"This is where I pick you up." Tomy pulled the bike up onto the walk. "If you want, I wait. Is okay."

"No, it's fine. Go ahead. I can take a cab back."

"What about tomorrow? If you like, I pick you up at the hotel. There is still much more to see. Maybe I take you north to the Cu Chi Tunnels in Ben Dinh. Is hour's drive and very important for you to see. It's where Viet Cong hide."

"Sounds good. I'll meet you in front of the hotel at ten o'clock."

Chapter Five

Tomy disappeared into traffic, and I looked back at the shops. It could have been any street; I had left in such a rush that nothing looked familiar. The sidewalks were teeming with shoppers. I stuffed my hat in my backpack, just in case one of the shopkeepers might recognize me as the woman who had run from Nguyen's store that morning. Then I pushed my way between the shoppers and down the street until I saw a flashing neon sign with the words *Jewelry Store*. In front of the store was the shoeshine stand I had tripped over that morning. I hurried toward the door. I was certain I had found my way back.

As I got closer, I noticed a sign had been placed in the window. Quán Đóng Cửa. The door was locked. In any language, the sign meant the store was closed. Still, I pushed on the door, and with one hand on the handle, I rattled the lock. But the door wouldn't budge.

"Store closed." A shoeshine boy, dressed in loose-fitting long shorts, a t-shirt, and sandals, stood up from behind his stand. "You look for someone?"

"I'm looking for Ahn. He works for Mr. Nguyen."

"No more. Nguyen is dead."

"Dead?" I took a step back and feigned surprise. "W-w-what happened?"

"Someone shoot him. Police investigate. You ask them. Store closed now. You should go."

I placed my hand flat against the door. I couldn't give up. If I couldn't get inside and search the store myself, there had to be someone who could.

"Do you know Ahn? Do you think he might come back?"

"Why you ask me?"

"It's just…" I lowered my voice and stepped closer to the shoeshine stand. "I need to talk to Ahn. It's important."

"Why you want to talk Ahn?" The shoeshine boy looked at me suspiciously. If he recognized me, I saw no sign of it in his eyes. Even so, I wasn't about to risk saying something that might jog his memory, and I chose to lie instead.

"I was here yesterday. Ahn sold me a bracelet. I think I left my credit card."

"Sorry." The boy shook his head, pulled a rag from his back pocket, and started to wipe down his stand. "Store closed. Ahn not here."

This wasn't the first reluctant witness I had ever questioned, and I sensed he knew more than he let on. I took my backpack from my shoulders, reached inside for my wallet, took out a ten-dollar bill, and then dropped it into an open can next to the shoeshine stand.

"Yes, but maybe you can help me?"

The boy picked up the ten-dollar bill, folded it over, and put it in his pocket. "What your name?"

"Kat Lawson." I took my business card from my wallet and handed it to him." I'm a reporter. I'm here working on a travel feature on tourism in Vietnam. I'm staying at the Majestic. If you see Ahn, could you give him my card and ask him to call me?"

The boy glanced at my card. "If Ahn come back, I tell him. If he find credit card, he call you. You not worry."

I left the shoeshine boy in front of Nguyen's shop, hopeful he would find Ahn and give him my business card. Ahn would know when he heard I had come back to the shop looking for a lost credit card that it was a lie. If I was right and Nguyen's murder had been a warning to Ahn that the Saudis knew he had the diamond, Ahn wouldn't waste any time getting back in touch with me. As for Sophie? She wasn't going to be happy when she learned I had failed to meet up with Ahn, and that I still didn't have the envelope Nguyen was supposed to give me. What I had was the Saudi Diamond hidden in the heel of my shoe and an assassin who, if he thought I could identify him, would want to silence me. It was almost five thirty, and it was starting to get dark. I hurried away from the store and got as far as the traffic circle, where I hailed a cab. I wasn't about to step out into the street and risk being hit by a distracted driver, or stand on the edge of the roundabout and be some marksman's target. I had enough risks to contend with.

* * *

By the time I returned to the Majestic, the lobby was abuzz. The front desk was busy helping guests check in, while porters with their gold trolleys were loading suitcases onto their carts. Several of the hotel's guests had gathered at the bar for drinks. I was relieved to see that Tomy's friend, Davy Crockett, wasn't waiting for me, and I hurried past the bar toward the elevator. I was anxious to get to my room and call Sophie to tell her that Ahn appeared to have taken flight, and I had struck out.

I had barely closed the door to my room when I heard the room phone ring. I hoped it might be Ahn, and I could set up a time and place to meet. I tossed my backpack on the bed and raced to the phone.

"Hey there, Legs. Are you going to join us tonight?"

I recognized Crockett's southern drawl and relaxed my grip on the phone.

"Join you for what?" I asked.

"Oh, come on now. Don't tell me you don't want to see my pretty face again. Give me a chance to buy you that drink I promised."

I tilted the phone's mouthpiece away from my face and exhaled. *The sooner I could get rid of this jerk, the better.*

"I'm sorry, I'm—"

"Yeah, yeah, yeah, I know. You're busy. But I figure, you being a journalist, that you must have gotten the invite to tonight's meeting. The Red Poets' Society? Rex Hotel."

I sat down on the edge of the bed. Whoever Crockett was, the fact that he knew about the Red Poets' Society and that I had received an invitation to tonight's soiree got my attention. "I did. But, how did you know?"

Crockett chuckled. I sensed a tone of sarcasm in his laugh and bristled.

"This really is your first trip to Nam, isn't it? Tighten your belt, babe, we're going to have some fun."

"I'm sorry. Fun? Did I miss something?" I didn't appreciate that Crockett

33

had assumed we would have fun. Crockett was not the type of man I wanted to have *fun* with. Nor did I appreciate that he thought I needed his guidance in any way.

"My dear, in case you hadn't noticed, this is a communist country. When you register at a hotel, you fill out a form. Everyone does. It all looks routine. Name. Age. Occupation. By now, your name's on a watch list. Probably several. You can't expect privacy. Not here."

I paused. I wanted to tell Crockett to take a flying leap, but thought better of it.

"I see. So, this Red Poets' Society, you're a member?" Crockett didn't strike me as a spy or anyone the FBI or the CIA would have hired. He was way too unorthodox, at least in comparison to those few agents I had met in New York while interviewing for the job. But he was ex-military, and from the brief conversation I had with him at the bar, I sensed not much happened inside Ho Chi Minh City that he didn't know about.

"Tell you what, why don't you get yourself all dolled up and stop by tonight? I'll explain more when I see you. The Rex Hotel. Top floor. Nine o'clock."

Crockett hung up, and I picked up the invite I had left on the bedside table. I wasn't at all interested in meeting Crockett, but if members of the Red Poets' Society had sent me an invite because they wanted to see me, I wanted to see them as well. But not on an empty stomach. I hadn't eaten all day. I was nervous about meeting Nguyen and didn't have anything but a bag of nuts and some fruit from a fruit basket I had in my room before I set out to meet with him. The shock of his murder had killed my appetite, but now, eight hours later, I was starving, and I needed something. I picked up the bedside phone, called for room service, and ordered a bowl of ramen.

While waiting for my dinner to arrive, I took my backpack off the bed and headed to the shower for the second time that day. The heat had been insufferable, and my clothes clung to me like wet wallpaper. I turned on the water, waited until I thought there was enough force to drown out the sound of my voice, and then sat down on the side of the tub. I was about to reach into my backpack and call Sophie when my cell phone rang.

"Hi, Soph—"

"Did you get hold of Ahn?" Sophie sounded anxious.

I exhaled.

"He wasn't there. The shop was closed. But I met someone who knows him." I explained how I had run into the shoeshine boy whose stand I had stumbled over that morning when I ran from Mr. Nguyen's jewelry store.

"Did he recognize you?"

"No. But I gave him my card, told him I was staying at the Majestic, and asked if he would pass it on to Ahn.

"That's not good enough, Kat. We need that package. People's lives depend on it. You need to call me as soon as you know anything. Anything at all. I'll be waiting. And don't mess this up. We can't afford any more screwups."

"It wasn't me who screwed up, it—"

Sophie hung up. I sighed and put my head in my hands. I had been in the country less than twenty-four hours, witnessed a murder, had a Saudi diamond necklace hidden in the heel of my shoe, and had good reason to believe I had been invited to a private party so that I could be observed. *What else could go wrong?*

* * *

My dinner arrived by seven p.m., and along with a glass of wine I had taken from the small refrigerator in my room, I did my best to enjoy it, then showered and selected a simple, loose-fitting black cotton shift from the closet. Something that didn't yell *notice me* or cause Crockett to think I had dressed up for him, but would be appropriate for a book club, or as Sophie said, a nest of spies. Black seemed appropriate. Crockett would be disappointed I wasn't all dolled up, but I was in no mood to encourage him. The last thing I needed to do was to fight off his advances. I had enough reason to be looking over my shoulder without worrying about Crockett. *Best to blend in and dress discreetly.* I slipped into my dress, pulled my hair tightly up on top of my head into a sensible bun, and fastened it with the silver hair clip–the one with the switchblade hidden inside. Then, I looked into the mirror, added a simple pair of silver studs, a large pair of black glasses, and slung my backpack casually over one shoulder. Sans any lipstick and voila! Kat Lawson. Middle-aged, no-nonsense travel reporter on assignment. I had to look twice in the mirror to recognize myself.

Downstairs, I checked with the concierge to see how long the walk would be from the Majestic to the Rex Hotel. Rather than take a cab, the cooler night air would make a nice walk while giving me a chance to look over my shoulder to see if anyone was following me. The concierge took a tourist map out from beneath the desk and outlined the walk with a yellow felt-tip pen. The Rex Hotel was ten minutes away, and at that time of night, the streets were well-lit. I shouldn't have had much trouble.

The city's vibrant nightlife was in full swing as I headed up Dong Khoi, a historic boulevard with glimpses of the city's colonial past mixed with high-end designer boutiques. The blur of headlights from cars and motorcycles, amid the beeping of bicycle horns and the warble of police sirens, all felt foreign to my Western ears, yet triggered a memory—a heartache I had long since forgotten. I rubbed the ring finger on my right hand, the small wedding silver band Eric had given me, and paused to look in the window of one of the boutiques. Whatever this feeling of the past that swallowed me, I couldn't shake the feeling I was being followed. Behind me, a young couple walked arm in arm, and behind them, a single man, with a phone to his ear. Eyes straight ahead. I studied him. Average height, middle-aged, white. Maybe Russian. Could be American or at least a Westerner. As he passed me, he jutted his chin, a friendly nod, and walked ahead. He wasn't Russian. He wouldn't have acknowledged me if he had been. Probably just some lonely tourist or businessman, out for an evening stroll. As a reporter, I had learned to ask questions and read between the lines. Later, after I started working undercover, I learned even more about how to read body language. Nothing about the man indicated he was following me. I was overreacting, thinking too much about the past and not focusing on the present.

Much as I tried not to, my thoughts returned to Eric. He had been stationed at Cam Ranh Air Force Base, a thousand miles northeast of Saigon, but the sights and smells. The way he had described them. They all felt familiar. Occasionally, Eric would get a chance to come into Saigon, and when he could, he would call me. In the background, I could hear the sounds of the city. The last call I got from Eric was when I was in class at the university. The Dean of the Journalism Department had come into my class, asked for me by name, then instructed me to follow him back to his office. It was highly unusual. I had no idea why until I arrived at his office, and he stepped aside and nodded to the phone on his desk. *You have a call.* I feared the worst. Why else would the Dean come to get me out of class? But then I heard Eric's voice, and my knees went weak. I slumped down into the chair behind the desk. Eric told me he had been calling all over trying to reach me. He was due to leave the city and go back to his air base, and he wasn't about to leave until we spoke. He told me he had called the house first, then my folks, and when they told him I was at school, he got the Dean's number and called the university. That's the way Eric was. When Eric wanted something, he made it happen. I smiled at the memory. Eric loved Saigon. He talked about the people. The congestion and the excitement of the city. The old men, too old to fight, who befriended the Americans and wanted us to win the war, and the women, with their large, white, cone-shaped hats on their bikes, going to market. The food—hu tieu, a pork and seafood noodle soup, was his favorite. Communication back then wasn't always the easiest; there were no cell phones, and the mail wasn't always reliable. Sometimes I would get two or three letters in one day, and then for a week, there would be nothing. I'd run barefoot to meet the postman, and he'd shake his head. *Not today. Maybe tomorrow. You keep positive.* I had pushed so much of this aside. But now, as I headed for the Rex Hotel, so much of what I thought I had buried and forgotten was creeping back.

I had never told Sophie about Eric. Few people who knew me had any idea about my early life or my brief marriage. It wasn't something I ever wanted to talk about. I was barely twenty-one when Eric got orders for Vietnam, and we ran off to Vegas to get married. I never took Eric's last name. He was shot down before I graduated, and it was just easier not to change my college transcripts. Sophie had no idea. She never knew I had been a member of a group called the Waiting Wives, wives who waited for their husbands' return from war, or anything about the women and their families who were my friends and kept me company during those empty holidays, and with whom I spent birthdays. How I waited and prayed for a war that none of us wanted to end, and hoped that Eric would come home. Most of all, Sophie never knew about the black government car that pulled up in front of my home four days before Christmas or the news that forever changed my life.

Sophie didn't know that seven years after the war ended, the Pentagon had changed Eric's status from MIA to KIA. She didn't know that, along with Eric's parents, I had buried an empty coffin, or that I had moved the slim silver band I had worn on my left hand to my right. She didn't know I had a life I refused to talk about. Nor did she have any reason to suspect my widowed status, because I had never mentioned it, and there was no official record. Our quickie Vegas wedding, while legal, had left us no time to file the proper paperwork. We promised each other we would do that when he came back. The only record was the gilded paper certificate, which I had folded away with Eric's memory at the bottom of my jewelry box. Sophie had no idea about Eric because I had never told her, and Sophie was in a rush to find someone she could send to Vietnam. The mission was urgent. She needed someone she could trust, someone experienced who could get in and out without a problem. The FBI didn't need an agent. They needed a courier, and with my background as a journalist, I was the perfect fit.

Chapter Six

The Rex Hotel was a magnificent post-modern structure that took up an entire city block and was lit up like a birthday cake, with yellow lights beaming from its windows and rooftop garden. I paused in the lobby long enough to take in the ambiance of the five-star hotel, with its high ceilings, marble floors, sweeping spiral staircase, and colorful floral arrangements, all of which were very classy. Judging from the accents I could hear around me, Rex's clientele was a very international crowd, a virtual United Nations of tourism: Russians, Koreans, French, English, and Americans.

I crossed the lobby to the elevators. It was almost nine-thirty, and while I hadn't wanted to be the first to arrive, I didn't want to be the last.

When the elevator doors opened, I found myself on a rooftop garden decorated with strings of white lights, potted plants, small tables, and an outdoor bar. The air was clouded with cigarette smoke. For all of Vietnam's rigid rules restricting human rights, smoking wasn't one of them, and the view of the city and river below was blurred with a grey haze of tobacco smoke. Small groups congregated around the bar while an audio system cranked out a soulful rendition of *Summertime* with Kenny G.

Crocket was seated by himself at the end of the bar. I suspected he had chosen the seat because it gave him a direct line of sight to the elevator door. He spotted me as the doors closed behind me and tipped his glass.

"So, looks like you decided to come after all." Crockett swaggered toward me with a glass in hand, leaned in, and kissed me behind the ear. "How about I get you that drink I promised? What'll it be?"

I could smell brandy on his breath. He had already had a few too many. I pushed him away and nodded curtly.

"I'm fine, thank you. I don't need anything. And you don't need to take care of me."

"Who said anything about taking care of you? I'm just tryin' to be polite." Crockett hunched his shoulders and raised his hands. "The least you can do is let me get you a drink, and then you can do all the socializin' you like. I'll leave you alone. I promise."

"Fine. A Chardonnay, then."

"Eh! Come on. You can do better than that. You're here in Vietnam." Crockett scrunched his face. "Let me get you a real drink. Drink of the house. A B-52."

"I don't think so." I shook my head.

"Trust me, you'll love it. Irish cream layered with Kahlúa and Grand Marnier, set on fire. Give it a try. Help you fit in."

I glanced around the room. Stiff. Forced smiles. Eyes that scanned the room, never making contact. Eyes that I felt were checking me out as much as I was searching to see who they were.

"Maybe so, but it's my first night here, and it's been a long day. I need to take it a little easy. I'm still adjusting to the time change."

"Suit yourself. But you don't know what you're missin'." Crockett winked.

"Oh, I'm pretty sure I do." Whatever ideas Crockett had about tonight, it wasn't going to happen. "And a Chardonnay would be just fine, thank you."

"Okay, then. The lady wants a Chardonnay, and Chardonnay is it. But a place like this? Book club and all. It seems to me that a gal like yourself might find it to your liking. Might even want to let your hair down a bit."

"Book club?" I ran the palm of my hand against my head and glanced around the patio. "This doesn't look like any book club I've ever been part of."

"I guess you didn't see the book table in the corner?" Crockett pointed to a Vietnamese bookseller who sat slouched with his nose in a book behind a small table at the far end of the bar. He looked as though he didn't expect to be disturbed. And, from the lack of any interested onlookers, I suspected his presence was more for effect's sake than sales.

"I must have missed that. So, is there a reader tonight?"

"Reader?" Crockett squinted.

"Is someone scheduled to read? Poetry maybe? I mean, this is the Red *Poets'* Society."

"Wouldn't know." Crockett shrugged. "I'm not an author. I come for the liquor and stay for the company. Never know who you're going to meet here."

I rolled my eyes. "Not to be rude, but I'm not surprised. You don't strike me as much of a poet."

Crockett grinned. "You always so quick to judge a book by its cover?"

I held up my hand. "I'm not judging—"

"No problem if you were." Crockett slapped the palm of his hand to mine and squeezed it. "You're right, this isn't your typical book club."

"Really?" I lowered my voice. "So exactly what is this Red Poets' Society?"

"How about I let you stew on that while I go get us a drink?" Then nodding to the book table, he added, "I'll meet you at the bookseller's table. We can talk privately there and maybe get to know one another a little better."

* * *

I wandered over to the bookseller's table. The small man behind it was wearing a thin pair of wire-rimmed glasses that he slid down the bridge of his nose. He looked up at me curiously as though he hadn't expected to be noticed.

"Excuse me, do you speak English?"

"I do. How may I help you?"

"I was wondering if there would be a reading tonight?"

The bookseller shoved his glasses back in place and shook his head. "This must be your first time here. There is no reading. There never is. People come. They visit. They have a few drinks. Sometimes they buy a book. Mostly not. But perhaps I could interest you in something."

I looked down at the table. Piles of used paperbacks, worn and dog-eared, in an assortment of languages. Vietnamese. Russian. English.

The bookseller moved several books around until he found one he liked and handed it to me. It was a worn paperback with a black-and-white picture of the author on the cover.

"This is Tan Da. He is Vietnam's first modern poet. It's in English. He writes about Vietnam's folklore and legends. He gives his readers a window into the soul of Vietnam. I think you should read."

I offered to pay the bookseller, but he shook his head, then looked back at the book he had been reading. Before I could ask again, Crockett returned from the bar carrying two flaming blue B52 cocktails on a silver tray. He put the tray down on an empty table next to the bookseller and waited for the flame to extinguish itself.

"What can I say? They were out of chardonnay."

"Why is it I find that difficult to believe?"

Crockett grinned, picked up the cocktails, and tried to hand me one. I put my hand up and shook my head. Crockett shrugged, put my drink down, and took a sip of his own.

"You figure out who we are yet?"

"We?"

"I wasn't aware you were including yourself in the group."

"Nobody here is who they say they are."

"And you?" I asked. "Just who is Davy Crockett?"

"What do you care? As long as the booze is good and women are loose, I'm happy."

"Give me a break." I started to walk away.

"Oh, come on, Legs. The night's still young. You haven't told me what you think of this place."

"You want to know what I think of this place? I think there's a wine closet full of red and white wines behind that bar. And you? You're nothing more than a lonely, washed-up expat looking for an excuse to get drunk and go home with any woman who would have you. But I'm not interested. So, if you'll excuse me, I think I need to do a little mingling. Goodnight!"

⁎⁎

I left Crockett at the table with the bookseller and wandered over to the bar where three Russians stood, engrossed in an animated conversation, slapping each other on the back while they drank their vodka Russian style, ice-cold from shot glasses. I might have hung out at the bar, hopeful I could observe the room from the position of my barstool, but the Ruskies were loud and obnoxious, and as they finished each drink, they pounded a fist to their chests, burped loudly, and poured another. I swiveled on my stool, hailed the bartender, and ordered myself a glass of white wine—not at all the impossibility Crockett had indicated—and, with my drink in hand, moseyed toward the patio's perimeter, where I stared out at the city lights.

"Are you alone?"

I turned around to see an older, gray-haired woman sitting by herself at a table behind me. Her hair was cut boyishly short, and she wore thick, round tortoise-shell glasses that gave her a very plain, studious look. Around her neck, she had a slim leather strap attached to a small bag, big enough for a cell phone, and a notepad. Poking out of the top of her bag was the tip of a pen. I figured her to be a reporter.

"Not to be a bother, but I saw you come in. You're welcome to have a seat if you like." She motioned to the empty chair across from her and smiled.

I thanked her and sat down.

"My name's Eddie Charles. I apologize if I seem forward, but I couldn't help but notice you were talking with Davy Crockett." Eddie smirked. "I thought he might have had you trapped. Nice ditch by the way."

I rolled my eyes and glanced across the room to the book table. Crockett was still there. The King of the Wild Frontier was chatting it up with the bookseller.

"I imagine every woman in this bar's been cornered by Crockett at one time or another."

"Crockett's harmless. Been around for a while. But then, so have most of us here. I was here during the war as a correspondent, stayed to the end, and then came back in ninety-five to work for Nike. What about you?"

"Kat Lawson. Travel Reporter." I extended my hand. "I'm here with *Journey International.* I'm doing a story on tourism."

"You don't say?" Eddie scratched her ear. "Small word. I know your publisher, Sophie Brill. We were at Radcliffe together. It was an all-girls school and a small class. All of us are highly motivated. Sophie was our class president. So, how is Sophie these days?"

"Fine," I said. My voice caught in my throat. Coincidences make me nervous, and much as I didn't like Crockett, he had been correct about my registration at the hotel. I was sure every person in the room knew who I was. My picture, my occupation, and no doubt my listed reason for being in Vietnam had been widely distributed among various watch groups. And Eddie, whether she knew Sophie or not, I suspected had been assigned to watch me or watch out for me. I took a sip of my wine. "Did you know Sophie well?"

"Not really. We had a few classes together. It's been a long time, but I do remember she was a very talented artist. Is she still painting?"

"I don't know." I had been to Sophie's office in New York when she had hired me. It was a large office, and there were several paintings and sketches on the walls, mostly abstracts. I didn't know if she had painted them, but I worried I was treading into unsafe territory and might slip up and say something I shouldn't. I pushed the conversation into Sophie's more recent past with the magazine. "She retired as a museum curator a few years ago and then founded the magazine. She told me, travel's always been her passion."

"Well, then," Eddie sat back in her chair, her eyes still glued to mine, as though she could read my thoughts. "You must give her my regards when you speak with her again. Although you should know, we were never close, more like friendly competitors. But that's ancient history now. What's more important is that you got our invitation and aren't partying it up in some nightclub."

I stroked the stem of my wine glass. "I'm not much for nightclubs. Particularly not on my first night here. But I did find your invitation interesting, especially the name. The Red Poets' Society. I take it you're a member?"

"There is no official membership, and we're not much of a book club. Sometimes, someone will walk out of here with a book, but mostly not. Our hosts, Vietnam's ruling party, the Chính phủ, along with the Russians and the Chinese, organize these meetings as a way of keeping track of their people, expats like me, and any visiting dignitaries. Tonight's meeting is nothing more than a watch party. They watch us. We watch them." Eddie's eyes swept to the far end of the bar where a group of men, both Asian and Anglo, stood with their drinks in hand.

I glanced over my shoulder. "How do you know who's who?"

"You don't. Sometimes you get surprised."

I took a sip of my wine. "So, then you're a—"

"Spy? I wouldn't tell you if I were."

I chuckled and raised my glass to her. "I wouldn't expect you to. But I am curious. You said you were here during the war. Why come back?"

"Because I love it. I feel a connection. Haven't you ever felt that with a story? Knew you were a part of it and wanted to follow it to the end. The war didn't end the story for me. It was just the beginning. My career started here. I was here with *Rolling Stone*, a young stringer, anxious to get in on the action and make a name for myself. Back then, all you had to do was get a visa, convince some newspaper to give you a credential, get on a plane, and come. I didn't get my first press pass until I got here. I was one of the only female reporters in the field, and I had to prove myself. I did everything the men did. Went out in the field. Jumped out of planes. Slept in foxholes. Watched out for landmines and got shot at. I saw some horrific things. Talked to soldiers and attended briefings. Have you ever heard of the Five O'clock Follies?"

"No."

"The nightly press briefings. They took place here, in the basement of this hotel. When I first got here, I was naive. I believed everything I heard. Then I began to understand that some of those in the Public Affairs Office who wrote the briefings for the Five O'clock Follies had never been out of the city, much less in the field. They had no idea what was going on. But I did. I had spent time in the field. Sometimes, with Special Ops, Green Berets who lived in the jungle and were experts in guerrilla warfare. I saw firsthand what was happening. What we were up against. How we were being lied to. America wasn't prepared to fight a guerrilla war. Our bombing had little effect, and I started to write reports that showed a different side of the war. Stories the public wasn't getting. Believe me, I wasn't popular with the brass back then."

"Brass?"

"Military commanders, field grade and above, and the press officials who worked for them. You name it. But when photographers started to shoot pictures of flag-draped coffins on the tarmac, and Walter Cronkite broadcast that the war was at a stalemate, I knew what I did had made a difference. You're a reporter. I don't need to tell you that sometimes you have to work both sides of the street to get the story."

I stared down at my empty glass. I knew all too well that what Eddie said was true. When Eric first left, I wanted to believe the war would be over and he'd be home soon. That America would win the war, and our lives would go on. But after Eric's crash, after he went missing, and was then classified as dead, I no longer trusted anyone. Losing Eric changed my life. I wasn't afraid anymore. I started taking risks. I didn't want to be the journalist who sat behind the safety of some anchor desk. I wanted to be in the field, behind the scenes.

"But that's behind us now. These days, we're not shooting at each other. Instead, we're playing a game of mental chess. Every so often, a player or two will go missing, but for the most part, we just watch each other and make each other nervous."

"Which, if I understand correctly, is why I received an invitation to tonight's party. Somebody's curious about me." I pushed my glass across the table. "For all I know, maybe it's you who's watching me."

Eddie laughed. "Don't be paranoid, Kat. It's not flattering. Everybody watches everybody. In a communist country, information is currency. And right now, you're new here and being watched to ensure you're exactly who you claim to be. A travel journalist on assignment. Do what you came to do, and you won't have a problem. Visit the historic sights, take lots of pictures, and enjoy yourself. But, on a personal note, watch out for Crockett. The man can be a problem if you're not careful. Other than that, if you need anything, I'll give you my card." Eddie opened her small pocketbook and handed me her business card. "Call me if I can be of help."

Chapter Seven

It was after midnight when I returned to the Majestic Hotel. The lobby was empty, the bar had closed, and housekeeping had just started polishing the marble floors. The whirling sound of the floor scrubber nearly drowned out the receptionist's voice as I hurried past the front desk.

"Ms. Lawson?"

"Yes?" I approached the counter.

"You had a visitor earlier this evening. He was anxious to meet with you. I tried your room, but you weren't there." The receptionist took a small, folded piece of paper from beneath the counter and handed it to me. "He asked me to give this to you."

"Thank you." I turned my back and unfolded the note as I headed for the elevator. Then stopped as I read.

Ms. Lawson,
I have your Credit Card. Please come back to the store in the morning.
I will meet you there.
— Ahn

I glanced over my shoulder to see if anyone was watching, then crumpled the note in my hand and hurried to the elevator. Sophie would be pleased to hear I had contacted Ahn, and I couldn't wait to tell her. Once back in my room, I went immediately to the shower, turned on the water, waited for the room to steam up, and then dialed Sophie's number.

"I've been waiting for your call, Kat. What's happening?"

"Ahn sent me a note. The shoeshine boy must have gotten hold of him. I had a message waiting for me when I got back to the hotel. He wants me to come back to the store in the morning. But first, I need to know what's going on. What am I walking into? What was Nguyen involved in?"

Sophie didn't say anything. In the background, I could hear the squeak of her cane-backed chair, and I pictured her with her elbows on her desk, one hand on the phone beneath her ear, as she considered what she could or wouldn't tell me.

"Sophie? What's going on?"

"To be honest? I'm not sure, Kat."

"That's not helping, Sophie. I need some assurances. Or at least an explanation of what this is all about. You can't expect me to go back to Nguyen's store and risk getting caught without giving me some idea of what to look out for."

"You know the rules, Kat. I can't do that. But maybe you know more than you think. Are you certain you couldn't identify the assassin? I realize you wouldn't know him, but did you get a look at him? Was he Asian? White?"

I closed my eyes and tried to recreate the scene. It had all happened so fast. It was early. The store hadn't officially opened, but Ahn had seen me standing outside and asked me to come in. I remembered thinking that was a little unusual, but so far, the locals all seemed to be very gracious, and I quickly dismissed any thought that Ahn was being anything but helpful. I told him I was there to see Nguyen. Ahn said the jeweler was in the back, getting something from the safe, and would be out in a minute. I remember putting my backpack down by my feet while I waited. The envelope I was to deliver to Nguyen was still inside the lining of my backpack, and aside from Ahn, the store was empty. I planned to wait for Nguyen to come out from the back and tell him I had a special delivery for him. Just as I had been told to do. I figured once I mentioned the delivery, he would know why I was there and dismiss Ahn. I would then take the envelope from inside my backpack and place it on the counter. Once Nguyen placed his envelope on the counter and I had it in my custody, I would slip it into my backpack and leave.

But for some reason, Nguyen was taking his time. I was feeling antsy, and I started to look at the jewelry beneath the glass. That was when I saw the gold four-seasons bracelet, exactly like the one Eric had given me, and I backed away from the counter. Ahn must have noticed and asked if I might like to see something different, and pulled the Saudi blue diamond pendant out from beneath the counter. I was holding the pendant in my hand when Nguyen came out from the rear of the store. I recognized him from the pictures Sophie had shared with me when she explained my assignment. I remember the look of surprise on his face. At first, I thought it might be that he hadn't expected an Anglo woman to be making a delivery. But then, I realized it wasn't me Nguyen was looking at, but someone behind me. A man had entered the store. Nguyen must have known who it was because the look on his face went from surprise to shock, and he started to run. The next thing I knew, I heard a gunshot. Nguyen stumbled, fell to the floor, and struggled to stand. The assassin pushed me aside, jumped over the counter, then ran to where Nguyen lay on the floor and fired point-blank into his chest. Ahn took off, and for a split second, the assassin looked up at me. I thought he might fire, and that this was the end, but instead, he stuffed the gun into the waistband of his pants and ran out the back of the store. All I could remember was that the assassin was wearing the same type of bucket hat that Tomy had worn that morning.

"I don't know if he was white, black, or Asian. Other than the fact that he was wearing a white bucket hat that covered his eyes. I can't tell you anything more than that. I can't even tell you what he was wearing. It all happened so fast. I thought he was going to shoot me."

"All right, here's what you're going to do. You're going to go back to the store in the morning, exactly like Ahn asked. He's reached out to you because he knows you have the Saudi Diamond. I doubt he had any idea what Nguyen was involved in, or why you were there. But when you walked into the store, my guess is Ahn was looking for an opportunity."

"What opportunity?"

"He needed a mule."

"Oh, come on, Sophie. You think I'd fall for that? I was an investigative reporter. I did stories about unsuspecting people used as mules to bring drugs across the border all the time."

"This is Vietnam, not Tijuana, Kat. I doubt you'd know the difference between an authentic diamond and a fake. And we're not talking about anything in bulk. We're talking about a single item. Listen to me, Kat. Ahn was setting you up. Perhaps, if he thought you might be worried about it, he would tell you the necklace was a copy and offer you a very good deal. How would you know? Or maybe, he would have bribed you to bring it back through customs. Either way, Ahn needs to get the Saudi Diamond out of Vietnam before the Saudis know he has it. Believe me, it's much easier to have you bring the diamond home and have it stolen from you once you're back stateside than for him to try to smuggle it out of the country."

"But what about customs, wouldn't they stop me and confiscate the necklace the moment I came back to the U.S.?"

"Not necessarily. Customs isn't particularly concerned about Americans bringing jewelry back from Southeast Asia. They expect it. Lots of couples are honeymooning, bringing back souvenirs. A lot of it's not the good stuff anyway, so customs isn't looking. Certainly not for individual pieces anyway. If you had a trunkful of loose diamonds, maybe. They're more concerned about drugs and sex trafficking. And right now, if Ahn thinks you've got the diamond, he'll be desperate to talk to you."

"So, you want me to use him."

"You're in a unique position, Kat. It's too late for us to send anyone else in, and as far as Ahn's concerned, you did take the diamond."

I exhaled. "I didn't *take* the diamond. You make it sound like I stole it!"

"I'm sure you'll work that out with Ahn."

"You're asking for a lot, Sophie. What if it turns out the assassin was a Saudi, and he murdered Nguyen by mistake, or he meant to shoot Ahn, and when he saw me, panicked? What if he knows I've got the diamond? What if he's watching the store and he sees me go in?"

"We don't think that's what happened."

"Who's we, Sophie?"

"You don't need to worry about that. Worry about getting the envelope we sent you to bring back. Go back to the store, meet with Ahn, and see if you can find it. If you have to tell Ahn that you were there to meet with Nguyen and to pick up an envelope, do it."

"What if he says he doesn't know anything about it?"

"Call his bluff. He's got to know something. The store's not that big. Tell him if he doesn't find the envelope and give it to you, that you'll turn the diamond over to the Saudis and tell them where you got it. That ought to motivate him."

"You're asking me to take some chances here. What's in this envelope that's worth so much?"

"Like I said, you don't need to know, and it's better that you don't. Just get him to look around for the envelope Nguyen was supposed to give you. It's got to be in the store, maybe it's in the safe. We need it. Lives depend on it, Kat. Get it, and we'll talk."

I sensed Sophie was ready to hang up.

"Wait. One more thing. I met someone. She says she knows you. That she's an old friend."

"Who?"

"Does the name Eddie Charles mean anything to you? She said you went to college together. She's working for Nike now and said she was a reporter here during the war."

Sophie paused. "That's a name I haven't heard in a long time, Kat. I knew Eddie had gone to Vietnam as a war correspondent during the war, but I had no idea she was still there. I suppose I shouldn't be surprised. Eddie's always been a woman of mystery. But I have to warn you. Eddie and I were never friends. I never trusted her, and you'd be wise to remember that."

Chapter Eight

I called Tomy the first thing the following morning and told him I needed to beg off our tour of the Cu Chi Tunnels in Ben Dinh. I explained I had been out late the night before, and between the jetlag and the lack of sleep, I wanted to go back to bed. Tomy was disappointed, but I promised we could meet later. We agreed to meet in front of the hotel at around one p.m.

Meanwhile, I doused the lights in the room and dressed in the dark. If there were cameras in the room, without light, it would have been next to impossible to see what I was doing. From the closet, I chose a long, sleeveless cotton shift, slipped into my sandals, and then grabbed my backpack. I gave one final thought to transferring the diamond from the heel of my shoe to my backpack, thinking it might be safer, but decided against it. If anyone were following me—the Vietnamese, the Russians, or some Saudi investigator—it'd be far too easy to bump into me on the crowded streets and make off with my backpack, and then where would I be? I'd not only be out the envelope Sophie had given me to drop off at Nguyen's store, but the diamond as well. I couldn't risk that. My safety and the success of the mission depended upon my making the delivery, and I didn't dare expose myself to any unnecessary risk. I needed another hiding place, and I had a pretty good idea of what might work.

I opened my backpack, took everything out, and placed it on the bed—camera, guidebook, notepad, pencils, pens, hat, water bottle, a bag of nuts, and a few hard candies. Then, I reached inside where the lining next to that part of the backpack that embraced my back had been modified to accommodate the hidden manila envelope. If anyone had picked up my backpack or looked inside, the secret compartment looked like it was nothing more than cushioning to add an extra degree of comfort for the wearer. Giving a slight tug to the lining, I opened the secret pocket, took out the manila envelope, and hugged it to my midriff. The envelope, a standard legal-sized manila folder, was less than an inch thick. Inside were four thin stacks of one-hundred-dollar bills, laid side by side, with four passports snugly packed on top. The entire package was no more than a couple of pounds, and—since I'm tall and long-waisted—if I turned the package sideways, it could easily fit beneath my clothes without appearing as though I was trying to hide anything.

Stripping off my shift, I worked quickly, taking a pillowcase from the bed and tearing it into two long, silky strips. Knotting the strips together, I wrapped them securely around my midsection like a money belt, then took the envelope and shoved it between my stomach and the silk wrap. One extra tug to the silk ties, and my homemade money belt fit like a corset. I slipped back into my shift, added my macrame belt on top of my dress for a little extra security, and checked the mirror. Other than looking slightly thicker around my middle, my secret money belt was undetectable. With the strap of my backpack loosely over one shoulder and my camera strung around my neck, I looked like any other tourist. I grabbed a city map from the dresser, noted the location of Nguyen's jewelry store from the hotel, and decided that, despite the early morning hour, it would be best to take a cab.

I was surprised when the cab dropped me off to see how busy the street was in front of Nguyen's store. It wasn't yet eight o'clock, and already small three and four-wheel delivery vans were dropping off their wares, merchants were setting up their outdoor stands, and a few early-morning shoppers were sorting through the morning goods. I reached into my backpack for my wallet and paid the cabbie. I was less than half a block away from the jewelry store when a firm hand grabbed onto my elbow.

"Hey there, Legs. Slow down."

I turned to find myself face-to-face with Crockett.

"What are you doing?" I tried to pull away, but Crockett put his arm around my shoulder and whispered in my ear.

"Saving your life."

"What?"

Crockett squeezed my arm and pulled me closer. "Keep moving."

I elbowed Crockett, but he pulled me closer. To anyone watching, we might have looked like drunken lovers the morning after as we pushed by carts with baskets of fresh flowers and fruit stands that lined the walkway. As we got further down the street, a police cruiser sped by us with lights flashing and came to a stop in front of Nguyen's store. Crockett tightened his grip on my arm as two policemen got out of the car. From inside Nguyen's shop, two more cops emerged with the shoeshine boy between them, his hands tied behind his back. I hesitated as we passed, but Crockett grabbed my face and, with his fingers on my cheeks, turned my head to his and kissed me on the lips as he pushed me forward.

I jerked my head free and looked back over my shoulder. The police were shoving the shoeshine boy into their car.

"What's going on?"

"Shut up and keep walking."

"But—"

"Ahn's dead. And you would be too if you had walked into the shop as you intended. So, keep walking. I'm about to ruin your reputation, and you'll be glad I did."

With my head locked in the elbow of his arm, Crockett pulled me closer to him and kissed my ear.

I stumbled along, trapped beneath Crockett's grip, until we turned down an alley, and I was able to slip out from beneath his shoulder. "I'm not taking another step. Not until you tell me what's going on?"

"Keep your mouth shut and come with me. I'll explain everything. But not here. It's not safe." Crockett reached for my hand and pulled me further down the alleyway. I stumbled behind him.

"Where are you taking me?" Other than being in an alleyway, crammed with bicycles, mopeds, and shabby apartments stacked one on top of the other, I had no idea where I was.

"The Fish Doctor."

"What fish doctor? What are you talking about?" I yanked my hand free and refused to take another step. Not until Crockett told me what was going on.

"Have you ever had a fish pedicure?"

"No. And why are you here? What's happening?"

"We need to talk. Follow me. That is, unless you'd prefer to fend for yourself with the Saudis."

Crockett started to walk away. I glanced behind me. Several men had entered the alleyway. They could have been anyone. Russian. Vietnamese. Or the assassin who had killed Nguyen the day before. I wasn't about to wait around and find out.

"Hey, wait up. How do you know about the Saudis? How do you know about any of this?"

Crockett turned around and put his hands firmly on my shoulders. For a second, I thought he was going to shake me. Instead, he pulled me close in a bear hug and whispered in my ear. "Listen to me, Legs. Ahn's dead, and you're in danger." I pulled my head away and stared into his eyes. "Sophie called last night. She told me you were going to meet Ahn at the jewelry store this morning. We put a man outside Nguyen's shop this morning. He saw the shoeshine boy follow Ahn inside, and thirty minutes later, the boy called the cops and reported he had found Ahn's body."

Suddenly, all the secret cells, those agents whose identities Sophie had refused to share with me, started to take shape, an underground network of spies and informants. Whether I liked it or not, I realized I was staring into the face of the man who had put it all in place, and if I hoped to get out of Vietnam alive, I was going to have to deal with him.

"Now here's what's going to happen. I'm going to stop talking, and you're going to hug me, so if anyone's watching, they'll think we've had some lovers' spat. Then I'm gonna turn around and walk away. So, make up your mind, you either come with me or stand here and make yourself a target."

Crockett let go of me and walked away.

I took one look behind me, realized the three men coming toward me could have been anyone, but I wasn't about to stand around and find out. I weighed my options. Either I followed Crockett or risked dealing with the three men coming my way.

"Fine," I said. "I'll go with you!"

Chapter Nine

Crockett got as far as the end of the alleyway before I caught up with him. He didn't stop for me and walked stiffly ahead until he came to an open door covered with beads beneath a sign marked Doctor Fish. Sweeping the beads aside, he nodded to me to enter.

Inside, two Vietnamese women, dressed in traditional clothing—a long, split tunic over silk trousers—stood up and smiled politely. One pointed to a jacuzzi-sized tub and said something in Vietnamese. Crockett answered in Vietnamese, and the second woman nodded politely and crossed the room to a bookshelf crowded with books, magazines, and a small transistor-sized radio. She turned the radio up to full volume, and a soulful female voice blared from the speaker, accompanied by the sharp plucking sound of a zither.

I grabbed Crockett's elbow. "What's going on? Why are you following me?"

Crockett pulled away. "Take your shoes off, put your feet in the water, and we'll talk."

I glanced back at the door where one of the women stood. She gestured to the tub, and I reluctantly turned and walked ahead of Crockett.

"You better have a good explanation for this."

I sat down on the side of the tub, removed my shoes, and stuffed them inside my backpack. I wasn't about to leave my sandals with a million-dollar Saudi Diamond hidden inside, where they might be stolen. I pulled my backpack onto my lap and fluttered my feet in the water while Crockett kicked off his shoes. Within a matter of seconds, hundreds of tiny fish swarmed my feet and nibbled at my toes.

"Bet you never had a pedicure like this." Crockett rolled up the bottom of his pants, sat down, and dangled his big feet next to mine. I floated my feet in the opposite direction.

"Feels good, doesn't it?" Crockett scooped up a handful of water and splashed his face. "Those little guys, the Vietnamese call 'em fish doctors. The proper name is Garra Rufa. They nibble away the dead skin around your toes."

I wasn't in the mood for small talk, and with arms around my bag, I leaned as far away from him as I possibly could. "Who the hell are you?"

"That all depends on who you ask." Crockett stretched his arms above his head, and for a moment, looked stone sober. But I knew better. I could smell the whiskey on his breath, and it wasn't from last night. I had known men like Crockett, worked with reporters who could drink twenty-four seven and still walk a straight line. "But as far as you're concerned, I'm the man you were never supposed to meet. But unfortunately, you've got yourself into a nasty situation, which jeopardizes the operation you were here to help us with. And now, in addition to the Marxist minders you've got following you, which, by the way, we expected, you've likely got the Russians thinking that you're the one who shot Nguyen."

"Me? Shoot Nguyen? Why would anyone—"

"Because you were one of the last people to enter the shop, and from the information we're getting from our undercover inside the police department, the bullet that killed Nguyen came from an American-made pistol. A Colt forty-five."

"But I don't have a gun."

"I know that, and you know that. But the Vietnamese and the Russians? They don't. Which is why, by now, you're probably on their radar. As for the Saudi Blue Diamond, you told Sophie about? We have no idea whether the Saudis are aware that Ahn had it in his possession or not. But if they did, they may be looking for you, too."

I wiggled my toes in the water. If what Crockett was telling me was true, then things would be much worse than I expected.

"So why haven't I been arrested?"

"That's a good question, and frankly, I don't have the answer. It could be nobody saw you leave Nguyen's store, or if they did, they're not talking. There isn't a local in all of Ho Chi Minh City who's going to step forward with an eyewitness account. People around here don't do that. They run the other way. As for the Vietnamese and Russians, they may want to wait and see what happens."

"Why do you say that?"

Crockett screwed his face. "You know I can't tell you that. But I can tell you we don't think the Vietnamese had any idea what was going on inside Nguyen's store. They had no reason to keep an eye on it. As far as they're concerned, Nguyen was just another Vietnamese merchant doing business here in the city. And, if you're lucky, they didn't know you visited Nguyen's store the morning of the shooting. The Vietnamese keep tabs on visitors, but not that closely. Not unless they're suspicious of you from the get-go. And you weren't all that unusual. Just another Westerner here on business. That's why we hired you. As for the Russians, that's a different story. They may or may not have thought anything was wrong inside Nguyen's store. But we know they're dirty, and they weren't about to share what was going on with Nguyen with their hosts. Communication between the Russians and the Vietnamese only goes so far. And as far as we can tell, nobody but you knew what happened inside the store after the shots were fired. Word coming from our sources inside the Russian camp is that Ahn triggered the alarm after Nguyen was shot, and when the police got there, they found Nguyen dead on the floor."

"So, it's possible, then, that the Russians didn't see me."

"I'm not saying that. All I'm sayin' is that they're not talking. And when the Russians aren't talking, we get worried."

"What about the shooter? Didn't anyone see him *bolt out* the back door?"

"We haven't heard anything."

"Yeah, well, I saw him. He jumped the counter, and for a second or two, I thought he was going to shoot me."

"That's too bad because it means the shooter might have gotten a good look at you, as well. Which isn't good." Crockett kicked the water, and several of the doctor fish swam away, then returned. "I have to say, for someone we thought we could send in who nobody would notice, you've managed to complicate things."

"Well, thank you for that." If I weren't worried that my reaction might attract the attention of our Vietnamese attendants, I would have taken a handful of water and splashed it in Crockett's face.

"Don't take it personally. I would have made the delivery myself, but it might have blown my cover. We all agreed it would be better if we brought in a new face. Somebody no one knew. And now, thanks to this mess you've gotten yourself into, things have become more complicated."

"Explain complicated." I squeezed my backpack against my corseted money belt and wondered how much more complicated things could get. "And start with Nguyen. I think I deserve to know something. What exactly was he involved in? And why were we paying him fifty thousand dollars and giving him four US passports?"

Crockett folded his hands in his lap. "Nguyen's been working with the Russians, smuggling young girls and boys out of the country since the war ended. Some of 'em for sex. Others he sells as slaves to work in rich people's homes back in the States. Whatever happened between him and the Russians, Nguyen wants out, and he wants to take what's left of his family with him to America. I won't get into how, but he approached one of our agents and said he had information he'd sell in exchange for asylum and eventually citizenship."

"And you made the deal?" I hated the idea of dealing with anyone who had been involved in kidnapping young children and selling them into a life of prostitution or slavery. It sickened me. And not because it was just something I had read about, but because I had seen it firsthand. When I was still working for the newspaper in Phoenix, I had covered a story about a young Asian woman who had shot and killed her adopted father. It turned out that the victim, a high-profile Phoenix businessman, and his wife had allegedly adopted the young orphan girl after visiting Thailand and arranged to bring the girl back to the States, where she could be educated and have a better life. At the time of the alleged adoption, the girl was fourteen. Four years later, I had been called to the scene of a murder. Amy, not her birth name, but the name her adoptive parents had given her, was barely able to speak. Her mother, Francine, explained that Amy had gotten hold of her father's gun and, 'gone crazy.' Further investigation revealed that Amy had been secretly brought into the country, not as their daughter, but as a household servant. A servitude from which there was no escape. Amy was never allowed to leave the house, have friends, or go to school. Neighbors reported they had never seen the girl. And it was no wonder. Amy, it turned out, was not just a household servant, but a slave, a sexual distraction for the husband. And despite her desperate situation and evidence to prove the injustice of it all, Amy was serving twenty-five years to life in an Arizona prison south of Phoenix. Sometimes justice can be cruel.

"We need to know who's buying and who's selling. It's not always pretty, but if we understand who the players are, we can put a stop to some of it. And right now, we know there's a group of kids, a couple of them as young as three or four, the rest of them, twelve, thirteen tops. All of 'em kidnapped from rural villages either here in Vietnam, Cambodia, Thailand, or China and hidden somewhere in the city, and we need to find them. And fast."

"You think you can do that?"

"Once Nguyen got the money we promised him, he was going to give us the location of where the kids are hidden. Which might have worked, except Nguyen was shot. Until this morning, we still thought it might be possible for you to complete the job, retrieve the envelope from Ahn, and hand it over to us. Ahn had to know something, or at least he had to have seen something. We figured that if you went back and met with Ahn, bartered with him for the envelope Nguyen was going to give you, that we could still get the information we needed." Crockett splashed his face again. "Except, someone murdered Ahn this morning."

"And you know this because you had someone watching Nguyen's store."

"Yeah. You bet we did. Sophie called last night and told me you were planning to go back to Nguyen's store this morning. She said you had given your business card to the shoeshine boy, and he had passed it on to Ahn, who then sent a message to your hotel to arrange a meeting. We suspect the shoeshine knew something about the Saudi Diamond and that he went back to the shop to meet with Ahn. Whatever happened, whether the Russians saw you talking to the shoeshine boy yesterday and intercepted the message or had been watching the store, we don't know. But we do know that the shoeshine boy called the police to say that when he arrived at Nguyen's store, the door was open, and when he went inside, he found Ahn's body."

"How did he die?"

"From what I hear, it looks like there was a struggle, and Ahn was strangled. Once I got word that Ahn was dead, it was too late to call Sophie and hope she'd have time to stop you. I had to do something. I wasn't about to let you walk inside the store. It was too risky."

"So, you followed me."

"If I hadn't followed you, you would have walked into Nguyen's store and gotten yourself killed. And if you had, and the police were to find that envelope with several thousand dollars of American bills in your backpack along with US passports, it would have blown this case wide open. But, as it is, I still think you might be of use to us."

"How so?"

"I need to get out more, and I need a believable cover. I think together we can save your cover, while I get what information we need."

"How's that?"

"Simple, you're here to write a travel feature. You and I hook up. We help each other. You include me in your travels. Let me tag along. It'll allow me to get close to some people and locations where I might otherwise look suspicious. And believe me, nobody's going to think it odd that we've hooked up. I've got a reputation."

"I'll bet you do."

"Look, we were together last night at the Rex Hotel. People saw us. You and I shared a drink. We talked. And whether you knew it or not, I followed you back to your hotel."

"You followed me?" I couldn't believe I'd been so careless.

"Believe me, I made sure everyone saw me. Then this morning, you called your driver and told him you wanted to sleep in. What do you think people are going to think? You're an attractive, single female journalist staying at a hotel where I frequent the bar. Nobody would be surprised." Crockett leaned closer and kissed me lightly on the shoulder.

I pushed him away. "Slow down there, Cowboy. Maybe nobody would be surprised in your world. But in mine? This isn't happening. I'm not about to hook up—"

"Relax, Legs. Nobody said anything about sleeping together. And, if it makes you feel any better, you're not my type. Too skinny for my tastes. It's a job, that's it, and I need you to make it look good. Think about it. You're not some rookie journalist the FBI hired. You've been around the block. You're a good reporter. Sophie wouldn't have hired you if you weren't. I also know you're a single woman who got fired from the last decent job she had, and—"

"I wasn't fired!"

"No? Look, I don't give a damn about your past; it doesn't matter to me if you were Saint Teresa or some hooker from the Bronx. You could be wearing a scarlet letter for all I care. What matters is that kids' lives are at stake. We needed someone with a good backstory. You were perfect. A middle-aged, single female reporter who needed a job and liked to travel. And from what Sophie's told me, you're a doggedly determined investigator."

"You don't need to sell me. I know who I am."

"Good. Then you know you've got a choice. You can call Sophie, and she'll tell you that you have two options: either work with me or go home. As for the Saudi Diamond, there's not a damn thing Sophie can do about it. Not from New York. You got yourself into that one. For all I know, you grabbed it and thought maybe you might get away with it."

"You think I stole it?"

"Maybe. But I'll tell you this, whatever you did, whether you stole it or pocketed it because you were scared, this job doesn't come with any guarantees. You screw up in the field, it's on you. There's only one thing I care about, and that's the kids. And somethin' tells me that you're enough of a reporter that you're not going to walk away from a story like this. And if we're lucky and don't get ourselves killed, you can sell this story to the *New*

York Times, and maybe you'll get some damn Pulitzer Prize. As long as you leave my name out of it, I don't care."

I slapped my hat on my head. "I need to talk to Sophie, and it's getting late in New York. So, if you'll excuse me, I think it's time I left you here and got back to the hotel."

"Not a problem. I'll be at Majestic's bar if you need me. In the meantime, Legs, if I were you, I'd be careful."

"Believe me, I intend to. And the name's not Legs. It's Kat."

Chapter Ten

I left Crockett standing barefoot at Doctor Fish and got as far as the traffic circle, where I hailed a cab. I wasn't about to walk back to the hotel. With everything Crockett had just told me, I didn't trust that I wouldn't step out into traffic. I wasn't thinking clearly, and I didn't want to stand out in the open if I had a target on my back. Not after Crockett had told me the Russians, the Saudis, maybe the Vietnamese, and possibly the shooter might all have me in their crosshairs. I was angry and frightened. I had accepted an assignment that should have been a simple drop-off. Instead, I had witnessed a murder—a murder I might well be accused of doing—and I had unwittingly become part of an undercover operation involving child trafficking. I needed to talk to Sophie. I wanted to hear her tell me I had to work with Crockett, an arrogant, egotistical, sexist man, who I suspected looked at me as an expendable asset he planned to use and throw out. I didn't trust him. If Crockett and his group had been watching Nguyen's store so closely, why had they been surprised by the shooting? And Nguyen and the Russians? If they had had a falling out, why didn't Crockett know? I wasn't about to put my life on the line for someone I wasn't sure about. The adrenaline was already coursing through my veins. I wanted in. However, I wanted it to be on my terms, and I was eager to return to the hotel and make the call.

Unfortunately, my timing was less than perfect, and as the cab started to pull up in front of the Hotel, I noticed Tomy and Sam had arrived ahead of me. They were standing by the curb, smoking. Next to them was a rusted yellow Peugeot truck with balding tires that looked as though it had gone through the war. Not wanting to be seen getting out of the cab, particularly after I had told Tomy I planned to sleep in, I instructed my driver to pull up around the corner and let me out down the street.

I took my camera from my backpack as I walked around the corner of the hotel.

"Did you find your credit card?" Tomy spotted me and tossed his cigarette on the ground.

Credit card? I gripped the strap of my backpack. Did Tomy know I had lied about my credit card? Did he know that I had just come from seeing Crockett? Or that Ahn was dead? I looked down at the ground. I didn't want him to see in my eyes that I was lying. "Yeah. Everything's fine, thanks."

I slipped my camera back into my backpack. Why hadn't I asked Crockett when I had the chance if Tomy and Sam worked for him? When Crockett referred to 'us', was he including Tomy and Sam as part of his team? Or were they spies for the Russians or the Vietnamese?

"Sorry, I'm late. I wanted to get a picture of the hotel from the river. Could you give me a couple of minutes, please? I need to go up to my room for a second. I'll be right back."

* * *

As soon as I got to my room, I went to the bathroom and started the shower. Again! If my Marxist minders were listening, they would think I was either the cleanest person in all of Ho Chi Minh City or that I was on to them. Either way, they weren't going to hear my end of the conversation. I pulled my cell phone from my bag and dialed Sophie's number. It wasn't midnight in New York, but I knew she would be waiting for my call.

Sophie picked up on the first ring. "How did it go with Ahn?"

"It didn't." I paused and caught my breath. "Ahn's dead."

"What?"

"The police were there before I got to the store. Someone murdered him." I sat down on the edge of the tub and kicked off my shoes. "I'm fine, by the way." I noticed she hadn't asked. "But, this Davy Crockett guy, he intercepted me before I got to the store. Why didn't you tell me about him before I got here?"

"Calm down, Kat."

"Yeah, well, it's a bit hard. Two people are dead, and this Crockett guy, just who is he?"

"He's a Special Agent. He's undercover. You were never supposed to meet him."

"Yeah, well, I have and—"

"Listen to me, Kat. You know how this works. This was a simple assignment. You drop by Nguyen's shop, give him the envelope, and pick up another one. That was it. Once you had the envelope, you were to call me, and I would have instructed you where to drop it off. End of story."

"Well, that certainly is not the end of the story now. What am I supposed to do? You expect me to work with Crockett?"

"Look, Kat, nobody expected Nguyen to be shot, and if Ahn's dead, things have gone from bad to worse. You need to get hold of yourself."

I squeezed my eyes shut and exhaled.

"The good news is that Crockett knows who you are. Originally, he wanted me, but I'm too old for this kind of work. Once I told him about you, he approved of you. Sight unseen. And, if he thinks he can keep this operation moving forward, you need to listen to him. More importantly, your life may depend upon doing exactly as he says."

I fisted the phone in my hand and leaned against the bathroom wall. "Do you trust him?"

"To be honest?" Sophie stopped talking, and I found the silence chilling.

"Sophie? What's up?"

"I wouldn't know Crockett if I ran into him, Kat. We've never met in person. It was the agency that put us together. An informant in the field provided my name to him, and the agency subsequently called, instructing me to expect a call. Other than that, the agency doesn't provide pictures of agents with their bios. I don't get to pick and choose who I work with. But he's in charge of the operation there because someone higher up thinks he's qualified."

"And that's supposed to make me feel better? You know he's a drunk."

"He's who we have, Kat. Drunk or sober, Crockett knows people. He's been there long enough to know that nothing's ever concrete. Situations. People. They change. Sometimes it's a revolving door. There's a thin veil between the good guys and the bad guys. Agents and double agents. Sometimes what looks bad on the surface ends up being good."

I looked up at the ceiling. This wasn't an argument I was going to win. "So, how am I supposed to know who to trust?"

"Kat, listen to me. I'm not there, but Crockett is, and if he thinks you can still be of some help, you need to trust him. But be careful. Politics makes for strange bedfellows, and double agents in that part of the world are deadly. Keep your eyes and ears open."

Sophie's warning regarding double agents wasn't lost on me, any more than Crockett's warning that I needed to be careful who I talked to. I glanced at my watch. It was almost one-thirty. I needed to hurry before Tomy or Sam started to grow suspicious and wonder what might be keeping me. For all I knew, Tomy and Sam worked for the Russians or might be double agents and worked for Crockett as well. I would have to be extra careful with what I said or revealed about myself.

I stripped off my dress and peeled the money belt I had made from my waist. I was hot and sticky from the early morning humidity. I took a damp washcloth, sponged myself off, then pulled on a sleeveless t-shirt and a pair of cotton cargo pants. I couldn't go to the Cu Chi Tunnels wearing a pair of wedge sandals, and I didn't dare leave the Saudi diamond in the room. I needed to keep it on my person, so I removed the diamond from inside the heel of my sandal and slipped it into a small zip pocket inside my pants. As for the envelope, I put it back into the hidden pouch inside my backpack, then threw in my camera and notepad. Twenty minutes after I had said hello to Tomy and Sam, I was on my way back downstairs and ready to go. Hopefully that I wasn't putting myself into the hands of my enemy.

Chapter Eleven

"Sorry for the change of schedule. I needed the extra sleep this morning."

I squeezed into the Peugeot's front cab with Tomy at the wheel and Sam crouched into the bed of the truck behind us. If Crockett had called Tomy and told him where I had been this morning, I saw no recognition on Tomy's face. Nothing to indicate that Tomy had any idea I was lying about sleeping in or that he knew I had seen Crockett.

"No problem." Tomy put the Peugeot in gear, and we rocked unevenly away from the curb. I took hold of the grab strap above my shoulder and glanced back through the open window at Sam. If Tomy and Sam were members of the Communist Party, the Peugeot, with its bent fenders and rusted body, was a poor example of a car gifted to a member in good standing. It was far more likely that the Peugeot had less to do with their membership in Vietnam's communist party than it did with the black market and their ability to trade, steal, or swap what they needed to survive in a cash-strapped society.

"Is it a long drive?" My stomach knotted. If Tomy and Sam didn't work for the Russians or the Vietnamese, did they work for Crockett? Either way, leaving the city with two men I barely knew didn't feel right.

"No. Not long. Cu Chi Tunnels in Ben Dinh. Is short drive. Maybe one hour."

My mind was racing. It was Tomy who had insisted I visit the Cu Chi Tunnels. Was it a ploy to get me out of town?

"You okay?" Tomy glanced over at me.

"I'm fine. Just still a little sleepy, that's all." I held tight to the grab strap above my head, unsure if my guides were taking me on a sightseeing tour of the Ch Chi Tunnels or had something more sinister in mind and were driving me out of the city and into the jungle where I'd never be seen again.

Tomy found an American music station on the radio and turned the volume up. *Purple Haze* by Jimi Hendrix. "This will wake you up."

The music was so loud I couldn't think. But it wasn't the music that caused my mind to blur, but the sudden adrenaline rush that always came when I chased a story, and trumped my fear and pushed me forward. I wanted this story, and to get it, I needed to know exactly who Tomy and Sam were. I shouted over the sounds of Jimi Hendrix and the squeal of his steel guitar.

"You like American music?"

Tomy kept beat to the sound with his fingers against the steering wheel, bobbing his head as he sang along.

"What?"

I shouted louder. "You like American music."

"I learn to like music during war. Was good then. Is good now."

I turned the radio down. "Tell me, why didn't you try to come to America when the war ended?"

So many Vietnamese who had helped our troops had been granted visas back then. I remembered watching CBS footage of the dramatic evacuation of Americans, and those Vietnamese lucky enough to escape, scramble aboard helicopters that hovered above the United States Embassy, desperate to leave before the Viet Cong entered the city.

Tomy turned the radio off and took a cigarette from his pocket.

"It not so easy. Not everyone who worked with Americans got out. For some, the price was too high. Too many people to leave behind. My father was old man, he begs me to go. But I cannot leave my family. My wife, my children. And Sam, his wife, is pregnant. So, we hide and try to blend in like Viet Nam Cong San, those guerrilla fighters loyal to the north. But is no good. The VC finds us, and we are sent to labor camps to learn to be good Vietnamese citizens. If you ask me then did I like American music? I would say I hate all things American. America is evil intruder into my country."

Tomy turned the radio back up, and I sat back. Tomy's answer wasn't the answer I wanted, but it was the answer I got. Rather than follow up with any more questions, I stared at the road in front of me and wondered how much the countryside had changed since Eric had been here. A motor scooter, its driver bare-chested and wearing army camouflage pants, sandals, and a straw cone hat, had a large wire cage of piglets strapped to the backseat. In front of him, another motor scooter transported baskets of fruit, balanced one on top of the other. Along the roadside, fields that had once been rice paddies sat fallow. I took my camera from my backpack and snapped several pictures. Everywhere I felt the scabs of war and the haunting presence of Eric's last days here.

"We're almost there." Sam pounded on the top of the cab with his fist, then poked his head through the truck's open window. "You see the sign ahead?"

Tomy slowed, and we turned off the highway beneath a sign marked Cu Chi Tunnels. We bounced along a dirt road through a thick forest of rubber trees until we came to a clearing marked with red Vietnamese flags. Finding a parking space, Tomy pushed the Peugeot's stubborn stick shift into park. The truck shuddered like a dog shaking fleas from its body as the engine shut off.

Sam jumped out of the truck's bed and opened my door. "You tell her yet?"

"Tell me what?" I asked.

Sam's accent was thick, and his English was not as good as Tomy's, but I could tell by the way he glanced nervously back and forth from me to the entrance of the outdoor museum that he didn't want to go any further than the parking lot.

"Is better you go ahead. I wait here with truck."

I didn't understand why Sam didn't want to accompany me to the entrance of the outdoor museum, but I could see as Tomy put his hat on and looked down at his feet, that he was uncomfortable as well.

"What's wrong?"

"This museum. I can go with you, but I cannot talk or answer questions. You understand? The museum guide will tell you story."

I nodded. But it wasn't until we were met at the entrance to the outdoor museum by a young Vietnamese woman who introduced herself as our guide that I understood. She walked ahead and proudly pointed out a US tank, scarred from battle, its hatch door open and decorated with Red Vietnamese flags. "We are small people, but stronger than the American forces who invade us."

Only then did I understand that this abandoned tank was a war trophy, one of several that my Marxist Minders wanted me to see. I took my camera from my backpack and began to shoot. This wasn't a tourist attraction staged for American tourists. It had been staged to show the Vietnamese their mighty defeat of the American enemy. Shell casings had been scattered on the dirt with the dummied remains of dead American GIs. My throat tightened. I didn't like looking at the scene in front of me, but having the camera lens between myself and the horrors my camera captured made it easier. As a journalist, I learned early on that if I was going to survive reporting on stories that might otherwise bring me to tears, I had to separate myself from what I saw and report only the facts as they presented themselves.

Our guide moved on and pointed to an open pit camouflaged with leaves, concealing a deadly trap of sharpened bamboo poles, known as Punji sticks. American troops on patrol in the jungle, looking for VC, would unknowingly step onto the leaves, fall into the trap, and suffer an agonizing death. Next was a crude-looking bamboo cage. During the war, tiger cages, barely big enough for a man to sit upright in, served as mobile jails for the Viet Cong. After capturing wounded American soldiers in the field, the VC would often march these cages with their human cargo inside through the streets. Locals would jeer and shove punji sticks smeared with poisons through the cage's branches, stabbing at their prisoners. Other times, the VC would release poisonous snakes and scorpions into the cages. Those prisoners who didn't die or weren't shot along the way were brought into larger prison camps, like the infamous Hanoi Hilton, where they were tortured and held as hostages. Some for as long as seven years.

Finally, our guide led us to a shaded area beneath the trees, where a 3D diorama of the Cu Chi Tunnels, with a glass cutaway, revealed a maze of narrow passageways hidden beneath the surface.

"This is how Vietnamese people win the war. Come look, then we go inside the tunnels, and you can see more."

I studied the diorama. It was like looking at a giant ant farm, a colony of interconnected corridors leading to large, irregularly shaped rooms. Our guide sidled up to me and explained these were classrooms, nursing stations, hospitals, sleeping quarters, and kitchens, complete with a pipeline that funneled smoke from the underground fires to the surface. A map attached to a mobile chalkboard showed one hundred and fifty miles of tunnel running from the Cambodian border to what was now Ho Chi Minh City.

Tomy tapped me on the shoulder and whispered. "We should go now."

"But?" I pointed to the line of tourists waiting to enter the tunnel.

Tomy shook his head and looked back in the direction of his truck, away from a line of tourists who were waiting to go inside the tunnel area. "Not here."

"Why? I thought you wanted to show me the tunnels?"

"You see tunnels, but not here. This is for tourists. I show you a better place. Not so many people. We go further inside and not have to wait in line. You see. Much better."

I didn't like the idea of going deeper into the jungle. My stomach knotted as I tried to think of a way to get out of going, but already Tomy was leading the way back to the truck.

"You coming?" Tomy reached for my hand and pulled me along.

So this was how Tomy and Sam planned to get rid of me. They were going to bury me in some pit in the middle of the jungle where I would never be found again. I glanced back at the line of tourists. It was hot, and the line was moving slowly. I slipped my backpack over my shoulder and patted my pants pocket where I had hidden the Saudi diamond. I could use the diamond to negotiate my freedom. If that didn't work, Tomy and Sam were small men, and I had my stiletto hair clip in my hair. If I needed to, I could protect myself.

When we got back to the truck, Sam opened the passenger door and looked up at the sky. "Hurry. It'll be dark soon, and rain is coming. We need to go now."

Sam hopped into the bed of the truck, while Tomy waited for me to get in and then slammed my door shut. I put my backpack on the seat between us and clung to the grab strap above my shoulder. Tomy started the truck, and the first thing I noticed as we headed out of the parking lot was that we were going in the opposite direction we had entered.

"We're not going back the way we came?"

"No. This is shortcut to other tunnel entrance."

If this were a shortcut, Tomy looked worried. Dark clouds had started to form in the sky above us, and Tomy's hands tightened on the wheel. His eyes darted anxiously behind us. He mumbled something in Vietnamese, and Sam answered, then tapped the palm of his hand on top of the cab, indicating we should hurry.

"Everything okay?" I asked. "It looks like it's going to rain. Perhaps we should go back to the city."

"No. It'll be fine." But the strained look on Tomy's face told me differently.

"You sure?" I would have welcomed any excuse not to go further into the jungle with two men who I feared might have been assigned to make sure I disappeared. "Maybe we could come another. I'm okay if we don't see the tunnels. I saw enough."

"No. Trust me. I know this area. I helped to clear it of landmines after the war. A little rain is no problem. You see inside tunnels. It'll be fine. I promise."

Mines? I hadn't thought about landmines, but they could be anywhere outside the city. If we wandered deeper into the jungle and I stepped on a mine, Tomy's mission would be accomplished. No one would ever know what happened. Tomy sped up, and I clung to the grab strap, my knuckles white as the truck bumped along the trail.

Suddenly, a loud thunderclap shook the ground. For a second, I thought we had hit a land mine. Instead, it was a heavy downpour. Rain, thick, grey sheets poured down on top of us and, within minutes, turned the jungle floor into muddy puddles. Tomy's windowless truck did nothing to shield us from the rain. Sam yelled for Tomy to stop the truck, grabbed a tarp from the truck bed, and, soaking wet, jumped into the cab next to me and covered the open back window with the tarp to keep the rain out.

"You okay?" I hugged my backpack to my chest.

Sam nodded. "Yeah, but we turn around. We get stuck out here, Tomy, we'll lose the truck."

"That sounds like a good idea to me." I glanced over at Tomy. "Maybe we can try again tomorrow?"

"Good idea." Tomy struggled to turn the truck around. Little rivers had begun to trickle in the ruts of the Peugeot's tire tracks, and we slipped and slid, splashing through muddy puddles until we rejoined the highway.

On the drive back to the city, I wondered if it was the monsoons that had made Tomy and Sam change their plans not to go on to show me the *other* tunnel. Maybe they were just two concerned local guides afraid of losing their truck in the rain. Whoever they were, I knew they had been tunnel rats during the war, working with our GIs to help navigate the weaponized maze beneath Vietnam's jungles. I had heard conflicting stories about those who had worked as guides. Most were war heroes who helped our troops, and a few, whose loyalties were compromised by the VC, had set our troops up and led them into small villages in the jungles where they were massacred, like the scene I had just seen outside of Ben Dinh tunnel. At the end of the war, hundreds of Vietnamese military and diplomatic officers who had been helpful to our cause were airlifted from the top of the American Embassy. The question was whether Tomy and Sam had chosen not to escape and later been captured by the VC, as they had said, or if they had been spies for the VC all along and were in bed with their communist minders today?

Chapter Twelve

A block from the hotel, the rain got heavier, the streets were flooded, and traffic had come to a standstill. Rain pelted in through the doors where the windows should have been. Tomy took the plastic tarp Sam had draped over the open back window and handed it to me.

"Here. Take this. The Majestic is just around the corner. We can pick you up again tomorrow if you like. There is more we can show you."

"I'll call." But even as I said it, I knew I wouldn't. Tomy's explanation of his wartime role didn't clarify whether he and Sam had been aligned with the VC or if they might still be loyal to Vietnam's Communist Party today. Not until I knew who Tomy and Sam worked for would I put myself in a situation where we were alone again.

Holding the tarp over my head, I dodged puddles as best I could and hurried in the direction of the hotel. I was almost at the front door when I felt my cell phone buzz from inside my backpack. Hoping it wasn't Crockett and that it might be Sophie calling with good news. I ducked under the sidewalk overhang and reached into my backpack for my phone. Hopefully, she was calling to tell me Crockett and his team—whoever they were—had found the shooter, and my role as an undercover courier was no longer needed.

But it wasn't Sophie. And it wasn't Crockett calling to check up on me.

"Ms. Lawson? My name is Mr. Le." The caller's English, despite his thick Vietnamese accent, was perfect. Too perfect. "I believe you're looking for your credit card?"

I knew, despite the caller referring to himself as Mr. Le, that he wasn't using his real name, and the excuse of a lost credit card was one that both the caller and I knew was a lie. Other than telling Tomy I had lost my card so he would take me back to Nguyen's shop, there were only two people who knew there was no lost credit card. Both of them had my cell number and knew where I was staying. One was Ahn, and he was dead. The other was the shoeshine boy.

"I'm sorry, who did you say you were again?"

"Mr. Le. I work for Vietcombank."

I played along.

"You found my credit card?"

"We did." Le explained that someone had turned in my credit card and was able to get my cell phone number from the credit card company, so he might call and arrange to return the card to me in person. "It's unfortunate when tourists lose a credit card. It can ruin your holiday. How about we meet, so I can return it to you?"

Based on Mr. Le's erroneous claim that he had my credit card, I was certain that the man I was talking to had to be the shoeshine boy, and that he had made contact with Ahn, and likely knew why I wanted to meet with him.

"Perfect. I'm at the Majestic. If you like, I could meet you in the lobby in a few minutes." If Crockett was right and the police had released the shoeshine boy because they didn't have enough on him to arrest him for Ahn's murder, then a public place felt like a safe bet.

"No. Not now. It's too late. But tomorrow. There's a Vietcombank a block from your hotel. Meet me there. Nine o'clock good for you?"

"Nine o'clock's perfect." I thanked Mr. Le and hung up. There was only one reason why Mr. Le wanted to meet with me. I had the Saudi Diamond; he wanted it, and I knew Mr. Le had to be the shoeshine boy. *Checkmate.* I smiled to myself, folded the wet tarp over my arm, and approached the Majestic's front doors.

Despite my very wet and bedraggled look, the doorman at the Majestic Hotel recognized me.

"Welcome back, Ms. Lawson. Please, come in." The doorman opened the door and took the wet tarp from my arm. "Mr. Crockett asked me to be on the lookout for you. He wanted me to apologize. He's been detained and can't join you for drinks tonight. However, he's left a nice bottle of wine for you." The doorman nodded to the bar.

Of course, he did. Anything to keep up appearances.

Begrudgingly, I wandered over to the bar where Crockett had arranged for a bottle of red wine and a dozen red roses to be placed in front of the stool where he usually sat. I picked up the card.

Legs,

Sorry to miss tonight. Enjoy the wine. I'll make it up to you tomorrow.

I promise,

Davy

I put the card down on the counter, slipped the bottle beneath my arm, and started back across the lobby.

"Aren't you forgetting something?"

I stopped and turned around.

"The flowers?" The barkeep gave me a knowing wink, picked up the roses, and held them out to me. "You've made quite an impression."

I bit my tongue, walked back to the bar, smiled, and took the flowers. Then headed for the elevator. *Damnit. If Crockett was going to try to romanticize our relationship for his benefit, I was going to have to go along. But on my terms. Not his.*

* * *

By the time I got back to my room, I was starving. I hadn't eaten all day. I tossed the flowers Crockett had left for me at the bar in the trash, put the wine bottle on the dresser, and ordered room service. Crockett and his plan to use me as his cover to get close to the Russians was the last thing I wanted to think about. I had a plan of my own in mind, and if I was going to meet Mr. Le in the morning, I saw no reason why I should include Crockett in any of it. Le had made contact with me, not Crockett. And Crockett had made it very clear that when it came to the Saudi Diamond, I was on my own. He wanted nothing to do with it. He had even accused me of stealing it. As far as Crockett was concerned, I had made a stupid mistake, and he wasn't about to help me.

I opened the bottle of wine Crockett had left for me and poured myself a glass. Crockett was committed to finding the kids, and I had no doubt, he would use me until I was no longer necessary, and then kick me aside. But if I could short-circuit the operation and bypass Crockett altogether, get the envelope Nguyen was supposed to give me, or better yet, the location of where the kids were hidden, our rescue operation would be back on track. The Saudis would be off my back, and I could finish up my travel feature for Sophie without any concern of being caught in anyone's crosshairs.

The problem was the shoeshine boy. He didn't work inside the shop, and I had no idea how much he knew. But it seemed logical since the boy had offered to carry a message to Ahn that the two men were friends. But how close? Had Ahn shared with the boy that he had given me the diamond? Had the boy gone to meet with Ahn, and an argument ensued, and the boy murdered Ahn? I dismissed the thought. Crockett was probably right. The police questioned him and let him go because he was a nobody, and locals don't volunteer information that might get them into trouble. Which made me wonder, if the shoeshine boy hadn't murdered Ahn, might it have been the Saudi assassin? Had the shooter meant to shoot Ahn when he shot Nguyen, and when he saw me, panicked and left? And if so, come back to finish the job?

My mind was full of questions. How close were Ahn and the shoeshine boy? They appeared to be around the same age, in their early to mid-twenties, and were similar in height and build. Other than the way they dressed, there was little discernible difference. Ahn had been dressed as a shopkeeper's assistant, wearing a short-sleeved cotton shirt and Western-style pants, whereas the shoeshine boy was dressed in shorts, a T-shirt, and sandals. But the fact that the boy knew Ahn and worked outside Nguyen's shop made me think their relationship might have been more than a casual acquaintance. Could the boy be part of Ahn's scam to fence the diamond? Did either Ahn or the boy know about Nguyen's involvement with trafficking minors? Did the boy have access to Nguyen's shop? Was I walking into a trap?

Before I knew how much time had passed, I heard a knock on the door.

Room service entered with my dinner, rolled a table into the room, and placed it in front of the window. A fancy silver-domed cloche covered my meal. The attendant asked if I wanted the blinds open or closed. I said open and sat down at the table. He opened the blinds, took off the domed cloche covering my food, placed it on the table, then politely excused himself.

Alone in the room, I stared out at the city lights. I had ordered the hotel's specialty, a Pho soup made with rice noodles, thin slices of chicken with mushrooms, and bean sprouts. The savory scent made my mouth water. I poured myself a second glass of wine, took a sip, and watched the raindrops as they spattered on the window. Tomorrow, I would meet with Mr. Le, a man who had something to trade, whom I was convinced Ahn had told about the Saudi Diamond and knew I had it. And, if I was correct, Mr. Le, aka the shoeshine boy, knew more about Ahn and very possibly what was going on inside Nguyen's shop than either Crockett or the Russians suspected. If all went well, I'd use the Saudi Diamond to convince him to sneak back inside Nguyen's shop to search for the envelope Nguyen was going to give me. Once the boy found the envelope and gave it to me, I would happily give the Saudi Diamond to him and be rid of it. I didn't want it. I hadn't intended to take it in the first place, and as far as I was concerned, it was bad luck.

Chapter Thirteen

I woke up before sunrise the next morning and decided it would be a good idea to go for a run. I wanted to locate the bank where I planned to meet Mr. Le and familiarize myself with side streets in case I was followed and needed to escape. The skies were still grey, the rain was little more than a drizzle, and while the streets looked puddly-wet, they were nothing I couldn't navigate. I dressed quickly, wrapped my corseted money belt around my waist, pulled on a t-shirt and a pair of running shorts, hid the Saudi Diamond inside a slim interior pocket, and then slipped on my tennis shoes. As I left the room, I grabbed my cell phone and stuffed it along with my room key into my fanny pack.

Outside, the heavy rains had caused flooding, and I had to pick my way between puddles as the wind began to kick up. I was five minutes from the hotel, almost to the bank, and within sight of Vietcombank's ATM when my cell phone rang. I stopped to take the call.

"Ms. Lawson." I knew from the accent it was Mr. Le.

"Yes?"

"I need to reschedule our appointment. The storm has made it impossible for me to come into the city today. Unfortunately, I took your card with me when I left the bank yesterday. I'm so sorry. But if we can make it tomorrow, the rain should clear up by then, and everything should be fine. Same time? Same place?"

What choice did I have?

"Everything okay?"

"Yes, it's fine. The summer monsoons can surprise you, but it's nothing we're not used to. I'll see you tomorrow."

* * *

By the time I got back to the hotel, what had started as a gentle drizzle had turned into a torrential downpour, complete with thunder and lightning that shook the streets and lit the skies. While I did my best to dodge puddles as I ran back to the hotel, I was soaking wet when I arrived. My hair matted to my head, my clothes drenched and sticking to my body. The doorman handed me a towel.

"Well, look who showed up." Standing just inside the lobby doors with his cowboy hat in his hand was Crockett.

"Get out of my way." I gave him my best don't-mess-with-me look and tried to step around him.

Crockett stepped in front of me. "Sorry, I can't do that."

"What are you doing here?"

"Oh, come on, Legs. Ya still mad about last night?" Crockett put his hand under my chin and raised my face to his. "Give me a break, I came to apologize and take you to breakfast."

I slapped his hand away from my face and started to move away. "I don't eat breakfast."

Crockett grabbed my arm. "Well, you do now." Then, pulling me close to him, he whispered. "We need to talk. Go upstairs. Get yourself all prettied up, and I'll meet you in the restaurant. And hurry it up. I'm hungry."

* * *

Crockett was seated in Catinat Lounge by the time I got downstairs. He had ordered an American Breakfast, had wolfed half of it down, and mopped what remained of runny eggs and bits of bacon on his plate with a piece of toast. He looked up at me, licked his fingers, then wiped his mouth with the back of his hand.

"Try the buffet. Got everything you need. Good Asian spread, too. As long as you don't mind the same food mornin', noon, and night."

"I'll be fine with coffee and a croissant, thank you. I don't need anything more." I sat down, poured myself a cup of coffee from a carafe on the table, and took a patisserie from the basket. "So, why are you here?"

Crockett put his elbows on the table and reached across for my hand. "You and I need to go on a date tonight."

I tried to pull my hand away, but he held it firmly between his hands and whispered. "Smile, people are watching. We need to make this look convincing." Then, with a forced smile, he added, "We're friends. Remember?"

I offered him a polite, albeit insincere, smile and placed my hands on my lap. There were many aspects of my life that I could control. Unfortunately, selecting my handler was not one of them.

"And where exactly do you plan on taking me?"

"A place called the Water Puppet Theater. It's a kids' show, but a lot of tourists go there as well. I received a tip last night from a friend of mine, Eddie Charles. You had drinks with her at the Red Poets' meeting."

"Friends, huh? Strange she didn't mention you two were friends."

"Eddie's a client. Has been for some time now."

"Really? A client?" I took a sip of my coffee. If Crockett had a client list, I suspected it wasn't just a list of those he had sold insurance to, but a working list of contacts he trusted to mine information for him in the field, and I wanted to know who was on it. If both Tomy and Sam were on Crockett's list, that might explain how we had come to meet. As for Eddie, my impression was that she definitely had worked undercover at some point and might even have been a double agent.

"I told you, I sell insurance. I'm a broker." Crockett stood up and took his cowboy hat from the back of the chair. "And this evening's important. So, get yourself all dressed up. I need to get eyes on some people without being obvious. Eddie will join us. Meet us at the bar. Six o'clock."

"You think you're getting close?"

Crockett shrugged. "Maybe."

"You're a drunk, Crockett."

"I may be. But I'm the drunk in charge. And I need you with me tonight."

I didn't bother to stand. Crockett had made it very clear I was here only as long as I was of use to him. Turn him down, and I had no doubt, he would tell the Saudis I had stolen the diamond from Ahn, and I'd be on the next plane to Saudi Arabia. Either that or Crockett would arrange to have me flown home with orders for the FBI to never use me again. I didn't want to lose my head, and I couldn't afford to lose this job. If Crockett needed me to play kissy-face and pretend to be his girlfriend, I could handle that. But the Saudi Diamond? That was my ace in the hole. And if tonight's little outing didn't turn out as expected, I still had my meeting with Mr. Le tomorrow.

I raised my index finger. "I will be there."

Chapter Fourteen

The minute I entered the lobby and saw Crockett and Eddie sitting at the bar beneath the amber lights of the chandelier, I knew I was about to enter a deeper, darker world of espionage than I had ever been. In a world where nothing was as it seemed, in a country riddled with hidden tunnels and gleaming high rises, I was about to play a role where everyone was being watched, and people were never who they pretended to be. Frustrated as I was with Crockett, the idea was seductive, and the risk of never knowing if the next step I took might bring me closer to our target or expose me, thrilled me.

Crockett acknowledged me with a wink as I approached the bar. I smiled confidently. Due to the rain and the concern that one of my communist minders, some Russian thug, or even worse, some Saudi assassin, might be following me, I had decided it would be best not to leave the hotel. I spent the afternoon taking advantage of the Majestic's luxury spa and visited a small boutique next to the lobby, where I picked up a long, red, silky tunic.

Tall and tan, and with my dark hair loose about my shoulders, heads turned as I slowly sashayed across the room. Crockett was pleased. I looked exactly like he wanted me to. I had prettied up. I was dressed and ready for an evening out and had given careful consideration to what to wear. Beneath my long, slit-to-the-thigh red dress—that even had me looking twice in the mirror—I had fastened my corseted moneybelt. On top of my dress, I belted a long floral scarf to help camouflage my slightly thicker middle. Although from the look on Crocket's face, it wasn't my middle he noticed. Nor was he aware I had hidden the Saudi Diamond securely in my shoe, or that inside the small bag I carried was my camera, phone, and—because I didn't trust Crockett or going out without some protection—my stiletto hairclip.

"You clean up nicely, Legs." Crockett stood up, leaned in to kiss me on the cheek, and offered me his stool.

I dodged his kiss and settled myself on the barstool next to Eddie.

"Can I get you a glass of wine?" Crockett raised his hand and signaled the bartender. "Glass of chardonnay for the lady, and another round for my friend and me." Then, to me, he asked. "Chardonnay, right?"

"If we're not in a rush, why not?"

Eddie bumped my shoulder. "It's still early. We have time, and there are a few things you should know before we leave to go to the theater."

The bartender brought our drinks, and Eddie and I turned on our stools to face Crockett, who stood between us. With our backs to the bar and glasses in hand, we huddled together, toasted our drinks, and spoke in whispered tones.

"Did you bring your camera?" Crockett glanced at the bag in my lap.

"I never go anywhere without it."

"Good. Because I'm going to need you to take some candid shots tonight. There are some people we're expecting to show up, and I need to get photos of them for verification."

"Won't that look suspicious?"

"It shouldn't. I'm taking you out, showing you around the city. It ought to be easy enough for you to get some pictures. Anyone following you, or me, for that matter, knows you're a travel journalist on assignment. If they had any questions about our little outing tonight, it'll only help to cement the fact that I'm doing favors, showing you around, and hopin' for a few personal favors in return." Crockett took a sip of his drink and rested his hand on my shoulder.

Much as I didn't like it, I left Crockett's hand on my shoulder, placed mine on top of his, and dug my nails into his hand, a subtle reminder he better not slide his hand down my back.

"And what about her?" I nodded to Eddie.

"What about me?" Eddie shrugged. "We're old friends, expats who meet for drinks now and again. Nobody will think it odd."

I wasn't so sure. Eddie may have convinced Crockett she had his back, but Sophie had warned me about Eddie, and until I knew she wasn't the double agent I suspected she might be, I wasn't about to be so quick to trust her.

* * *

It had stopped raining by the time we left the bar at the Majestic. Crockett called a cab, and as we pulled up outside the Water Puppet Theater, I noticed the outdoor patio entrance. It had been elaborately decorated with red lanterns and little white lights. Cast members with their puppets on long poles stood inside the courtyard, doing a kind of mini-performance to entertain those waiting for the show to start.

While we waited on the patio, I shot several pictures of the performers with their puppets. Crockett scanned the crowd, then hustled Eddie and me toward the door. A theater attendant showed us our seats and, noticing the camera around my neck, pointed to a sign on the wall indicating no pictures were allowed. I glanced over at Crockett and shoved my camera back into my bag.

"Don't worry. The night's young." Crockett took my hand and held it, and as he did, his grip grew tighter. I started to pull my hand away, then realized Crockett was signaling me.

To our left, an usher escorted three pale-faced, Slavic-looking men with three young Asian girls to a row of seats directly ahead of us. The men were obviously in no way related to the girls. The girls were too young to be escorts and dressed erotically, in tiny tank tops and short skirts that barely covered the tops of their legs. Two of the men I recognized had been at the bar at the Rex Hotel, where I had gone for the meeting of the Red Poets Society.

Crockett leaned over and whispered in my ear. "Enjoy the show."

The house lights dimmed, and the red velvet curtains opened to reveal a shallow pool with puppets that appeared to float on the water. The crowd applauded, and the show began, accompanied by the sound of Vietnamese music. Without any knowledge of the language, it was easy to understand that this was a tale of courage, respect, and resilience. A classic Vietnamese folktale, like I had read in the book the bookseller had given me.

When the first half of the play concluded, the drapes came down and then went up again with the house lights to reveal the puppeteers who sat offstage in waist-deep water and moved their wooden puppets around on long bamboo poles beneath the surface. A small orchestra sat offstage on either side of the proscenium and played traditional Vietnamese music.

The crowd began to rise from their seats, but Crockett put his hand on my knee and signaled me to wait until the Russians and their young escorts started up the aisle. We followed the group outside, where several small carts had been set up for drinks and candy. Two of the Russians moved to the far side of the patio, one picked up his phone, and the other lit a cigarette. The third man stopped at one of the refreshment stands and bought a small bag of candy for the girls, then led them to an area close to where his cohorts stood, while he maintained watch.

Crockett took a pack of cigarettes from inside his shirt pocket and stood in front of me. With his back to the Russians, I could see them over his shoulder without being obvious. They were maybe fifteen feet away, far enough so that they couldn't hear us. But I didn't need to hear them to understand what was going on.

"You getting a good look?" Crockett cupped his hand to light his cigarette.

"Yeah."

"The big guy, the one talking on his cell phone, his name is Boris Mikhailov, and from the look on his face, whoever he's talking to has made him very happy."

My eyes tracked quickly from Crockett to Boris. The Russian pressed the phone tightly to his ear with his short, stubby fingers as he walked back and forth across the patio, looking up at the sky with a broad smile on his face.

"The other two, the skinny one, his name is Dimitry Andreeva, and the bald guy next to him that gave the candy to the girls, his name is Luka Nikikov."

Eddie grabbed Crockett's hand, took a cigarette from the pack, put it in her mouth, and mumbled, "She doesn't need their history, Davy. She's a reporter.

She can see for herself who these people are and what they're doing. You don't need to spell it out."

I watched the girls over the glow of Crockett's lighter. Two of the girls were barely out of puberty, long-legged, overly made up with lots of blue eyeshadow, and dressed in short miniskirts, stiletto heels, and thin, tight-knit tops that revealed their small nipples. The third girl couldn't have been more than four or five and was wearing a red sequined dress that barely covered her little body, exposing a pair of lacy, white ruffled panties beneath. She held hands with one of the older girls and looked like she was afraid to let go.

"This is a Russian operation?"

"Looks that way. There's an influx of Russians here since the fall of the Soviet Union." Crockett took a drag on his cigarette and exhaled from the side of his mouth. "They're all looking for ways to make money, and they don't care who they kill or hurt to do it."

I glanced at the girls. "But if you know that, and these girls are their hostages, why don't you call the police and have them arrested?"

Crockett snorted and looked down at his feet. "You think like a Westerner. You think these girls don't have papers. Passports? Visas? They may be forged, but nobody cares about these kids. They're lost children. The Vietnamese aren't going to care. And the Russians here are their guests. They have a long relationship. They helped the Chinese during the war, and they stayed on after. The only way we're going to break this ring up is to find where they're hiding these kids and catch them in the act."

I reached into my bag for my camera, but Crockett stopped me.

"Wait. I need you to get a picture of Eddie and me together. And make sure you got the Russians in the background."

I stepped back and framed the shot, made sure I had the Russians in the background, then took three or four pictures of Crockett with Eddie, and several more candid shots of the girls on the patio. Satisfied I had gotten the pictures Crockett needed, I slid my camera back into my bag.

"Tell me something. How did you learn Nguyen was connected to the Russians?"

"Let me tell her." Eddie took a final drag on her cigarette, blew a ring of smoke, and dropped the butt on the ground, then smashed it with her shoe. "It wasn't Crockett who found out. It was me. I told you I was here during the war. So was my son."

"You had a son?" Sophie hadn't mentioned that Eddie was married or had children. Another mystery Sophie had either missed or didn't know.

"He was a handsome kid. Barely eighteen when he got drafted. My husband had died the year before, and when Mark was called up, I didn't want to be alone. I did everything I could. I picked up a job as a stringer for *Rolling Stone* so I could stay close. Mark was with the 9th Infantry. Like a lot of GIs, he got involved with a pretty girl. Turned out the girl was Nguyen's sister. Her name was Mai. That's how I got to know the family. Mark was killed in sixty-eight. He had been here less than a year."

"I'm so sorry. That must have been terrible."

"It was, and at the time I thought of going back to the States, but Mai was pregnant, and six months later, she gave birth to my grandson, Bao."

"So, you stayed?"

"I did. And it wasn't easy, especially not for Mai. She had to hide the baby. If the Viet Cong thought any of the villagers had offered aid to the Americans, they would massacre the entire village. Nguyen was fearful they would find Mai and the baby, and refused to let them live at home. One look at the baby, and anyone would know his father was an American. The Vietnamese have a name for these children. They call them bui doi. Children of the Dust."

"What did you do?"

"I did the only thing I could do. I took them in. I had an apartment in Saigon. It was relatively safe for those of us in the city, and I thought I could bring them back to the US. I tried to get papers, but it was impossible. My son was dead. Mark and Mai had never been officially married, and when the war ended, it was chaos. You've seen the newsreels. Saigon fell, and within twenty-four hours, seven thousand people were evacuated. By the time I knew what was happening and got back to my apartment, Mai was gone. My neighbors, who had worked with Americans, had small children and orders to evacuate. There was no time to pack. We all fled. I carried my neighbor's child in my arms while my own grandson was lost. Once I got back to the States, I tried desperately to find some way to learn what had happened, but I never could. It wasn't until ninety-five that Vietnam opened its doors to foreign investors, and Nike set up a shop and hired me to do PR. The first thing I did when I got back was to find Nguyen. By then, he had moved from his family's village to a small rural area close to the Cambodian border. He was twenty years older, married, and had children of his own, and he wanted nothing to do with me. Mai, he said, had died in a labor camp."

"And the baby?"

"Bao was seven years old when the war ended. He and Mai had lived with me up until then. After that, the VC found Mai and sent her to a reeducation camp, and Boa was sent to live in an orphanage. Then, shortly after I came back to Vietnam, Boa found me. He had applied for a job at Nike as an interpreter. He speaks Vietnamese, English, and Russian."

"Russian?"

"There were more than ten thousand Russian troops in Vietnam during the war. Most of them were stationed in the North. They acted as consultants." Eddie made air quotes around the word. "Russia never admitted to having soldiers here, but you didn't have to look far to see how influential they were. Their tanks and anti-aircraft guns were everywhere."

"I remembered reading reports about that."

"Were you a protester?"

"I was studying journalism at the time. We were sent out to cover the protests on campus. I had friends on both sides." I neglected to say anything more. I wasn't about to reveal that the real reason I hadn't protested was that my husband was MIA. Or that, as the wife of an Air Force officer who had been shot down, those of us in the unlucky club had been told to stand down while the government negotiated for what we all hoped would be an end to a hopeless war.

"So, you know something about the war and the Russians' involvement. What you may not know is that after the war, some of the Russians stayed and came south. That's how Boa got mixed up with the Russians. They picked him out of an orphanage. They had to know from just looking at him that his father was American, and when the Russians learned he spoke English, they sent him off to Mother Russia to be educated. He was there until the Soviet Union officially collapsed in ninety-one and then came back. Several years later, he found me, and we were reunited. My grandson was the reason I learned what Nguyen was up to. Boa had tried to reconnect with his mother's family, just like I did. But Nguyen told him not to come around again. That he was bad luck and didn't want him near his wife and daughters. Bao said he knew something was wrong. The Russians in that area were trafficking drugs and children from Thailand and Cambodia. Then, a couple of years ago, we learned that Nguyen had moved his wife and daughters to Ho Chi Minh City to open up a jewelry store. There's only one way that happens."

"You think Nguyen made a deal with the Russians?"

"What else could he do? He has a wife and young girls. It didn't take much to figure out that Nguyen must have told the Russians to leave his wife and young daughters alone, and he'd do whatever they needed him to do if they did."

"And they rewarded him with a jewelry shop in Ho Chi Minh City?"

"Not at first, but after a while, you bet. Nguyen was part of their underground train, responsible for transporting kids across the country without being seen. And after a while, for whatever reason, Nguyen decided he wanted out."

"And you think the Russians shot Nguyen because they discovered he wanted out?"

Crockett exhaled a ring of smoke out the side of his mouth, then dropped his cigarette and crushed it. "We don't know for sure who shot Nguyen. We're not hearing anything from inside the Russian camp, and I'm not speculating. Could have been anyone."

I bit my bottom lip and glanced back at the young girls. "How did you know the kids would be here tonight?"

"We got a tip from one of our field agents."

Eddie's cell phone rang; she glanced at the caller ID, then back to Crockett to let him know the call was expected, and excused herself to take the call.

"So, that's it? We just stand here and watch these kids, knowing what's about to happen to them, and don't do anything?" The idea that Crockett, Eddie, and I were so close to these kids and couldn't do anything enraged me. "There must be something we can do. They walk away, we'll lose them forever."

Crockett put his arm around my shoulder. "Trust me, Legs, we're getting closer, and when we make a move, we'll cut off the head snake and save a lot more lives than just these three."

"So what do we do now?

"Right now? We go back into the theater and enjoy the show. You saw the look on Boris's face when he was on the phone. Something's happened. They're getting ready to rock and roll."

Eddie returned, but her demeanor had changed. She looked worried. Sallow. Her face drained of color. Whatever the call, it wasn't good news.

I touched her shoulder. "Are you okay?"

"I'm fine." She brushed my hand away. "But I think we need to return to our seats. The show's about to begin."

Eddie walked ahead of us into the theater, and we took our seats, but the Russians didn't return, and neither did the girls. The red velvet seats in front of us remained empty, and when the house lights went out, Crockett leaned over and whispered in my ear.

"Stay here with Eddie. Take a cab back to the hotel, and don't talk to anyone. I'll call you in the morning."

"Where are you going?"

Crockett didn't answer. He motioned with the tip of his finger to his lips, then turned, walked quickly up the aisle, and out the door.

Eddie pressed her lips together and looked over at me.

I mouthed, "What's going on?"

Eddie squeezed my arm. "You've been made. We need to leave. Now."

Chapter Fifteen

Outside, Eddie hailed a cab, and as we waited for the car to arrive, she told me I needed to go home, that it wasn't safe for me to be in Vietnam anymore.

"This country will destroy you. Crockett will use you until he doesn't need you anymore, and then he'll toss you out. He won't protect you. Go home."

"But—"

"You've been made, Kat. Go back to the hotel, pack your bags, and leave. Do it tonight. Don't wait. These people don't fool around."

I felt as though Eddie had slapped me in the face. I couldn't believe the words coming out of her mouth. Where was the woman who had been so interested in helping me? Who had given me her business card and wanted to show me around. Whoever or whatever had caused Eddie's sudden change, I wasn't convinced the reason the Russians had left the theater at intermission was because they had recognized me.

"Eddie, what's going on? There's something you're not telling me. What is it?"

"Trust me, Kat. You don't want to risk it. You're a long time dead."

Dead? Was Eddie trying to warn me or threaten me? Whatever it was, I was certain it had nothing to do with her claim that the Russians had made me. Maybe I was wrong, but I had seen no evidence that the Russians had even noticed me. And as uncomfortable as I was with playing Crockett's girlfriend, I didn't catch so much as a sideways glance that would have indicated the Russians were suspicious of me or my relationship with Crockett. I was confident my cover was secure and had nothing to do with the Russians' sudden exit from the theater. A far more likely excuse was the phone call Boris had received while outside on the patio. Even Crockett said he thought the Russian looked as though he had received good news and would soon be on the move. If the Russians were on to me, Crockett would have said something and not sent me back to the hotel, telling me to wait for his call. Instead, he had left me with Eddie, whose sudden change in attitude worried me. But whatever had caused her to want me out of the way, I wasn't about to start taking orders from her

Eddie didn't say another word once we got into the cab, and we drove in silence until the cab pulled up in front of the Majestic Hotel, where I let myself out and slammed the door behind me. I didn't bother to say goodbye, and I wasn't about to go home. Eddie's warning frightened me. I felt a sense of desperation about her. But whatever had caused Eddie's change in attitude, I was certain it had nothing to do with my well-being, and the only way I was going to find out what it was about me that threatened her was to do a little digging into her background.

* * *

The lobby was nearly empty as I entered the hotel, and I went directly from the elevator to my room on the third floor. Despite Sophie telling me not to call, I was anxious to talk to her and took extra precautions to ensure our call wasn't overheard or that I was being watched. Instead of just turning on the shower, I stood on the toilet seat, closed the bathroom vent, and, to make sure I wasn't seen, threw a bath towel over the mirror, then sat down on the edge of the tub. With the bath water running, I dialed Sophie's private line and pressed my cell phone to my ear. Somewhere in New York, some eighty-eight hundred miles away, Sophie's phone was ringing. Seconds felt like minutes as I listened to the hollow cranking sound of the phone's ring.

"Come on, Sophie, pick up. We need to talk."

Finally, after what felt like five eternally long rings, Sophie answered. "Hello?"

"Sophie, it's me, Kat."

"Kat? Why are you calling me? It must be nearly midnight there. You know I can't help you. What's— "

"I'm not calling for your help, Sophie. I'm calling because I have something important to share with you. Did you know Eddie Charles had a son? His name was Mark. He would have been born about the same time Eddie left college. He got drafted and came to Vietnam. Eddie followed him here. He died, and—"

"Slow down, Kat. What's going on? Where did you get all this?"

"Eddie told me."

I could hear the squeak of Sophie's cane-backed chair as she rolled away from her desk, and I pictured her with the phone to her ears and her eyes closed.

"Sophie?"

"Well, that certainly might explain a rumor that was flying around when we were in college and why I never heard from her again."

"Is she an agent?"

"Not for us, she's not. After you called the other night, I did a little digging around. Eddie doesn't work for the FBI. Never has. But she was a journalist, and she might have sources and information she shared with people in the field. She might have been an informant."

"Maybe on both sides?"

"I wouldn't be surprised. For the right amount of money or in the right circumstances, people have been bought. In my experience, Eddie's always been out for herself. I've never trusted her."

"What happened between you and Eddie? Why don't you trust her?"

"It's an old story, and it happened a long time ago. However, if it helps you to know, Eddie and I applied for a study abroad program during our senior year. She won. I lost. The rumor was that she had an affair with the professor in charge of the program. I didn't believe it at the time, but shortly after Eddie got the grant, the professor left his wife and later the university. As for Eddie, I never heard from her again or anything about her until you mentioned her name to me. In hindsight, I always thought she might have complained about me to the program's professor in charge and done what she could to secure the scholarship. I don't suppose she mentioned any of that?"

"Not at all. What she did say was that when Mark got drafted, she got herself a job with *Rolling Stone.* She was here in Vietnam reporting on the war when Mark was killed, and she stayed on until the war ended. It turns out that Mark had a baby with a Vietnamese woman, and Eddie tried to bring that child and Mark's wife back to the US, but couldn't. Eddie went home, continued her search as best she could from abroad, and then, when things opened up here in Vietnam for international business, Nike offered Eddie a job, and she came back."

"What's Crockett say about her?"

"He hasn't said a lot, only that she's a client. To anyone watching, the Russians or the Vietnamese, their relationship would look nothing but professional. Eddie's an expat, and Crockett's her insurance broker. But according to Eddie, she's more than a client. A lot more. She claims she's the one who discovered the Russians were using Nguyen to traffic kids to the States."

"So Eddie's the link to this whole operation. She's why we know about it."

"It looks that way to me. And up until Crockett abruptly left the theater tonight, I thought we were all on the same page."

"And now she wants you out of there."

"She thinks the Russians know who I am, that I've been made."

"And you don't think so?"

"No. But something happened at the theater. I don't know what it was, but suddenly she got nervous and told me I had been made, and that I needed to leave. She even threatened me."

"What exactly did she say?"

"Her exact words were, You're a long time dead."

"Damnit, Kat, you need to get out of there. If Eddie's not working with you, she wants you out of there for a reason, and I've no idea why. Come home. It's not safe. You're in way over your head."

"I'm not leaving Sophie. I can't. You should have seen those kids with the Russians at the theater. There was a little girl, barely three feet tall, maybe four or five years old. She looked frightened. I could see it in her eyes. She was wearing a little red sequined dress. You know what happens to kids like that?"

"Get out of there, Kat. I don't know what's going on with Eddie, but I don't trust the woman, and you shouldn't either. As for Crockett, if he sent you back to the hotel, there's a good reason. Maybe he wants you out of sight, or maybe he doesn't need you anymore. Whatever it is, I don't like it. Come home."

"No."

"It's not your problem, Kat."

"You're wrong, Sophie. It is my problem. I'm making it my problem. And until those kids are free and walk away, I won't leave. This isn't about a paycheck anymore. It's about doing what's right for those kids."

I didn't wait for Sophie to reply. I hung up, ripped the towel off the bathroom mirror, and stared at my reflection in the glass. I couldn't live with myself if I didn't do everything I could to stop the Russians.

Chapter Sixteen

The thought of changing hotels and going somewhere Eddie couldn't find me crossed my mind, but it was pointless. It was too late, and even if I could sneak out without being seen and registered at another hotel, my passport and ID would be recorded and reported to the authorities by noon the next day. But if I stayed put and Eddie couldn't get hold of me, she might think she had frightened me off and that I had flown home without checking out. As for Crockett, he had been very explicit that I return to the hotel and wait for his call. But for what? I was feeling not only out of the loop but very unsettled. Somewhere between Eddie's threat, Crockett's very adamant request that I return to the hotel and stay out of sight, and my meeting with Mr. Le the following morning, I was becoming increasingly concerned for my safety and ever more doubtful about whom I could trust.

If Le knew Ahn had given me the Saudi Diamond, did he want it for himself? Or had the Saudis somehow figured out that I had the diamond and coerced Le to set up a meeting so they could steal it back? I clung to the idea that if Eddie couldn't find me, the Russians weren't sure who I was, and the Saudis didn't know I had the diamond, that I might be able to convince Le to recover the envelope I had been sent to get from Nguyen, and then I could give it to Crockett. All I had to do between now and then was to stay alive.

I returned to the bedroom, took my notepad from my backpack, and made a few notes about tonight's play at the Water Puppet Theater. If anyone were to stop me and go through my belongings, they would find my reporter's pad full of notes and comments about the places I had seen and planned to see, and know that I was nothing more than a travel reporter on assignment, with a notebook full of places to go, things to do, and what to eat. Satisfied I had entered everything I could think of into my journal, I closed my notepad, put it back into my bag, and did my best to close my eyes and try and catch a little sleep.

At 5:45 a.m., I woke up to the sound of a ringing phone. The room was dark, and I was groggy and disoriented. Before going to bed, I had pulled the blackout curtains shut, and when I heard the phone, I reached for the bedside table, then I realized it wasn't the bedside phone ringing at all, but my cell phone. I felt for my backpack at the end of the bed and found my cell inside.

"Hello?"

"Ms. Lawson?"

I recognized the voice as Mr. Le.

"Yes."

"We need to meet now. It's not yet sunup. But we need to get an early start."

"Start?" I pushed my hair from my face. Le hadn't mentioned anything about us going anywhere. "Where are we going?:

"I'll explain when I see you. Meet me in front of Vietcambank, and come alone. It's five minutes from your hotel. How soon can you be there?"

I threw the bedcovers off my legs and got out of bed. "Is this really necessary? Can't we just meet here? In the lobby—"

"No!" Le's voice was firm and quick. "There is something you must see. Please. Hurry."

"Fine. Give me fifteen minutes."

I clicked my phone off and stumbled to the bathroom, splashed cold water on my face, and looked in the mirror. *Showtime.* I had no choice. It was too late to turn back. Crockett was playing by the book. He hadn't tried to rescue the kids when we saw them at the theater and would likely still be going through channels to determine where they were hidden. If he were lucky enough to find them, he would then need to decide how to best execute a rescue. And if the happy look on Boris's face at the theater was any indication, the Russians were close to closing the deal, and there was no time to waste. As for Eddie, if she had any idea what I was about to do, she would have stopped me. I had one chance, and I needed to take it. I threw on a pair of cargo pants and a T-shirt, and, since it was wet outside, put on my tennis shoes and slipped my sandals with the Saudi Diamond hidden in the sole inside my backpack, along with the envelope Sophie had given me. Taking one last look in the mirror, I swept my hair from my face and secured it with the stiletto hairclip, then grabbed my macrame belt and tied it around my waist. Ten minutes later, I was down on the street, map in hand, with my camera around my neck, looking like an early-morning tourist.

* * *

Outside the hotel, it was quiet; the sun had yet to come up, and the street was still damp from last night's rain. I was alone as I approached Vietcombank's ATM. The only other person on the sidewalk was a small Asian man, dressed in a Western-style business suit, wearing dark glasses and a straw fedora that he had pulled low over his brow. Upon seeing me, he dropped the cigarette he had been smoking and put his hands in his pockets.

"Mr. Le?"

The man turned his head quickly to the street, then back to me.

"Did you come alone?"

"Yes," I said. Taking the initiative, I stepped closer. "And I believe we both know that I have something you've been looking for."

Le glanced nervously back at the curb, then nodded. "Yes, I think you do. But we mustn't talk here. Come. Follow me."

I had no idea where Le was taking me, but I followed him to the street where he had parked a motorcycle.

"Get on. We can talk on the bike."

I threw my backpack over my shoulder and settled myself on the back of the bike. Le patted my leg as he started the engine, then darted out into the street and through the city, skirting thoroughfares in choice of back alleys, and along a narrow road that paralleled the Đồng Nai River. Fifteen minutes later, with the city behind us, Le slowed the bike, turned onto what was no more than a footpath, and headed down to a small embankment along the river.

I clung to the side of the seat. "Where are we going?"

"You see."

What I saw were thatched-covered houseboats sitting low in the water, crammed one next to the other like weeds wasted along the riverbank.

"You live here?" I stared at the boats. Children dressed in short pants and mothers with babies clinging to their breasts stared back.

"Come quick." Le stopped the bike, got off, and nodded for me to follow. "We go inside. I explain everything."

A small boy, maybe two-and-a-half years old, dressed in short pants and barefoot, ran toward us. "Ba!Ba!"

Le scooped the boy up in his arms and laughed, then nodded for me to follow him up a thin wooden plank from the riverbank to one of the boats. Onboard a flimsy awning, strung from four bamboo poles, provided shade and a small amount of privacy. A small, very pretty woman, not even five feet tall, bowed as we boarded.

Le nodded to the two child-sized wooden chairs that had been positioned face-to-face beneath the blue tarp. Taking one chair for himself, with the small boy at his side, he waited for me while I settled into the chair opposite him and dropped my backpack at my feet.

"I have a confession to make, Ms. Lawson. My name is not Mr. Le, and I do not work for a bank. But I suspect you already know that."

I crossed my arms and looked him directly in the eye. "You're the shoeshine boy. I tripped over your stand the morning of the shooting. And the only reason you had my number is because I gave it to you to give to Ahn. I knew right after you called me and mentioned the credit card that it had to be you."

"My name is Pham Duc. Pham is my family name. You can call me Duc. I brought you here so we could talk." Duc put his hand on the boy's shoulder, then smiled at the woman. "And this is my son, BiAhn, and my wife, Kiều, Mr. Nguyen's youngest daughter."

I glanced over at Kieu. *Was it safe to talk in front of her?*

Duc saw the concern on my face. "Don't worry. Kiều does not speak English. But, I will tell you, my father-in-law was a very desperate man. He did some very bad things. During the war and afterward, too. But he does them to survive. I believe you know what I'm talking about."

I wasn't about to say anything. If the police had released Duc because they didn't think he had anything to do with shooting Nguyen, they might have been following him because they suspected he knew who had, and I might have walked into a trap.

"I don't know what you're talking about."

"I think you do. But don't worry. We're safe here. Please, let me explain. Nguyen told me someone would come that day. He was expecting you. I was his security, the shoeshine boy outside his shop. No one knew I was his son-in-law. Not even the Russians, who my father-in-law worked for. We were very careful about that. It was my job to protect him."

I raised my hands. "Then you must have seen the man who followed me into the store. He shot Nguyen; you must have seen him."

"I heard shots, and I saw you flee." Duc shrugged. "I saw nothing more."

"Because it would be dangerous if you did."

"Not just for me, but my family as well. If whoever shot Nguyen knew who I was or where Kieu and I lived, they would shoot us, too. It's why we left the city and are in hiding."

"But who were you protecting Nguyen from?"

"Who do you think?"

"My guess is the Russians. You were Nguyen's security guard for a reason. You knew what he was doing, and that he was worried the Russians would find out that he wanted to escape."

"So, you think the shooter was Russian?"

"You don't?"

"I didn't see him. My back was turned when he entered the shop."

"But you called the police—"

"No. I didn't call the police. The police came because Ahn set the alarm off. I didn't talk to the police. It would be very dangerous for me. I didn't want the police to know anything about me. I didn't talk to anyone about what happened in the store that morning until you came back the next day, looking for Ahn, and told me you had lost your credit card. It was only then that I knew you were not who you said you were."

"How did you know that?"

"Because you gave me your business card, and when I called Ahn, he told me you came in and had asked for Nguyen."

I straightened myself in the chair. "What else did he tell you?"

"He said he was showing you a diamond necklace when the shooter came in. He thought you took it, and he was very frightened. It would be very dangerous if anyone were to know you have it."

Duc explained that Ahn's brother was part of a group of Thai officials who, after arresting a Thai house cleaner for stealing jewels from the Saudi royal family, had then switched the stolen jewels for copies and returned them to the Saudi Royal family. However, the Saudis hadn't been fooled, and the situation escalated rapidly, quickly becoming an international incident. The Saudis launched an investigation and sent several agents to Thailand who tracked down and killed three Thai officials, including Ahn's brother, but not before Ahn had managed to smuggle some of the jewels out of the country. It didn't take long before Nguyen realized that Ahn was using the safe inside of his jewelry store to hide some of the jewels and suggested that, for the right price, Ahn could keep some of what he had smuggled out of Thailand, provided he shared in the profits.

"So, let me guess. You came back to the store when you thought I'd be there with Ahn because you wanted the diamond."

"You're very bright, Ms. Lawson. And you're right. I do want the diamond."

I sat back. "You murdered Ahn!"

"No." Duc shook his head. "You did."

"What? Why would you think such a thing?"

"Why wouldn't I?"

My head was spinning. Is that what you told the police when they questioned you after Ahn's murder?"

"Relax. Ms. Lawson. I didn't tell the police anything."

"But I saw you talking to them the morning Ahn was shot. I was on my way to the store when I saw you."

"Of course you did. I called and reported the crime. What else could I do? The door to Nguyen's shop was open. So I went in, and that's when I found Ahn inside the safe. He was dead."

"And that's what you told the police?"

"I left out the part that I thought you had been there earlier. But I had to tell them something. Two murders in as many days were suspicious. They took me to the station and questioned me. I had no reason to kill Ahn, so they let me go. But not before they suggested that if I remembered anything, I give them a call. You know how one's memory comes and goes. Could come back any time."

How had I not seen this coming? Duc was blackmailing me. I either give up the diamond, or Duc would turn me in. I had nobody to blame but myself. I had walked right into a trap. It was the perfect setup. I hadn't killed Ahn, but I had no evidence to prove otherwise. The necklace alone would be plenty of motive, and I would be in a difficult, if not impossible, position to prove my innocence.

I pushed back. I hated what I was about to say, but I needed to do something.

"You're going to have problems convincing the cops I killed Ahn. Because I was with someone the night before. All night long. He was with me the morning Ahn was murdered. His name's Davy Crockett, I'm sure if the police ask, he'll vouch for me."

Duc's jaw dropped. I had surprised him. I didn't wait for him to speak. I continued with my argument. It was my only way out.

"You know what I think? I think you're desperate. You don't know who murdered Nguyen, and you're frightened because if it was the Russians, and they find out that you're Nguyen's son-in-law, they'll come after you next."

"Stop! I don't know what the Russians know. I don't know if they sent an assassin to shoot Nguyen, or if maybe the Saudis sent someone to shoot Ahn and shot Nguyen by mistake. All I know is that things are not safe here for my family. The Russians are bad people. Nguyen had made a deal with an American agent to help him and my family escape to America. Cash.

Passports. But now, with Nguyen dead, I don't trust anyone. My family and I need to move quickly. I can't count on the Americans to help me. They take too long. Too many channels to get approval."

"I get that. It's scary, but—"

"No, you listen to me. You have the Saudi Diamond, I know it. Ahn told me. You give the diamond to me, and I won't tell the police you killed Ahn. If not, things won't go so well for you. I'll tell the police you asked me to call Ahn and set up a meeting, and they'll find the Saudi Diamond on you. Once I tell them what I know, you'll have a hard time proving you didn't murder Ahn or Nguyen."

"And what are you going to do with the diamond? Aren't you worried the Saudis will think you stole it?"

"No. I'll tell the Saudis I knew Ahn had it, and that I found it after Ahn died. All they want is the diamond back. They don't care about Ahn. I'll tell them I want a reward, that I want to leave the country. They'll help me and my family escape. You give me the diamond, and I won't turn you in."

"No." I shook my head. "I want something in exchange."

"What?"

"I came here to give Nguyen an envelope, cash in exchange for information about a Russian sex trafficking ring. Nguyen was supposed to give me an envelope in return with a map showing where the kids were hidden. You get me that envelope, or some proof of where the kids are hidden, and I'll give you the diamond, the cash, and the passports I was prepared to give Nguyen."

"Okay." Duc held his hand out. "You give me Saudi Diamond and cash now, and I'll tell you where the kids are."

I dropped my head and closed my eyes. I wasn't about to give Duc the diamond now. For all I knew, if I did, he would take a knife, slit my throat, and throw my body in the river. Although I didn't think he would murder me in front of his son.

"I'll give you everything I was going to give Nguyen, but not here. I don't have the diamond with me. But I can get it, and I'll give it to you. But you need to take me to where the children are hidden."

Duc nodded. "That's fair. But you must go now. I'll not take you back to the hotel. I don't want to risk being seen. Instead, you can take a boat. It's easy. When you leave here, turn left and walk along the riverbank. You'll come to a clearing. There you'll find several small boats for hire. Take a river tour. Do whatever you like, but don't go back to the city."

"Why not?"

"It's best you stay out of sight. If the Saudis know you have the diamond, they may be looking for you."

"And what about the Russians?"

"Like I told you, I don't know about the Russians. I only know you'll be safer on the river." Doc took a cone-shaped hat from the wall. "Here, wear this. No one will recognize you. I'll call you sometime before the sun sets and tell you where we can meet."

I put the hat on my head.

"And then you'll take me to where the kids are hidden."

"Yes, but remember, my life, the life of my family, and the lives of the children the Russians are trafficking are in your hands. Be careful who you talk to. No one must know what you plan to do. Trust no one. People disappear here. You don't want to be one."

Chapter Seventeen

I left Duc and his family and walked along the Đồng Nai River's muddy riverbanks, past the cramped houseboats covered with tarps and the houses built on stilts, until I came to a clearing. The river was wide and flat, not at all blue but a brownish green, and busy with small boats. No two vessels were alike, either in shape or size. Some boats sat low in the water, laden with fresh fruits and vegetables on their way to market, or piled high with fish nets on their bow as they trolled the river. Others were crowded with families wearing straw, cone-shaped hats, mothers tending to their children, while men in short pants stood at the rear of their small crafts, using long poles to guide their slow journey. Each was a picture of life along the river, an ancient tradition that had remained unchanged for hundreds of years.

After walking several kilometers, I came to a small clearing in the reeds.

"Hey, Lady, you looking for a ride?"

"Tomy?" I pushed the reeds aside. A canoe was moored next to the riverbank. "Is that you?"

Sitting in the middle of a canoe with his hands on either side of the boat was Tomy. He shuffled forward, being careful not to stand, and offered me his hand.

"How did you find me?" I stepped back. Unsure if I was about to be kidnapped, or worse.

"We followed you."

"We? You mean you and Sam?" I looked behind me. "Where is he?"

"Over here."

Sam stepped out from beneath the shadows of a large rambytan tree. In one hand, he held a knife, and for a second, I panicked, thinking he might be about to kill me. Instead, he smiled and held up a red spikey fruit he had picked from the tree. Using the knife to peel the skin from the fruit, he cut what looked like a small white onion in half, threw the seed aside, and handed me a piece.

"Here, take a bite. It's quite good."

I was hesitant. I had heard stories about GIs who had eaten Rosary Peas, innocent-looking little red fruits they found in the jungle that were highly toxic. A single seed could be fatal. I was skeptical. I wasn't sure if the fruit in my hand was poisonous or just something I'd never seen before.

"What is this, a peace offering or my last meal?"

"Don't look so worried. It's harmless." Sam popped the other half of the fruit into his mouth and grinned.

I sniffed the white bulb, then took the smallest bite. It tasted like a green grape. I wiped my mouth. "How did you know I was here?"

Sam pointed to the boat. "I'll let Tomy explain it all to you. But not here. Put your hat on and get in. It's best if we keep moving."

I wasn't about to argue. If Tomy and Sam had followed me, so could the Russians or the Saudis. I stepped forward, and Sam helped me into the canoe, then pushed the boat away from the shore and jumped in. As we settled into the boat, Tomy moved from the bow to the back and, with a long pole, began to gently guide us down the river. I waited to speak until we had reached the middle of the river and were far enough away from land that any listening device couldn't pick up our conversation.

"How long have you been following me? And I'm not just talking about today. When did you first start?"

Tomy was silent, slowly digging the long pole into the river before he answered. "Why do you need to know?"

"Let's just say I'm curious. Has it been since I arrived at the airport or since Nguyen was shot?"

"You ask dangerous questions." Tomy switched the pole to the other side of the canoe. "It's best you not know."

"Really? Because I'm beginning to think you may not be the only one following me. So, what is it? Who do you work for? The Russians? The Vietnamese? The Saudis? Or is it Crockett?" I splashed river water onto my face, then held the back of my hand to my forehead and stared at Tomy. "And while you're at it, just what happened to that Pidgin English the two of you've been speaking. What was it an act?"

Tomy and Sam exchanged a look, then, after what seemed to be an impossibly long time, while the water skimmed beneath the boat and the scene along the shoreline changed from small villages to a thick jungle, Tomy started to speak.

"Davy asked Sam and me to keep watch over you. We didn't want to appear too obvious. So, yeah, the broken English? It was all part of playing a role."

"So, it was no accident then that you rescued me in the traffic circle the morning Nguyen was shot. You were watching me all along, just in case."

Tomy didn't answer, and I began to realize as we drifted with the river's current that we were headed downstream, away from the city.

"Why aren't you taking me back to the Majestic? What's going on?"

"Davy thought it would be best that you not go back to the city today. He wants you to spend time along the river visiting tourist sites. He thinks it's best if you look like you are researching for your travel story. You're safer that way."

"Davy!" I wrapped my arms around my backpack. "Every time I hear that name, there's trouble attached to it. How did you know where I was?"

"Sam saw you leave the hotel this morning, and when he saw you on the back of Duc's bike, he called Davy."

"You know Duc?"

Sam answered. "I didn't know it was Duc when I started to follow you. But when you got to the houseboat, I saw a little boy run up to Duc—that's when I knew. We've been looking for Duc. He's married to Kieu, Nguyen's youngest daughter."

"How do you know them?"

"Tomy and I, we're from a small village south of Saigon. The same small village where Nguyen grew up. Nguyen was from a large family. He was the oldest brother, and like all men back then, he was a soldier and was gone a lot. After the war, he moved away and got married. I didn't see him again until he opened the jewelry store here in Ho Chi Minh City. But we were never close. I didn't like him."

"Why not?"

"I was friends with Nguyen's younger sister, Mai. She was very pretty, and during the war, she had an American boyfriend. His name was Mark. He was a soldier in Davy's unit and a friend of ours."

"Small world," I said.

Tomy picked up the conversation. "It's about to get smaller. Sam and I both knew Mark and Mai. I met Mark because I worked as a guide for Davy. Unfortunately, Mark was killed during the war, and Mai was pregnant. When Nguyen learned about the baby, he threw his sister out of the house. He told her she could never come home again. He was afraid that if anyone told the Viet Cong about the baby, the VC would know Mai was involved with an American, and they'd kill everyone in the village. Things like that happened. There were spies everywhere."

"Wait a minute." I took my hat off and rested the back of my hand against my brow. "I know this story. This is Eddie's story. I've heard it before. Eddie Charles. She was a reporter, and she worked for—"

"*Rolling Stone.* We know her. She was a good reporter."

"And her son Mark was in Crockett's unit?"

"Yes, and after the war, Mai was sent to a re-education camp where she was tortured and died."

"What about Nguyen? Was he sent to a re-education camp?"

"No. It's why Nguyen and I aren't friends. He betrayed his sister to the Russians. And ever since then, Nguyen's done exactly what the Russians wanted him to do."

"Like, look the other way when the Russians trafficked children through his village?"

Sam spoke up. "It wasn't easy back then. At the end of the war, people were hungry and desperate. They had lost everything. Family. Their land. The rice paddies were gone. People were starving. The land that was once lush, green, and fertile had been bombed and burned. It was contaminated with poisons. You couldn't grow anything. Nguyen had three daughters. Two of his older daughters died after the war. He was desperate to protect his family. A lot of people were. He would have done anything."

"And later," Tomy said, "after Nguyen had proved his loyalty to the Russians, they moved him to the city, where his life was much better."

"A reward, no doubt, for a job well done." The thought disgusted me.

"Perhaps, although by then, Nguyen had lost everything. His wife and two oldest daughters. It was just him and his youngest daughter, Kieu. Life was easier for those who moved to the city. There was food and shelter. Nguyen did whatever he could in exchange for getting the Russians to help him."

Tomy interrupted. "And as soon as Nguyen got to the city, he married his daughter off to Duc. Probably to keep her safe."

"And how did Nguyen meet Duc?"

"Duc was friends with Ahn, and Ahn was clerking in the store when the Russians brought in Nguyen."

I dangled my fingers in the water as we drifted along the riverbank. "I'm almost afraid to ask. But what happened to the previous owner?"

"I have no idea. But if he worked for Russians, they may have had a falling out."

I shook the water from my hands. "Okay, so Nguyen moves to Ho Chi Minh City, and his daughter meets the shoeshine boy, and they get married."

"What shoeshine boy?" Both Tomy and Sam asked in unison.

"Duc. He's the shoeshine boy outside of Nguyen's jewelry store."

"Duc was never a shoeshine boy." Sam looked at me, puzzled. "Why would you think that?"

"Because I tripped over his shoe stand after Nguyen was shot, and when I went back to the store to find Ahn. He was there, and—"

"And you thought he was a shoeshine boy." Sam shook his head, and from the surprised expression on his face when he looked at Tomy, I realized neither man knew that Duc had been masquerading as the shoeshine boy outside of Nguyen's store.

"Up until this morning, yeah." I explained how I had received a call from

Mr. Le claiming he had found my credit card, and that I knew right away he was the shoeshine boy. "When he took me to meet with his wife, he told me he was Nguyen's son-in-law, and that he worked as a shoeshine boy so he could watch the shop. If he's not a shoeshine boy, who is he?"

"Duc was Nguyen's bookkeeper. He was friends with Ahn and had worked as an accountant for the previous jeweler. We knew he married Nguyen's daughter, but he disappeared with his wife and son a while back, and we haven't been able to find him."

"Let me get this straight. The Russians take a shine to Nguyen because he's helped them to traffic kids from Southeast Asia around the world, and as a reward, or maybe to further their connection to their overseas clientele, the Russians move Nguyen to the city. They set him up in business after they got rid of the previous jeweler, who, for all you know, is buried somewhere along these riverbanks, and Nguyen marries his daughter off to Duc, who was the previous jeweler's bookkeeper and friends with Ahn."

"That pretty much sums it up." Sam took his hat off and mopped his brow.

"And because Nguyen didn't trust the Russians, he asked Duc to work as a shoeshine boy outside the jewelry store so he could keep watch and come to Nguyen's aid if he needed help." I was talking with my hands as I visualized Duc hiding in plain sight while stooped in front of the shoeshine stand outside of Nguyen's store.

"Nguyen had a right to feel nervous." Tomy continued to stroke the long pole into the river as we drifted further downstream. "The previous jeweler had disappeared, and once Nguyen got to the city, he could see the country was opening up to international business and tourism. It didn't take much for Nguyen to figure that if he sold the Russians out to the Americans, he might be able to negotiate citizenship for himself and his family. All Nguyen had to do was befriend someone who came into his shop, someone he could trust to put the deal together without the Russians noticing."

"And who was that, Tomy? Who did Nguyen talk to help put the deal together?"

"I think it's best if you ask Davy. He wanted me to call after we picked you up. You can ask him."

Tomy took his cell phone from his pants pocket, dialed, then placed the phone next to his ear. The sounds of the river rushing swiftly beneath our boat, along with the wild chatter of monkeys from beneath the jungle's thick canopy, drowned out any chance I had of hearing Crockett's voice. What I could hear was Tomy's response.

"Yes, boss. We have her." Tomy paused, then handed the phone to me. "Davy wants to talk to you."

"I'm sure he does." I took the phone and pressed it to my ear.

"Hey there, Legs, what the hell are you doing? I told you to go back to the hotel and wait for my call. I've got a case that's about to explode, and you've suddenly taken off. Why can't you stay put?"

"Maybe because Eddie threatened me and told me I had to leave. That I shouldn't trust you, or maybe it's because I don't trust you. Does it even matter?"

"Trust?" Crockett snorted. "What are you? A child? Look, Legs, in case you hadn't figured it out yet, trust around here is in short supply. Nobody trusts anybody."

"Which is why I'm taking care of myself, Crockett. You were very clear when I told you about the Saudi Diamond that I was on my own."

"So that's why you set up a meeting with Duc. Because you think he can help you?"

"Correction. I think he can help *us*. And while you're out doing who knows what—using me when you need to and keeping me in the dark when you're not—I see no reason why I shouldn't do what I can. You're running out of time, Crockett. And, like you said, I'm on my own. So, if Duc knows where the kids are, and if I have to use the Saudi Diamond to find them, why shouldn't I?"

"News flash, Legs. You're not in charge of this operation. I am. You don't get to make decisions. You go around trying to be some superhero here, you're going to get yourself killed."

"You think I'm trying to be some hero? You seem to forget, you're the one who told me I've got a target on my back. I'm not going to wait around in some hotel room for you to call so that you can use me as your cover and not tell me what's going on. Not when I've got information that might be useful in finding these kids before this whole thing explodes. So, if you want my help, you need to tell me exactly what's going on."

"Put Tomy back on the phone!"

"Ask me nicely, and I just might do that."

Crockett exhaled. I could feel his fury through the phone. "Woman, you are a piece of work. Look, there's a safe house along the river. Tomy will take you there. There's someone there you can talk to who will help shed light on the operation. But you need to keep it between us, because—"

"Yeah, I know, lives depend on it."

"More than you know. Put Tomy on."

I handed the phone back to Tomy. "Crockett wants to talk to you."

Whatever Crockett said, Tomy's expression changed from concern to surprise. His mouth fell open.

"You sure, boss?" Tomy shook his head, then put his phone back into his pocket.

"I don't know what you said to him, but Davy wants us to take you to the Safe House. But first, I need to make sure no one follows us, and we're going to take a little tour of the river. Make it look like you got up early to do a little sightseeing."

We drifted beneath the river's jungle canopy for another ten minutes, listening to the birds and the monkeys chirping, until the small tributary we followed joined the main river, and life on the river took on a more vibrant flow.

Boats of every shape and size navigated the river. Some were small, like our canoe, while larger junkets had evil-looking eyes painted on their bow. Tomy explained that the owners of these boats believed their vessels had souls, and the eyes helped the boat to see below into the water and protect those on board from the monsters beneath.

"Or to scare the crocodiles off." Sam laughed as he pulled his hand from the water and splashed me. "Used to be you couldn't go into the river without seeing one. These days, they've been hunted to extinction. Or so we like to think."

"But I wouldn't worry." Tomy used his pole like an oar and guided us further toward the center of the river. "Tourists aren't high on their diet."

"Let's hope not." I wrapped my hands tighter around my backpack and slouched deeper into the boat.

"Look," Tomy pointed ahead. "The floating fish market. We should visit. You'll like it. I promise."

The market, a huge floating barge in the center of the river, was like nothing I had ever seen. Small boats packed with fresh fruits and vegetables were tied up to the barge while other vessels backpaddled in the water, waiting for a space to come free so that they could moor alongside and come aboard. Boats and people were everywhere. The smell of fresh fish and the sounds of seagulls in the air. The market was the Grand Central Station of the river.

From the fish market, we floated further downriver, past small villages where women and children played on the shore and washed clothes in the water. I slipped my hat from my head, focused my camera on the riverbanks, and waved to the children. They waved back, some of them running barefoot on the shore and shouting. It all felt innocent enough until Tomy warned me. "Keep your hat back on your head and don't wave back. We don't need to call attention to ourselves. The less we're noticed, the safer we are."

Chapter Eighteen

ad I been rescued, or had I been kidnapped? Tomy's warning that I not wave back to the kids on the shore or call attention to our small canoe worried me. If we were being followed, I could understand Tomy not wanting me to be recognized. But I wasn't certain if I should be thankful that Tomy and Sam had picked me up or concerned that I was being taken further down the river and away from the city to some hidden safe house I knew nothing about. With all Crockett's talk about people not being who they said they were, and both Sophie and Duc warning me not to trust anyone, I was more than a little jumpy. I considered my options. The river was deep and wide, and the current fairly swift. But, while I might be able to swim to shore, I wasn't about to jump into a river where riverboats all had large eyes painted on their bow to ward off evil spirits or the occasional crocodile. It was a ridiculous thought. Even if I were right and I had been kidnapped and could swim to shore, I would be lost in the middle of the jungle. Better to wait to see what this safe house was all about.

Tomy continued to navigate further downriver, leaving behind small villages and large expanses of empty jungle. As we rounded a bend in the river, Tomy dug his long pole deep into the water and steered us toward the shore, thick with jungle vegetation, Jackfruit trees with yellow fruit the size and shape of footballs, rubber trees, and flowering vines of blue and yellow flowers. Ahead of us, a single thatched-roof hut stood on bamboo stilts. Beneath it, a small boat had been tied to one of the supporting bamboo poles.

"That's the safe house?" I expected a safe house to have some type of guarded protection. A speedboat in the river with a couple of plainclothed guards, but this had nothing. The house was nothing more than a bungalow on stilts with a covered balcony.

Tomy leaned back on the pole, slowing our boat's movement in the water, while Sam reached over the bow and paddled toward the house. As we got closer, Sam jumped out of the boat and, grabbing the boat's rope, waded through waist-high water to an open space between the boat moored beneath the house and a small grassy area where he tied the rope around the base of a rubber tree.

"Let's go." Sam held out his hand.

As I stood, the boat rocked, and I stooped to catch my balance. With my backpack slung over my shoulder, I clung to the boat's wooden sides. Sam took my hand and helped me as I leaped from the canoe onto solid ground, then sought refuge beneath the cool shade of the rubber trees.

Tomy tossed the pole into the bottom of the boat, then leaped from the boat onto land. "You wait here with Kat. I'll go find Buddy."

While Sam and I waited in the shadows of the trees, a monkey swung from the balcony above our heads and scampered off into the jungle.

Sam laughed. "Buddy must have kicked Koko out."

"Who's Buddy? I asked.

"The man you're here to see. That was Koko. He's not good with company. Buddy probably told him to get lost."

Moments later, Tomy leaned over the balcony. "You can come up now."

I followed Sam up a wooden staircase to the veranda, where Tomy stood in front of an open door. Sam stepped aside, and Tomy nodded for me to go in. In front of me was a sparsely furnished room with a large open window that faced the river. A straw mat was on the floor in the center of the room, and a small wooden chest of drawers was against a wall. A few dishes and a jug were on top of the dresser. To my right, a second door in the center of the wall was closed.

"Please, come in." A slender young man, I estimated to be in his mid to late twenties, with dark, curly hair, blue eyes, and Asian features, stood in the center of the room. He greeted me with a quick bow and extended his hand.

"Do you know who I am?"

I took his hand. "No. But, I'm Kat—"

"Lawson. Yes, I know who you are. Davy Crockett called me a couple of hours ago and asked me to meet with you."

"Crockett called you?" Crude as conditions were, I didn't expect cell service in such a remote area.

"Don't look so surprised. I don't have much here, but I do get good reception. My name is Nguyen Bao. But my American friends call me Buddy."

Buddy dropped my hand and pointed to the straw mat in the center of the room. Then, speaking to Tomy in Vietnamese, Buddy filled two glasses from the jug on top of the chest and offered one to each of my guides. Sam and Tom then retreated to the balcony. With the jug in hand and two more glasses, Buddy joined me on the floor.

"My grandmother's name is Eddie Charles. Davy tells me you've met, and that's why he wants me to talk with you." Buddy placed the glasses on the mat between us and sat cross-legged with the jug in his hand. "He thought if you knew my story, it would help you to understand how important it is for you to stay out of sight."

Buddy filled both glasses with rice wine, then took a sip from his glass before he continued.

"I was born in a village south of Ho Chi Minh City in January 1968. I don't know the exact date. My mother was in hiding. My father was an American soldier. He died in the war. My mother told me I had his eyes. Her name was Mai. She was Nguyen Tuân's sister. You know this man, he is the jeweler you came to meet. He is also my uncle, although he never accepted me into the family. My mother was banned from her family because she had an American boyfriend, and my uncle feared for his safety should the Viet Cong find out about me or my mother." Buddy put the glass down and sighed heavily.

"I've heard some of this story. I'm sorry, it must have been very difficult for you."

Buddy poured himself a second glass of wine.

"Then you know, it was Eddie who rescued my mother and me and brought us to live with her in what was then Saigon. She hoped to bring us back to the United States, but it couldn't happen. My father had never married my mother. And when the war ended, my mother and I had to flee. But there wasn't time to plan or to pack. Things happened so fast. I was just seven years old. Soldiers came and took my mother. I never saw her again. I was sent to an orphanage for what the Vietnamese call Children of the Dust. Half-breeds. The children of American soldiers were left to survive in a country where no one wanted them or cared if they lived or died. But I was lucky. Because I could speak English and Vietnamese, a Russian soldier found me in an orphanage and sent me to Russia. It wasn't unusual. After the war, other Vietnamese children were sent to Russia for school. It was considered prestigious. And because of my blue eyes and Asian features, the Russians thought I might be useful to them. So I was sent to a very special school, an American school deep inside Russia." Buddy stopped and filled his glass. "Do you understand what I'm saying?"

I shook my head. I had no idea what he was talking about. "An American school in Russia? I don't understand."

"It wasn't just a school. It was a city. With everything American. Soda fountains. Jukeboxes. American-style homes. It was a model American city."

"I've never heard of such a thing."

"You weren't meant to. It was a secret. A spy school, designed by the Russians for spies in training."

I put my glass down and reached for my backpack. I wanted to take notes. Buddy put his hand on top of mine.

"No. No notes. You listen. Later, if you like, you can write whatever story you want, but I won't risk you being caught with notes of what I'm about to tell you.

I pushed my backpack aside and folded my hands in my lap. "Okay. You get sent off to a Russian spy school that looks like an American city. Then what?"

"I got a good education, and until 1988, I thought I was going to be a Soviet spy. I was a good student, and the best students were sent to the United

States to spy. But then the Soviet Union fell apart, and everything was in chaos. No one cared if I lived, or died, or where I went. So, I came back to Vietnam. It was the only home I knew." Buddy took a sip of his wine. "But I didn't come alone. My friend, Alexi, was my teacher, and we came together. And when we returned to Vietnam, we found a small group of Russians who had never left, and they took us in."

"After what you had been through, you must have felt some sense of home with the Russians when you got here. I can understand that."

"But it wasn't good. Times were difficult. People were starving. To make a living, some of the Russians are doing some very bad things. There was a lot of drugs and human trafficking. I wanted nothing to do with these people. I had hoped, if I came back to Vietnam, I would find my mother, and we could start over. But it was too late. I learned she had died in a re-education camp, and that my uncle Nguyen had moved to a small village close to the Cambodian border. He had married and now had daughters of his own. I hated this man. He wanted nothing to do with me, and I wanted to destroy him. So I told the Russians about him. I think they will destroy him for me, kidnap his daughters, and ruin him, and then he will know the pain I know. But Nguyen is a tricky man. He shows the Russians a hiding place deep inside the Cu Chi Tunnel near his home. In exchange for leaving him and his family alone, he joins the Russians and helps them to traffic children. In some way, I feel responsible."

Buddy's eyes had started to tear. I looked down at Buddy's empty glass, then I leaned forward and filled it. "Go on. What happened after you learned what Nguyen was doing?"

"Nothing. There was nothing I could do. Several years went by, and I struggled to make a living. Then, in 1995, I heard Nike was looking for someone to work as a salesman. By now, I speak not only Vietnamese, English, and Russian, but also a little French. So, I applied for a job, and it was then that I found my grandmother. She had returned to Vietnam and was working for Nike, and she had been looking for me as well. For the first time in my life, I am happy, and I feel safe. I moved to Ho Chi Minh City to be with my grandmother, and I introduced her to my friend, Alexi. He comes with me from Russia, and we become like family."

"That had to be a welcome feeling."

"It was. Then one day, I heard Alexi tell my grandmother he had news about my uncle. Alexi tells her he was shopping with a Russian friend. They were looking for jewelry for the friend's wife when they visited Nguyen's jewelry store. Up until then, I didn't know Nguyen was in the city. Alexi said he heard his friend talking with Nguyen about his work with the Russians. Later, Alexi goes back to the store. He tells Nguyen he wants to find something nice for his wife. They talk, and Alexi tells Nguyen he overheard him talking with his friend about his *export* business with the Russians and wants in. He tells my uncle he could get him a much better deal than the Russians are offering."

"Better?"

"At first, Alexi says, Nguyen's not interested. He plays coy. Then Nguyen tells him the only thing better would be if someone could arrange for Nguyen and his family to escape, to leave Vietnam. Alexi tells him he can arrange such a deal. I was furious. I couldn't let that happen."

"Couldn't let what happen, Buddy?"

Buddy looked up at me from the glass he held in both hands. "You have to understand. My uncle ruined my life. He caused my mother's death. I had no one, and he didn't care. I wanted to destroy him. I wanted to—"

"Kill him." I put my glass down. "It was you. You were the one who followed me into the store. You shot Nguyen."

Buddy closed his eyes and nodded.

"Do the Russians know?"

"If the Russians knew I would be dead."

"Where did you get the gun?" I knew it was illegal for civilians to own handguns in Vietnam. Possession could mean up to five years in jail, and murder was punishable by death.

"It was my father's. A sidearm he carried in the field. When he died, his body was sent home, and he was buried at Arlington. But his personal effects, including his gun, were put in a trunk and given to my grandmother. During the war, when she was in the field, she carried it with her. Later, when she returned to Vietnam, she had it sent along with a few furnishings she was allowed to bring. It was illegal to bring a gun into the country, but she had hidden it inside a small secretary's desk. No one ever knew."

I wasn't surprised. Rules may have applied for some, but for Eddie, rules and regulations were for breaking, and for whatever reason, Eddie had figured a way to keep her son's gun.

"Where's the gun now?"

"You want it?" Buddy got up, went to the dresser, opened a drawer, and took out a forty-five. Then walked back across the room and held it by the barrel, the butt beneath my nose. "Here. Take it. I don't ever want to see it again."

I pulled my head back and my hands up. "Hey, I don't think I—"

"You want me to talk? You take the gun. Here, I'll put it in your backpack for you. Get rid of it for me, and we'll talk." Buddy unzipped my backpack and shoved the gun inside, then sat back down across from me. "We good?"

I exhaled. "Alright, but I've got a lot of questions. How did Crockett know you were here? Did you tell him?"

"No. My friend Alexi told him."

"What's Alexi's last name?"

"Petrova. But he's not Russian, he's American. He uses a Russian name because when we lived there, it was the name the Russians gave him."

"Okay, so Alexi. What did he do when you told him you shot your uncle?"

"He said I needed to disappear for a while. That if the Russians had any idea I had shot Nguyen, they'd find me and kill me. Alexi said he knew about the safe house, and he told me I should take my truck and go."

"And then what?"

"Then he called Davy and told him what happened."

I couldn't believe what Buddy was telling me. But if Buddy was correct, the Russians had an American informant working on the inside. Someone who had lived with the Russians and came to Vietnam with the fall of the Soviet Union. Someone the Russians trusted and was feeding Crockett inside information.

"Exactly when did Alexi tell Crockett about the safe house?"

"Yesterday. Before you went to the theater."

"You knew we were going to the theater?"

"Alexi told Davy the Russians were taking three of the girls out, and if Davy wanted to get a good look at them, he should go to the theater to see for himself."

"And Crockett knew this because Alexi works with the Russians."

"Yes, but he doesn't work with them. It's more complicated than that. They use him and he lets them use him."

"So, he's a spy? A double agent?"

"In this part of the world, everyone's a spy. He gets information from people who don't want to share it and gives it to people who need it. And when the Russians need help, Alexi does what he can to help. So, yes, maybe he is a double agent. Or pretends to be."

"Does Eddie know you shot Nguyen?"

"I didn't want her to hear it from Davy. I called her when you were at the theater last night. She filled me in on who you were. Until she told me, I didn't realize anyone else was in the shop. I was so angry. My only thought was that I needed to shoot Nguyen and get out. He didn't deserve freedom. I wanted to kill him. Now I guess, we'll never know where the kids are hidden."

Buddy emptied his glass again and was about to ask for another when my cell phone buzzed. I pulled it from my backpack and glanced at the screen. It was Duc, the call I had been waiting for.

"Maybe not," I said.

Chapter Nineteen

I told Buddy I needed to take the call and went to the balcony. Tomy and Sam had gone down beneath the house and were smoking. Koko had returned and was sitting on a tree branch opposite me, mocking me as I put my phone to my ear.

Duc sounded nervous. "Do you have the diamond and the envelope with the passports and money you were going to give Nguyen?"

"I do. But tell me, why do you need the passports if you're going to give the diamond to the Saudis and seek asylum there?"

"Insurance, Kat. I want the money, the Saudi Diamond, *and* the passports. Just in case."

"As long as you have the envelope Nguyen was supposed to give me, they're yours. Don't worry."

"Good. Meet me at the Saigon Port. From the city, it'll take you about an hour and forty-five minutes to get there. Wait for me outside the Cai Mep Terminal. Seven p.m. And make sure you come alone. If I see anyone with you, I'll call the police and tell them where you are and that I know you stole the Saudi Diamond. Believe me, if the Saudis think you stole the diamond and find it on you, you'll never leave this country alive."

Duc hung up.

I stared back into the face of the monkey. He screeched, and I jumped.

"You okay?" Buddy joined me on the balcony.

"I will be. But I'm going to need the keys to your truck."

"It's not much of a truck, but you're welcome to it." Buddy reached into his pocket and handed me the keys. "I hope you know what you're doing."

Tomy hollered from beneath the balcony. "Everything okay up there?"

"Yeah. But I need to get somewhere. Buddy's given me the keys to his truck, and I'm leaving. You want to drive?"

"Davy's not going to like that." I could hear Tomy coming up the steps. "He was very insistent that you stay put."

I took the gun from inside my backpack and aimed it at Tomy. I needed him to know. I wasn't asking.

"I'm sorry, but staying put is not an option."

Chapter Twenty

"This isn't a good idea, Kat. Davy doesn't want you anywhere where you can be found. It's not safe."

"Oh, yeah? Well, where do you think he is right now? It's five o'clock. My guess is he's at the bar at the Majestic. Maybe he's working. Maybe not. But I'm not waiting around. I've got a lead on where the kids are, and I'm going to act on it. If I'm right, I'll find out where the kids are hidden, and Crockett can take it from there."

Tomy held his hands up and slowly closed the space between us. "Give me the gun, Kat."

"No. I'm serious, Tomy. You take another step, I'll shoot. I'm not giving you the gun." I didn't want to shoot Tomy, but if I had to shoot him in the foot to stop him, I would. "You and Sam want to come with me, fine. If not, I'm taking Buddy's truck, and I'll find my way on my own."

I glanced over my shoulder at Buddy's truck below the railing. Tomy lunged forward and wrested the gun from my hand.

"You're not going to shoot anybody. But if you know where the kids are, Sam and I are in. Where do you need to go?"

"The Saigon Port. I'm supposed to meet Duc in front of the Cai Mep Terminal. He promised to show me where the kids are hidden."

"You trust him?" Tomy stuffed the gun in the back of his pants and nodded to the stairs.

"I don't trust anyone. But I have something he wants, so yeah, I do."

Tomy stopped and put his hand on the railing. "What? The Saudi Diamond?"

"How do you—" I caught myself before I could finish. "Crockett, right? He told you about the diamond."

"It's one of the reasons Davy wanted us to look out for you."

"One of the reasons? What's the other?"

"The Russians. Right now, the Russians have no idea it was Buddy who shot Nguyen. If it were up to Davy, he'd let them think it was. It wouldn't take much to convince them that Buddy shot Nguyen. The coroner's report shows Nguyen was shot with a Colt .45, and the Russians knew there was bad blood between Buddy and Nguyen. The problem is that Crockett can't risk losing Buddy because he owes Eddie, and he won't go down that path."

"Then the heat's on me?"

"Not really. As long as we keep you out of sight, you should be okay. Word on the street is that Ahn shot Nguyen."

"How did that happen?"

"Davy. He put the word out to the Russians that Ahn was stealing from Nguyen, and things got out of hand."

"So now the Russians think it was Ahn who shot Nguyen, and as long as I stay out of sight, I'm fine."

"That's the plan."

"But what about the gun? Where would Ahn get an American gun?"

"Ahn was a thief, Kat. Nobody would believe he didn't have a gun or access to one."

"And who do the Russians think murdered Ahn?"

"The Saudis."

"And if the Russians don't believe that, Crockett thinks they'll suspect me."

"Exactly. Which is why Davy wants you out of sight while he manages the situation."

"Well, he can manage the situation all he wants, but he's not doing a very good job, is he? He didn't know Duc was working as the shoeshine boy outside Nguyen's shop. And Duc's not calling Crockett and asking for his help. He called me. And if we don't find those kids before the Russians load them up on some boat and ship them off to who knows where, we'll never find them. So you either come with me or get out of my way. I'm going to meet with Duc, see the kids, and then I'll tell Crockett where they're hidden, and he can do his job. But until then, I'm not sitting around and waiting for Crockett to tell me what to do."

* * *

Buddy's truck was a battered, doorless three-wheeler made from scrap parts and held together with duct tape. The cab would have been a tight fit for one person, let alone Tomy, Sam, and me together. Nevertheless, we squeezed in like sardines with me in the middle. By three-thirty, we were headed south toward Saigon Port—about as fast as we could have pedaled.

It took us four hours to arrive.

The Cai Mep Terminal, inside the Saigon Port, was a busy commercial hub, and finding parking wasn't easy. We must have circled for twenty minutes before Tomy decided to drop me off while he and Sam looked for a parking space close enough to have eyes on the terminal entrance without being obvious. We had agreed they would stay in the truck and not do anything that might spook Duc, while I would keep my cell phone on so they could monitor my conversation and my location. If all went well, I'd return after having seen the kids. Duc and I'd then exchange envelopes; he'd have the cash, the passports, and the Saudi Diamond, and I'd have the map showing where the kids were hidden. Should anything go wrong, and I need help, Tomy suggested I use a code word. Rickshaw, he said. If I used it, screamed it, or even mumbled it into my cell phone, Tomy and Sam would come running. At least, that was the plan.

But by seven-fifteen, I was beginning to wonder if Duc was a no-show. I had been standing alone in the dark with my backpack, about ready to give up, when I spotted a group of dock workers who looked like they had just finished their shift as they walked in and out from beneath the big terminal lights toward a chain link fence surrounding the lot. I wouldn't have looked twice at the group if one of the men hadn't stopped at a fountain in front of the Cai Mep terminal entrance. He was dressed in long kakhi work pants, hard-soled shoes, and carried a hard hat in his hand. As he bent down to take a drink from the fountain, he turned his head in my direction.

"Duc?" I stepped closer to the fountain.

"Don't come any further," Duc pretended to take a drink, then stood up. "You have the diamond?"

I stood back and scanned the area in front of the terminal. The last dock workers had gone through the gate. We were alone.

"You got the map?"

Duc smiled and pulled an envelope from his pants pocket. "You show me yours, I'll show you mine."

"Let's not waste time. Once I see the kids and you give me Nguyen's envelope with the map inside, I'll give you what you came for."

"Alright. Follow me." Duc nodded in the direction of the shipyard. "The kids are in an old boxcar in the junkyard. There's a guard on duty, but he's due to take a break soon. When he does, we should be close enough for you to climb up to the top of the boxcar and see in. But remember, if I see any trouble—"

"Save it. You don't need to worry. I'm alone."

"We better be." Duc crouched low to the ground, his head and shoulders over his knees, then sprinted into the shipyard.

I waited until I knew Duc was out of earshot, then reached into my pocket for my cell phone. "Did you get that?"

Tomy's voice was hushed. "Got it. Kids in a boxcar in the junkyard. Be careful, Kat. You don't know what you're walking into."

"That's why I'm keeping my phone on. Stand by."

I slipped my cell phone back into my pocket and ducked low to keep my shadow as small as possible. I followed Duc through a maze of shipping containers stacked three to four levels high. Duc was small and spry, and as crouched as I was, I had to work to keep up as he navigated corridors barely wide enough for a bicycle to pass. We finally reached an area of the shipyard that looked abandoned—a dumping ground filled with the remains of bombed-out tanks, old aircraft parts, wheel wells, gurneys—items discarded for scrap metal after the war.

Duc glanced over his shoulder to make sure I was behind him, then crouched behind the remains of what had once been a Russian tank. Ahead of us, an armed guard stood in front of a lone boxcar, smoking a cigarette. Duc signaled, his finger to his lips. *Quiet.* Without daring to breathe, I pressed my back up against the tank while we waited until the guard finished his smoke. Then almost comically, we watched as he stamped out the butt of his cigarette, loosened his belt beneath his big bell, and wandered towards a porta-potty nearby.

"You ready?" Duc leaned back against the tank and took a deep breath. "Let's go."

I trailed behind Duc, avoided the neon lights, and dashed into the shadows toward the freight car. Relieved that we hadn't been seen or set off any alarm, I pushed my body up against the back of the car and pressed my hand against my racing heart.

"You're sure they're inside?" I whispered to Duc. The double doors on either end of the container were bolted shut, and I didn't see any air vents on the side of the car. It would be inhumane to hide anyone inside such a crude, airless container.

"They're here. But if you want to see them, there's a ladder on the backside of the car. Climb up and see for yourself. The air vents are on top. You can look down inside from there. Go ahead, take a look."

I looked back from the shadow where we hid at the end of the boxcar. A bright neon light shone directly on the ladder. "After you. I'm not moving until you do." I didn't trust that Duc wouldn't set me up or that I might be shot as I climbed up the ladder.

"No problem. You just need to be quick." Duc snuck around the end of the trailer, jumped up, and grabbed the bottom rail of the ladder, which was at least a foot above his head, then climbed up to the top of the boxcar. He leaned over the side and waved for me to follow. As quickly as I could, I grabbed the rail above my head and pulled myself up the ladder until my feet could find a rail. Then I scrambled to the top.

"Over here. Come, look." Duc stood above an open vent and pointed down to a light inside.

I stooped down to get a better look and peered inside. Three groups of children, more than I expected, a dozen in all, were huddled in small groups. At the far end of the car were five girls, all in their early teens. They looked as though they might have been drugged and sat stoically, their legs pulled up beneath their chins, their arms wrapped around their legs, and their heads bowed. Across from them, three boys had drawn a chalk rectangle on the floor and played a game with rocks. Further forward, three smaller children, no more than four or five years old, had curled up on a mat, while a fourth child, a girl in a sequined red dress, the same child I had seen at the puppet theater, sat next to them.

"We've got to get them out!" I grabbed Duc's arm and held tight.

"No. That's not what you asked me to do." Duc yanked his arm free, and I grabbed for him again, but this time I tripped as I tried to stand, and he backed away."

"Help me. Please! Duc, don't leave."

Duc shook his head. "That's not going to happen. I told you I'd show you where the kids were. That's all. Now you give me the diamond exactly like you promised, or I'll call the guard."

Duc took hold of my wrist and tried to pull me to my feet. But my defense training kicked in. I don't know who was more surprised. I'm five-ten. Duc was five-five and strong. We struggled. I turned, and with my back to him, elbowed him in the ribs. With my hands free, I wrestled his arm behind his back, secured him with my elbow in a neck lock, then pulled my phone from my pants. "Rickshaw!"

But before either Tomy or Sam could respond to my codeword, I heard voices speaking in English. Duc froze.

"You lied to me!"

"No. No, I didn't."

"Who did you tell?"

"No one!" I got down on all fours and pulled Duc with me, my arm and shoulder on his back. "Get down!"

Coming through the shipyard toward the boxcar were the shadowy figures of a man and a woman, each carrying a flashlight. The woman was small and slim, her grey hair catching the reflection of the low light. The man was taller, about six feet, wore a black baseball cap, and walked with a slight limp. I didn't dare raise my head to get a better view, but I didn't have to. As they got closer, I could hear their voices.

"You're sure no one followed you here?" I recognized the woman's voice instantly. If Eddie were to look up, she'd see me crouched on top of the shipping container. I leaned heavily on top of Duc and strained to hear the man's answer.

"No one knows I'm here. They have no idea I know anything about the kids or what they're doing. But I wanted you to see them. You need to get word to Crockett. The Russians plan to move the kids tomorrow night."

What was it about his voice? It sounded familiar. I raised my head to get a better look. The man took a cigarette from his pocket, lit it with his left hand, and in the glow of the light, I saw his face. A face I thought I'd never see again. A face that for years had haunted me.

Eric? It couldn't be. What was I seeing, a ghost?

"Eric?" I blurted his name aloud. I couldn't help myself.

Eric jerked his head. His eyes searched the yard around the container, but he didn't see me. Instead, in my shock, I had relaxed my grip on Duc, and he scrambled to the side of the boxcar, then jumped and started to run.

I stood up, clutched my cell phone to my mouth, and yelled, "Rickshaw!" Just as I was about to repeat the code word, I saw Tomy and Sam come running.

Tomy stopped and pulled the gun he had taken from me at Buddy's and aimed it at Duc. "Don't move!"

Shots rang. But not from Tomy's gun.

From behind the open door of the porta-potty, the security guard stuffed his shirt into his pants, then took off after Duc, firing off two more shots as he ran.

Duc fell to the ground.

"No!" I clambered down the ladder. Fifty feet ahead of me, Duc lay motionless on the ground.

Tomy grabbed my arm. "We need to get out of here."

I shook him off.

"Not yet! Where's Eddie? Eric!"

I ran toward the rear of the shipping container. My heart was pounding. I was frantic. I could barely catch my breath. And then I saw him. Standing in the shadow of the boxcar, the man I had gone to college with. The man I had married. The man I thought I had buried in an empty coffin all those many years ago stared back at me. The shock on his face stole the air from my lungs.

"Eric?" I didn't know whether I should throw my arms around him or hit him. Eddie stepped between us, and I pushed her away. "What are you doing here?"

"Katy?" Eric closed his eyes. Then opened them again.

"It's me, Eric. What—"

"Eddie, get her out of here. It's not safe. Katy, I'm sorry. This never happened. Go home!"

II

Part Two

My world is upside down!

Chapter Twenty-One

Eric disappeared into the shadows, and within seconds of our meeting, he was gone. So fast, I wondered if I had imagined his presence. Except that Eddie had latched onto my arm and pulled me, and insisted that I follow her. I refused and tried to break away, but Tomy and Sam got in front of me and blocked any chance of my going after Eric. I threw myself at them, flailing my arms, trying to break through their line of resistance.

"Stop it! Let me go! That's Eric. I need to talk to him.' I yelled his name, "Eric!" But I might as well have been screaming into the vast darkness. There was no response.

Eddie grabbed me by the shoulders and slapped me hard across the face. "Shut up! Move! We need to get out of here."

"Come on! Let's go." Tomy grabbed my hand and pulled me away from Eddie. "We don't have time to argue. Follow me."

I stumbled in the dark, tripping over scraps of metal, as Tomy pulled me behind him through the shipyard, dodging the large overhead lights until we reached an unlit area by the fence, with Sam and Eddie following behind us.

Tomy panted. His chest heaving as he pointed to the ground. "Sam, get us out of here." Tomy took my backpack and threw it to the ground, then nodded for me to sit down next to Eddie, while Sam knelt and began digging in the hard soil.

With my back against the fence, I wrapped my arms around my legs and whispered to Eddie. "What's going on?"

"Stay quiet." Tomy put his hand on my shoulder. "We'll talk later. Anyone finds us here, we're dead."

Sam finished digging, reached up next to me for my backpack, and pushed it under the fence. "You next."

Crouching down as low as I could on my knees and elbows, I shimmed beneath the wire fence on my belly. Eddie followed behind me, with Sam and Tomy behind her.

I stood up and brushed the dirt from my pants. From above, I could hear the sound of an advancing helicopter. Tomy took my hand and pulled me to the other side of a dirt road that paralleled the fence we had just crawled under. Silently, we stood in the dark as we watched the helicopter circle overhead, its spotlights sweeping the ground below.

Eddie crowed next to me. "I thought I told you to go home. What the hell are you doing here?"

"What do you mean, what am I doing here? What are you—"

"Listen to me." Eddie pushed my shoulder. "I'm the one asking the questions here. Not you. You're lucky that the security guard didn't shoot you. If he had shot you, it'd be an international incident. As it is, he's going to be busy trying to explain what happened. So why don't you start and tell me why you're here? I'd like to hear it from you first."

"I'm not saying a word. Not until you tell me why you were with Eric."

"Eric, who?" Eddie scrunched her face. "What are you talking about?"

"I'm talking about the man you were with. My husband. Eric. That's who he is, or who he was, anyway."

"Look, Kat. I don't know what's going on with you. Maybe you're having some kind of panic attack, but I don't know anybody named Eric."

"Don't lie to me! I know what I saw, and I saw my husband. He was an F4 pilot. He was stationed at Cam Ranh Airbase. His name was Captain Eric Stewart. He was shot down right before Christmas in 1972 and—"

"Okay. Okay, I get it. You *think* you knew that man. But that man, the man I was with. His name's not Eric Stewart."

"Then just what is it? And don't tell me I'm imagining it. He said my name. You heard him. He called me Katy. Nobody calls me Katy."

"Kat. Listen to yourself. You sound crazy."

"I'm not crazy. He knew my name. He couldn't possibly know my name unless he knew me. I think you've got some explaining to do."

"I think we both do. But not here. Go back to the hotel. Tomy, Sam, take Kat back to the Majestic. And this time, Kat, stay there. I'm going to talk to Crockett. You get some rest. We'll talk in the morning. I promise."

Sophie left us, and I didn't say a word all the way back to the parking lot. When we got to Buddy's truck, Sam opened the door and insisted I take the middle seat. He must have known, given the chance, I would have bolted from the truck, returned to the shipyard, and searched for Eric. I knew Eric had to be hiding there.

I covered my eyes with both hands and tried to remember the look on Eric's face. The shock. The surprise. The horror? It was all there, along with every memory I ever had of the man I fell in love with. The man I thought I knew so well. But who was this handsome stranger? This man, who stared back at me in total disbelief? If he hadn't called me Katy, a name no one but Eric ever used, I might have been convinced he was nothing more than an apparition. A ghost from my past, playing tricks on my mind. But I knew better. I wasn't crazy. I was scared and I was frightened. I had just seen Duc shot down in cold blood. The second man I had seen murdered since I had arrived. But I wasn't nuts. I knew what I had seen, and I wanted answers.

I thought back to my first conversation with Crockett. He said he knew GIs who had gone back to Vietnam after the war, and some who had never left. Men who hid in the jungles until the war was over. I didn't like the way Crockett talked, and I didn't want to hear his stories about GIs who had deserted their posts. I didn't get how any American GI wouldn't want to go home. I knew many wives and families of MIAs, who had hung on to hope, eager to see their men return. I couldn't imagine their emptiness, the betrayal, or the confusion if they thought their loved ones had chosen not to return. I didn't want to think Eric might have been any part of that. But I had to admit, it would have been possible for a young American to pass for a Russian and escape detection after the war. The Russians had been in Vietnam before, during, and after the war, and some had stayed on after the war and made a life here.

I glanced over at Tomy. "Is Duc dead?"

"He wasn't moving. It looked like a clean shot to the head. I'd be surprised if he weren't."

I felt like I was going to be sick and covered my mouth. Duc had been desperate. With Nguyen dead, all of Duc's chances to escape the Russians were gone. He had risked his life and his family to try and buy his freedom, and now he was dead. I felt awful. Desperate people do desperate things, and I was certain Duc had murdered Ahn and had been setting me up to take the fall. And he would have succeeded if Crockett hadn't spotted me approaching the jewelry store the morning of Ahn's death, and taken my arm and waltzed me past Nguyen's shop.

I looked over at Tomy. His eyes focused on the road ahead. "Did you recognize the man with Eddie?"

Tomy didn't answer, but I noticed his hands were tight on the wheel, his eyes glued on the road ahead.

"What about you, Sam? Have you ever seen him before?"

Sam shook his head and looked away.

"You know something. I know it. I'm not crazy. I didn't see a ghost. That man back there? He was my husband. He's alive. His name is Captain Eric Stewart. I saw him. He's not dead."

Tomy glanced over at me. "Kat, I'm sorry. I don't know a Captain Stewart, but I do know you're not crazy."

"Then tell me what's happening, Tomy? I need to know."

"It's possible you saw someone you knew. I'm not saying I agree with you, but during the war, when an American plane was shot down and we saw a parachute, everyone would be on the hunt. If we found the pilot or copilot first, they would reward us for rescuing them. Sometimes with money. Sometimes with jewelry. They carried it in their flight suits to negotiate their safe passage back to their base. But if the Viet Cong picked them up, it was a different story. The POWs the Viet Cong picked up would have been strip-searched and marched through the neighboring villages in cricket cages. There, the locals would taunt them. Spit on them and poke them with pungi sticks. Later, if they weren't killed, they would have been brought to a jungle prison or, in some cases, the Viet Cong would trade their prisoners to Russians in exchange for missiles that the Russians would give to the Chinese to help the Viet Cong in their war effort against the South. And some of those traded to the Soviets? They're here today. They came back when the Soviet Union fell apart."

"You think Eric's a Russian spy?" I couldn't believe the words coming out of my mouth.

"I'm not saying that, Kat. All I'm saying is that during the war, some POWs and MIAs were traded to the Soviets. If they were here today, we wouldn't know who they were or why. They could blend in without anyone knowing."

"Well, I know this much. The man I married, he'd never spy against us. He may have been captured, but if he had any chance at all of coming home, he would, and I'm not leaving until I know what it is."

* * *

It was past midnight by the time I got back to the hotel. I left Tomy and Sam at the curb and went directly to the elevator, anxiously pushed the button to the third floor, but I wasn't going to my room. I had no intention of going back to a room that was bugged. I desperately wanted to talk to Sophie, but I knew I needed a safe room—a place with no listening devices planted inside the walls, where I could speak freely. When the elevator doors opened, I walked quickly past my door and down the hallway to the linen closet. I had seen the maid come in and out of the room with fresh linens, and given the late hour, I hoped I might find it empty and the door open.

I jiggled the lock, and with very little effort, the door swung open. In front of me were stacks of fluffy white towels, sheets, and blankets. I closed the door, ran my hands beneath the piles of linens, and found nothing that resembled a hidden mic or camera. Then, I took a small stool, stood on top, and checked the air vent. Nothing.

It was noon in New York, and I knew Sophie would be eating lunch at her desk like she always did. I clicked the linen room door lock, sat down on the stool, and then dialed Sophie's number. When she picked up, I didn't wait for her to say hello.

"Does the name Eric Stewart mean anything to you?"

"Who?" Sophie paused. My call surprised her. "No. Why are you asking? What's going on?"

"I'm not sure. Maybe it's my fault. I didn't think about it before. It was so long ago, and—"

"Kat, slow down. What are you trying to say?"

"I'm trying to tell you that I got married when I was very young. I was still in college. The man I married was Eric Stewart. He was an Air Force Officer, a pilot. He was sent to Vietnam when I was still in college, and he was shot down on a bombing run over Hanoi in 1972. And he died here. Or so I thought."

"Wait a minute. You never mention anything about Eric Stewart. Why didn't you tell me about him before?"

"Because it never occurred to me. It was years ago, another lifetime. And I'm telling you now because I saw him, Sophie. He's alive, and—"

"Hold on. Are you telling me you were an Air Force wife during the Vietnam War? How is it I didn't know that?"

"Because there's no record. I was in college, I had just turned twenty-one, and things happened fast. Eric received orders on a Friday to go to Nam. By Saturday, we were in Vegas, and by Sunday, we were married. Monday morning, Eric was on his way to Cam Ranh Air Base. All I had when Eric left was a Vegas wedding certificate and a promise we'd do it up fancy with a big official wedding with all our friends and family when he came home on leave in six months. But he didn't come home."

"And you never filed the paperwork?"

"There wasn't enough time. In those days, if you got married in Vegas, both the bride and groom had to walk the license down to City Hall. By the time Monday morning came around, Eric was gone. He never even had time to file all the dependent forms necessary that would have given me a military ID. He used to say, 'If the Air Force wanted him to have a wife, they would have issued him one.' He planned to do what he could from his base in Vietnam, but we weren't worried. I told him to wait. I had a part-time job, and we had been sharing a cozy little apartment off base, near the university."

"And you never changed your name?"

"I was halfway through my senior year. My transcripts were all in my maiden name, and then—" I started to choke up. "Eric was shot down."

"I can't believe you never said anything about this, Kat. Do you realize—"

"Stop it. Don't lecture me. It was a long time ago. I had closed the door. I didn't think it would be a problem. I moved on."

"Well, you sure fooled me. None of this came up in our initial background check when we cleared you. I know the military is famous for losing files. They lost millions of military personnel files in a fire back in 1973 in Missouri. But there has to be some record. You must have gotten his paychecks or something."

"No. I didn't. Eric's checks were in his name and deposited directly into his account. And just like everything else, there wasn't time to go to the bank and fill out a bunch of forms. Wives weren't given access unless their husbands had authorized them to access the account. It wasn't easy for wives when their husbands were overseas. They had to leave Base Housing, where they had been stationed, and either go home or find an apartment close enough to the base so they could visit the commissary and doctors. Most of the Air Force wives I knew were young like me. We leaned on each other for support. We had to. A woman couldn't even get a credit card in her name without her husband or father cosigning for her."

"So you're telling me, you lived on this little part-time job of yours? That you never had a joint account or something that would have shown you were a military dependent?"

"Eric gave me a little cash before he left. He wanted to ensure I was okay while he was away, and until we could complete all the necessary forms that would have identified me as a military dependent and cosigner on his account. But I wasn't worried. I figured that whatever we could save, we could put toward a wedding. I was fine on my own, and when Eric was shot down, I finished college and got a good job. Whatever money was in Eric's account, I didn't want it. Eric's folks would have been his beneficiaries. He was their only son, and they weren't doing well financially. I always assumed whatever money was in his account when the DOD declared him dead belonged to them."

"That was nice of you."

"It felt like the right thing to do. So, in answer to your question, the only official record I had of our marriage was a Vegas marriage license. As for the Air Force, I never went back to the base in Phoenix. It was too painful. I didn't have a military ID. I didn't want any of the money the government was offering. It felt like blood money. And the paperwork? Eric's father handled it all. For me, it was too much of a reminder. A year after the settlement, Eric's father died, and his mother passed away five years ago. I lost track of his folks, and I didn't want to look back. I couldn't. The world had moved on, and I needed to as well."

Sophie coughed and cleared her throat. "And now you're telling me you think you've seen him?"

"I'm not saying I *think* I saw him. I *saw* him, Sophie! He called me by my name. He called me Katy. Nobody but Eric has ever called me Katy. Worse yet, he was with Eddie. They were together. They know where the kids are hidden, and he told her to get me out of there."

Sophie sighed. "You've stepped into this time, Kat. I'll have to call you back."

* * *

I spent a miserable night. I snuck back into my room and tried to sleep, but I couldn't. I thought back to every day I've ever had with Eric. We met on my first day on campus at ASU. He was a senior, and I was a freshman. I remembered the football games, the parties, and the fun we had. When Eric graduated, he went off to Officer Candidate School. I thought our relationship might have been over then. Eric was gone, and I was only nineteen. But Eric got assigned to flight training at Williams Air Force Base near the campus, and when he came home, it was as though he had never left. He used to tell me that when he'd return from a sortie, he would fly over the campus and tip his wings. What a heady feeling that was. Looking up at the sky and seeing a small group of F-4 Phantoms flying back to the base, and knowing one of them was Eric's plane. I was high on him as he was in the sky. Then, when his orders came and he was assigned to Cam Ranh Air Base, we got married, in a hurry. It was a crazy thing to do. We were in love, and Eric said he wanted someone to come home to, and I wanted something to hold onto.

When the colonel arrived at my house and told me Eric had been shot down, I didn't believe it. For a long time, I was in denial. I kept telling myself that Eric was away and he'd be home soon. But when Christmas came and went and the days stretched into weeks, and weeks into months with no letters or phone calls, I started to realize Eric wasn't coming back. My Waiting Wives group thinned out as their husbands started to return, and as the war began to wind down, I got more active with the MIA Wives. A few of those whose husbands had been missing got calls from the DOD telling them their loved ones had been prisoners and that they were coming home. But not me. A couple of MIA wives I knew flew to Clark Air Force Base in California, and their reunions were televised nationwide. *Operation Homecoming.* Valentine's Day, February 14, 1973. Thirteen months after Eric was shot down. I watched with tears in my eyes, hopeful that there had been some mistake and that I would see Eric come off that plane, jogging down the stairway, with a big smile on his face. But it never happened. Before he left, Eric made me promise that no matter what, we would live our lives to the fullest. And if he didn't come home, he expected me to go on. I waited seven years. I wore an MIA bracelet with Eric's name on it, endlessly hoping. I'd go to sleep at night thinking that maybe tomorrow the phone would ring and there would be news. But there never was. Not until Eric's father told me he had accepted the DOD's reclassification that Eric was no longer MIA but KIA, did I finally agree to bury an empty coffin.

Chapter Twenty-Two

I waited all night for Eddie's call. When the phone rang, I was asleep and still had on the clothes I had worn the night before. My cell buzzed from beneath my pillow, and I tucked the phone beneath my chin and pulled the pillow up over my head.

"Hello?"

"Chào buổi sáng. This is your wake-up call. Your Tai Chi class is scheduled to begin in thirty minutes at Saigon Central Park. We're next to the koi pond. Bye nhe, noi chuyen sau!"

Despite the Vietnamese greeting, I recognized Eddie's voice. I clicked off the phone, threw the bedcover on the floor, grabbed my shoes and backpack, and was out the door before the bed was cold

Downstairs, I pulled a city map from the concierge stand and checked for the location of Saigon's Central Park. It was a short thirty-minute walk from the hotel, and I welcomed the opportunity to stretch my legs and organize my thoughts. After last night, my mind was swimming with questions, and I was anxious for answers.

* * *

Saigon's Central Park was located in the heart of the city, and was a mini-version of New York's Central Park, with its perimeters surrounded by gleaming glass highrises, some still under construction, while the interior was green on green with a variety of trees and colorful, flowering bushes. I checked the map for the location of the koi pond and found it next to an ornately carved stone bridge with old-fashioned globe lights anchored on either side. Eddie was sitting alone on a bench by the edge of the pond, feeding the koi from a small bag when I arrived.

I paused long enough in front of the Tai Chi Class to give the impression, should anyone be watching, that I was interested, then feigned surprise to see Eddie sitting on the bench. With a quick smile to the class, I shrugged and then turned to join Eddie.

"Hi. What a surprise. You come here often?" I took the empty seat next to Eddie.

Eddie threw a handful of fish food to the koi, then whispered to me. "It's safe to talk here. The water fountain will mask our voices, but be careful, I know you're upset."

"Upset? That's the understatement of a lifetime. Is that what you think I am? Upset?" I could barely control my whisper. What came out was more of a squeak.

"I told you to go home. Do you have any idea the trouble you've caused? You're lucky the police didn't get to the junkyard in time to arrest you. You would have blown the whole operation—"

"Hold it right there!" I put my hand on top of Eddie's and shook my head. "I'm not taking orders from you. I'm here because I want to know what happened last night. How do you know Eric?"

"Sweetheart." Eddit pulled her hand from mine. "I don't know anyone named Eric. And my advice to you is to forget what you saw last night and go home while you still can."

"Home?" I choked on the word. "Are you serious? Do you think I could forget what I saw last night and go home? What are you, insane?"

"Kat, listen to me. It's what he wants you to do."

"I don't believe you. Eric wouldn't want me to go home. Not now. Not after last night."

"Kat, you nearly blew his cover. As a result, Duc is dead, and the Russian traffickers we've been following have moved the kids to another location."

I reached into Eddie's bag, grabbed a small handful of fish food, and tossed it into the water. The fish swirled around our feet as the fountain in front of us shot water sixteen feet into the air.

"I need to talk to Eric. And I'm not leaving until I do."

"That's not possible. Go home. Forget him. Forget everything you've seen. He's not the same man you knew."

Eddie wasn't going to budge, and unless I had something she wanted, I wasn't going to get the answers I wanted about Eric. But I did have something to bargain with. I had thought about it all night long. One of the first things Eddie told me when we met was that in this part of the world, information is currency. And I had plenty of it. The reason Eddie had returned to Vietnam was to find her grandson. Buddy was the only family she had, and I knew after visiting with him at the safe house that Eddie was vulnerable and frightened that the Russians would find him.

"What if I told you I had something you want. That I know about Buddy."

"What?" Eddie snapped. "How do you know about Buddy?"

"I know he's your grandson, and I know that he called you the night we were at the puppet theater. I also know he called Crockett earlier that afternoon and told him he needed to go into hiding because he shot Nguyen."

Eddie scoffed. "You can't possibly know that. It's not true."

"It is true, Eddie. I know because Buddy told me so himself."

"Where is he?"

"He's somewhere safe."

"Where?"

"I can't tell you that, and I won't. Not until you've arranged for me to meet with Eric."

Eddie reached for my right hand and stared at my fingers. "You want to know the reason why I sent you home that night after the theater? It wasn't because I thought the Russians had made you. It was because of that ring on your right hand." Eddie nodded to the thin silver band I wore on my ring finger. "It's a wedding band, isn't it?"

I pulled my hand away and covered it with my left hand. I had never taken the ring off, except to transfer it to my right hand after Eric had been declared dead. It was a simple silver band with a small diamond, barely a quarter carat, set in a heart between a set of wings. Eric bought it at the Base

Exchange. It was the last thing we did before we ran off to get married in Las Vegas. Our initials had been carved inside along with our wedding date, *June 12, 1972.*

"How did you know?"

"I used to see rings just like it for sale in the BX here in Saigon. I'm sure the BX had rings just like it back in the States. Your age. Seeing the ring on your finger? I started to wonder if there was another reason you might have volunteered for this assignment. You weren't our first choice, you know."

"What do you mean, first choice?"

I was the one who went to Crockett and suggested we use an outside messenger to deliver to Nguyen's shop. He needed to keep his cover, and I needed to keep my distance. I told him about Sophie—that we'd gone to college together and I knew she was familiar with the country. She had been an art historian and traveled to Vietnam after the war. I could have reached out to her back then when she was shopping for Asian artifacts for an international art show that never happened. In hindsight, I suspected she might have been working undercover for the FBI or the CIA. There were a lot of undercover agents around back then, but I wasn't comfortable with the idea. Besides, things hadn't ended well between us, and I wasn't ready. Still, I left it up to Crockett. He told me he had contacted Sophie through his handler in the US. He said Sophie had retired and wasn't traveling these days, but they had arranged an alternative—a young journalist hired to work for Sophie's new travel magazine.

"So, you're the reason I'm here."

"I am. But after we met, I started to think you might have a few reasons of your own for accepting the assignment."

"Like what?"

"You wouldn't be the first MIA wife to come looking for her husband. "

"You think I came looking for Eric?"

"I began to suspect that you might have. However, the story always ends the same way. Usually, it's a dead end. Occasionally, a few remains are found, and the family arranges for them to be shipped home. It's not pleasant. If there are survivors—and there may be—I don't know about them. But I do know Eric's story."

Eddie explained that she met Eric after Buddy had applied for a job with Nike. "He hadn't been working there that long when he introduced me to his friend, Alexi. I knew right away Alexi wasn't Russian. He was an American. Alexi Petrova, Kat, that's Eric's Russian name. He was a schoolteacher in Ukraine, where Buddy had gone to school."

"Eric was a schoolteacher?" My throat tightened. I could feel tears start to form behind my eyes. Eric had always wanted to teach school. He used to tell me that when the war was over and he came home that he wanted to return to the university and earn a teaching degree.

"In a sense, yes. He taught at an American school in Russia, but not the type of school you might think. Some of the teachers the Russians used were American POWs. They taught Russian children and adults to be spies."

"A spy school?" My voice caught in my throat. "With American POWs as instructors? How could that happen?"

"It was easier than you might think. During the war, the Viet Cong traded their American POWs to the Russians, who brainwashed them into believing they had been suckered into an immoral war. The Russians called them baby killers and mass murderers. It doesn't take much to break a man's spirit if you know what you're doing, and the Russians knew what they were doing. You take away a man's dignity. You strip him. Starve him. Deny him sleep and the comfort of friends, throw him into isolation, and then eventually introduce him again to what he thinks is a safe zone, and you've essentially reborn him. Made him exactly as you need him to be. It's the Stockholm syndrome on steroids."

"But Eric didn't stay in Russia. He came back to Vietnam." My voice was rushed, and my thoughts jumbled. "Maybe he came back to find his unit, maybe he—"

"No, Kat. Eric didn't come back to find his unit. He knew the war was over. By the time I met him, he had enough sense of his past to know what had happened and that he could never go home. And even if he did, there would always be some who would consider him a traitor, who would believe that he had defected and trained spies to spy against us. Once he got here, I don't think he wanted to go home."

"I don't believe that."

"Think about it. Too much had happened since Eric was captured. The war ended on April 30, 1975. The Soviet Union collapsed on December 26, 1991. That's nearly sixteen years, Kat. Watergate happened. The Beatles split up. John Lennon was murdered. Apollo 13. The space shuttle Challenger exploded. Race riots. The Soviets used all that and more to convince Eric how bad things were in this country."

"So you convinced him to stay and be a spy here?

"I didn't have to convince him. I just opened the door for him to meet people who could be of help and who he could help."

"Like Crockett."

"I'm not naming names. But don't be naive. If the world's balance of power is to stay in place, we in the West need information about those who would do us harm. The best way to do that is by seeking out those who could help us without being obvious."

"You mean like me, a travel journalist innocently dropping off an envelope, and hoping no one would notice?"

"On a much less sophisticated level, yes. What you tried to do was a simple enough job. Eric's work, however, is more involved and long-term. And highly secret."

"And Eric agreed to this?"

"He had contacts we needed. He had come from Russia, and he had even taken a Russian name. He worked at the American school and trained Russians to be spies. He was the right man for what we needed. He speaks English, Russian, and Vietnamese, and he's able to mix well with the Americans and their Vietnamese hosts without bringing a lot of attention to himself, and he's very close to the Russians."

"Is that how you ended up at the shipyard last night? Because Eric's close to the Russians, and knew where the kids were hidden?"

"Let me be very clear. He's not part of their operation, Kat. And up until yesterday afternoon, while he had been supplying us information about the operation, he didn't know where the kids were. It wasn't until he overheard

Dimitry Andreeva talking to Luka Nikikov about taking food for the kids that he called me to tell me he had a lead on where the kids were hidden and wanted to show me."

"So the two of you just showed up when I was there?"

"Believe me, if I had any idea you were going to be there, I wouldn't have risked it. But why were you there? How did you know where the kids were hidden?"

"I was following up on a lead of my own."

"And that lead, does it have something to do with the man who was shot last night?"

"His name was Duc. He was Nguyen's son-in-law. He worked as a shoeshine boy outside of Nguyen's store."

"No." Eddie shook her head. "That's wrong. Duc was Nguyen's accountant, not a shoeshine boy."

"That's what Duc and Nguyen wanted everyone to think. But Duc told me he was Nguyen's security. He worked outside the shop to keep an eye out. I'm surprised no one recognized him?"

"There are millions of people in Ho Chi Minh City. We can't know them all. As far as we knew, Duc and his family had gone into hiding, hoping that after Nguyen got the money and the passports, they'd all leave together."

I explained how I had tripped over the shoeshine boy's stand as I escaped Nguyen's shop after the shooting, and later, when I came back to find the clerk who had been helping me, I introduced myself. "At the time, Duc didn't tell me his name, only that he was friends with the clerk. He said the clerk's name was Ahn, and they were friends. Duc promised to set up an appointment for us to meet. But when Ahn was found dead, Duc called me and said he knew why I had come to the store the morning Nguyen was shot. Ahn had told him everything, and Duc wanted me to give him the money and—"

"And the passports you were supposed to deliver to Nguyen."

"I thought if I could find out where the kids were hidden, it'd make up for my not getting the map from Nguyen. But until I had proof of where the kids were, I wasn't about to say anything."

CHAPTER TWENTY-TWO

"You always go off on your own like that?"

"When I need to." I reached into the bag for a couple of tablets of fish food and threw them into the pond. "Tell me, does Eric trust you?"

"As much as he trusts anyone, I suppose."

"So what is he? Some double agent?"

"He's a teacher and a confidential informant. He teaches elementary school while spying on Russians for us. I'm sure if for no other reason than to make himself look good with the Russians, he spies on us as well. I wouldn't know."

"But Crockett would."

"Crockett's had him leak a few secrets of our own. It's all part of keeping up the masquerade. Nobody's what they seem. Everybody's got secrets. If I were still a working journalist, I would have written the story about how our POWs and MIAs were traded to the Soviet Union. But as you can imagine, it's not a story I could write without exposing those I care about. And I would hope you realize that means you can't write about it either. Too many lives, including Eric's, would be at stake."

I twisted the silver band on my right hand. "I want to see Eric. There are things I need to say."

"I'll see what I can do with Crockett. After last night, it's not going to be easy to get favors from him. But before you go, please, tell me, where's Buddy?"

"Crockett won't tell you?" I knew Crockett wouldn't share Buddy's location with Eddie. Not until the Russians were convinced Buddy had nothing to do with Nguyen's murder.

"No. Crockett and I don't always see eye to eye on things. But when it comes to Buddy, Crockett owes me, and he knows it." Eddie folded her arms and stared at the koi pond. "Just tell me, how's Buddy doing? Because if the Russians find him—"

"Don't worry."

"You have to understand that none of us expected Nguyen would be murdered. Least of all me. I had no idea Buddy was planning to shoot Nguyen. But when Buddy called me and told me what he had done and that he was in hiding, I panicked. If the Russians suspected him, Crockett had two choices. He either—"

"He either let them think it was Buddy who shot Nguyen, or they'd suspect me because I'd been in the store that morning."

"To be fair, we weren't certain if the Russians had seen you or not that morning. Even so, just to be safe, Crockett got word to the Russians through Alexi that Nguyen thought Ahn had been stealing from him, and that Ahn had shot Nguyen to shut him up. But you need to know this, Kat. If it came down to saving the mission, don't think for a minute that Crockett wouldn't sacrifice you if it kept the Russians from suspecting we know about their operation."

"And that's why you told me the Russians had made me. You needed to get me out of here. I suppose I should be thankful you were trying to save me."

"You should be. The fact is, whether you like it or not, the longer you're here, the more danger you're in. You need to go."

"No! I'm not leaving Vietnam. Not until I've seen Eric and talked with him."

"You know that's not possible. Crockett would never allow it. It's too risky."

Eddie was stonewalling me, and I knew if I didn't push back now, I wouldn't get another chance.

"What's risky is me going to the Russians and telling them where Buddy is."

Eddie scoffed. "Don't try to bluff me. How would you even know how to make contact with the Russians?"

"I found Duc, didn't I? You and your group didn't even know he was the shoeshine boy outside Nguyen's shop. You think I can't find three Russians I saw at the theater and whose names I know?"

Eddie took the fish food sack from her lap and stuffed it into her bag. "You're a fool, Kat Lawson."

"Maybe so, but I'm not leaving."

Eddie huffed. "I'll see what I can do."

"Don't take too long. And if you can't get me a meeting with Eric, I'm sure Crockett can. Tell him I know where the kids are and I'll be happy to share that information with him, but I need to see Eric."

Eddie stood up. "Go back to the hotel and wait for Crockett's call. But don't blame me if things don't turn out as you like."

Chapter Twenty-Three

I didn't like threatening Eddie. She was as desperate to protect her grandson as I was to see Eric. But until I knew what had happened to Eric, I wasn't about to leave Vietnam. I wanted answers, and I was going to get them. I lied when I told Eddie to tell Crockett I knew how to find the kids. If the Russians had moved the kids after Duc's shooting, I would be back to where I had started, without a clue. I had no idea where the kids were hidden or if I could find them. But the little girl in the red sequined dress haunted me, and I was determined I was going to find her. Sometimes it's easier to jump into the fire than try to escape it.

When I got back to my hotel room, I locked the door behind me, took my pencil and notepad from my backpack, and paced the room while I checked my notes. In the last few days, I had witnessed a murder, avoided walking in on a second, or—if I was to believe Crockett—barely escaped becoming a victim myself, and seen Duc shot in cold blood. I stopped and poured myself a glass of water, took a sip, and proceeded to read my notes, or more accurately, between the lines of what I had written. I had witnessed, or almost witnessed, three murders. I also knew who our Russian suspects were. I had seen them at the Puppet Theater, candidly taken their pictures, knew their names, and seen three of the children the Russians had kidnapped and planned to traffic to the U.S. But, close as I was to them that night at the Puppet Theater, I saw no evidence that the Russians had any idea or concern of my presence.

I tapped my pencil on my notepad. There was no reason the Russians would have had eyes on Nguyen's shop the morning of his murder. They weren't expecting trouble. Nguyen had been a loyal and trustworthy comrade to their cause. He had always done what they had asked, and in return, they had moved him from the countryside, where food was scarce and shelter difficult, and set him up in a successful business. The Russians trusted Nguyen.

Something wasn't right. If the Russians hadn't been watching Nguyen's store, had Crockett lied to me? Eddie had told me neither Crockett nor any of his team had any proof the Russians had seen me flee Nuguen's shop. I knew Tomy and Sam worked for Crockett and had been shadowing me that morning. But Russians? Had Crockett told me the Russians had seen me to scare me? Had he tried to blame me for the failure of the mission because neither Crockett nor his team had any idea Nguyen was on someone's hit list? It was Crockett who put the fear of a Russian tail into my head and convinced me that the only way for me to stay safe and help bring a successful close to the mission was to team up with him to provide mutual cover for our covert activities. With me as Crockett's beard, and Crockett as my all-too-anxious-to-please tour guide, we made a convincing team. At least until Buddy called Crockett and confessed that he had shot Nguyen.

Crockett protected Buddy, but Eddie feared he would give me up to the Russians if I didn't leave. Instead of Crockett letting the Russians believe I had been in Nguyen's shop the morning of the murder and shot him, Crockett sent word to the Russians through Eric that Nguyen's murder was probably caused by a disagreement between the old jeweler and his clerk. Overall, Crockett's plan worked. With me as Crockett's cover, we managed to get closer to the Russians, and Crockett didn't sacrifice me when he had the chance. Which meant I wasn't as big a target for the Russians as Crockett initially led me to believe.

I closed my notebook and sat down on the bed. If the Russians weren't suspicious of me, they weren't going to come after me, but I could go after them, and if I did—

My cell phone buzzed before I could finish the thought. I bit back a smile. It had been less than an hour since I had left Eddie in the park, and I would have bet the Saudi Diamond and all the cash I had in my backpack that the caller would be Crockett.

I let the phone ring three times before I answered. "Hello?"

"How about you and I take a little drive this morning? Somewhere scenic, maybe. There are still a lot of places I'd like to show you." Despite Crockett's disarming messaging, I sensed he was ready to explode. "Meet me downstairs in front of the hotel. I have a car parked outside."

* * *

Crockett's car wasn't a car at all, but an old, grey, and green camouflaged Army Jeep. For all I knew, it could have been the same jeep he had driven during the war, except the tires looked new, and the windshield, the only window in an otherwise open vehicle, had been replaced.

"Get in. We're going to take a little drive." Crockett looked spent. He was dressed in a pair of wrinkled khaki shorts and a t-shirt, and his hair was still wet from his morning shower.

I took hold of the grab bar and had barely swung into the passenger seat before Crockett pulled away from the curb.

"Hang on tight there, Legs. You and I have some things we need to get straight. Eddie tells me you want some answers. But I'll warn you, you won't like what I have to say about your ex."

"He's not my ex, he's—"

"Call him whatever you want, but if you give me any trouble, I'm warning you, I'll push you out of this Jeep so fast you'll be dead before anybody knows what happened."

'Well, good morning to you, too." I locked my seat belt in place and crossed my arms. *What a jerk!*

"We're way beyond *good morning*. Talk to me about what you were doing at the shipyard last night?"

"I had a lead on where the kids were hidden."

"Give me a break. How did you have a lead on anything? From the moment you walked into Nguyen's store, things started to fall apart. The only reason I didn't send you home then was because I thought maybe I could use you to get closer to the Russians."

"The only reason you didn't send me home was because you screwed up. You had no idea Nguyen was in danger, and you needed me—"

"Like hell, I needed you. Lady, you are no team player. Do you even know the trouble you've caused?"

"Don't you dare put this on me! I'm not the reason Nguyen's dead, and you know it. Thanks to you and your team, I was in the wrong place at the wrong time. Seems to me that if you had done a little more research, you might have known that."

"Don't get smart with me."

"Somebody ought to. You sure as hell didn't know Nguyen's son-in-law was working outside his store. But because I did, I have a jump on you and something Duc wants."

"Which is?"

"The Saudi Diamond, you fool. Duc figured out I had it, and he was willing to trade for it."

"And you took it upon yourself to facilitate this trade without calling me?"

"Hey, you were the one who warned me that when it came to the Saudi Diamond, I was on my own. You wanted nothing to do with it. You even accused me of stealing it. So why should I have asked you for anything? I figured if I met with Duc, he'd show me where the kids were, I'd give him the diamond, and then, because I *am* a team player, I'd tell you where the kids were. But things happen fast, and now—"

"Duc is dead, and you're wondering why the hell your ex-husband was there last night."

"Yeah! Let's start with that. I think I deserve an answer. Up until last night, I had no idea he was alive."

"Sorry." Crockett took one hand off the wheel and straightened his cowboy hat. I can't tell you that. And I won't."

If Crockett hadn't been driving, I would have punched him. Beat him with my fists, and years' worth of anger had been bottled up with nowhere to go. He had to tell me something. I wasn't about to sit back and accept that Crockett couldn't do anything. He could. And he would.

"Maybe you will if I tell you I know of a way to find the kids and take down your three Russian traffickers in the process."

"You?" Crockett laughed. "You think you have a plan?"

"I do. And unless you have other ideas, I'd say you're back where you started. You have no idea where the Russians moved the kids, or how to find them."

"Which I have you to thank for. If you had stayed in your hotel room like I told you to do, we wouldn't have this problem. Eddie and your ex would have found them. Alexi would have reported back to me, the Russians never would have known anything about Alexi, you, me, or anyone else, and the kids would be free."

"So that's your answer? You're not even going to hear me out?"

"Give me one reason why I should. You're a loose cannon, Legs. Everything you do backfires."

I fisted my hand. "You are an as—"

"Careful there, Legs." Crockett grabbed my fist. "Don't say anything you'll regret. The only reason you're still here is because I haven't decided what to do with you yet."

I bit my tongue. If my plan was going to work, I needed Crockett on my side, and he had to cool down. I didn't say a word, and for a few minutes, I managed to keep my mouth shut.

"You hungry?" It was Crockett who broke the silence.

"Not particularly." My voice was still tense.

"Well, I am." Crockett swung the Jeep into the parking lot of the Reunification Palace, directly across the street from Tao Don Park. "And I listen better on a full stomach. I hope you like Banh Mi. There's a place here in the park where we can get a pork and pate sandwich. We can talk there."

Crockett jumped out of the Jeep and walked ahead of me. *Arragont son of a bitch.* I scanned the area behind me and, seeing no one, hurried to catch up. The park seemed safe enough. Visitors were everywhere, walkers, some who had come to do tai chi, and young couples out for a stroll. Further into the park, Crockett stopped abruptly and took his hat off.

"You hear that?"

I rolled my eyes. I was impatient. Anxious. Whatever Crockett was up to, I wasn't interested. "What is it now?"

"Birds. You hear them?"

I shrugged. "Yes. Why? How is this important?"

"Follow me. I'll show you."

We walked another hundred yards deeper into the park, and Crockett stopped again.

"You don't know this country, do you?" Crockett raised his hands to shoulder height and gestured to an open area directly ahead of us. "You want to know this country, you need to know the people and their history. Take a look, and tell me what you see."

Ahead of me was open green space where a giant metal tree had been erected. I had never seen anything like it. Hanging from its metal branches were dozens of bird cages of every shape and size, and beneath them were small plastic chairs and tables where old men sat sipping coffee and hand-feeding the birds like nursemaids.

"What is this?"

This is my second office. It's called the Bird Song Café. I come here to listen. If you'd spent any time here, you'd know that the old men sitting beneath the trees bring their birds and birdcages every day so their birds can teach songs to other birds. This is also where I first met Alexi. I thought this might be a good place for us to start our conversation.

Crockett nodded to a food stand several hundred yards from the tree, then wandered over to it and ordered two pork and pate sandwiches along with a couple of beers. He opened the beers, handed me a sandwich and a bottle, and after taking a bite of his sandwich, started to talk.

"Okay, so tell me about this idea of yours. Just what is it?"

I took a sip of the beer. "You said it all along. The Russians here aren't hiding; they're in plain sight. Nobody's bothering them. And I don't think they're at all concerned about me. I think you told me they were because once you learned Nguyen was shot, you wanted my help. But to them? I'm nothing more than a travel journalist on assignment."

Crockett huffed and started to walk.

"And I doubt the Russians had any idea Nguyen planned to defect. He was a perfect pawn for them. Nguyen was friends with the Russians here during the war. He was a traitor to the South Vietnamese. He probably provided the Russians with women and whatever else they wanted. And after the war, he avoided any possibility of going to a reeducation camp because he turned his sister over to the Viet Cong and relied on his Russian friends to protect him."

"Bravo, Legs. You've done your homework." Crockett tilted his head to a pathway beneath a series of flowering trees.

"And we both know it wasn't the Russians who shot Nguyen. The Russians trusted Nguyen. He was loyal to them, or so he had led them to think." I unwrapped my sandwich and threw the wrapper in the trash. "And you knew that."

Crockett took a big bite of his sandwich and walked ahead.

"Hang on, I'm not done yet." I quickened my pace until we were walking side by side. "You were as surprised as I was by Nguyen's murder. You had no idea who the shooter was. But you had to wonder, if the Russians had shot Nguyen, how had you missed it? You were ready to scrap me right then, and you might have, except Sophie told you I thought I could still recover the information Nguyen was supposed to give me from Ahn. So you hung in there, hopeful that maybe I could pull it off. And then that day you rescued me from walking in on Ahn's murder, and we went to Doctor Fish? You knew if you scared me into thinking the Russians might have seen me coming out of Nguyen's shop or that they might be following me, you could convince me to work with you."

"A lot of good it's done."

"I think it has. Look, you knew the night you took me to the Water Puppet Theater, the Russians weren't paying any attention to me; they weren't one bit concerned about me. I was your cover, and we got pictures. Everything was going according to plan. But then Eddie got a call, and you did too. It was Buddy. He told me he called both of you that day. He had confessed to Alexi that he had shot Nguyen, and he was worried the Russians might suspect him. And why not? The Russians knew that after the war, Nguyen had turned Buddy's mother over to the Viet Cong. Mai died in a re-education camp. Her brother had abandoned her, and Buddy grew up an orphan. He blamed Nguyen for everything. It was only a matter of time until the Russians figured it out. And Buddy was scared."

"So now you know."

"And when the Russians didn't come back into the theater with the kids after intermission, you realized something was up. Eddie tried to tell me it was because I had been made, and I needed to leave the country. But it had nothing to do with that, did it?"

"You tell me, you've done a pretty good job so far."

"You left to check on Buddy. You were worried about him. So you had Eric spread a rumor that Nguyen was shot by Ahn after Nguyen accused Ahn of stealing from him."

"Did Eddie tell you that?"

"She did. She was worried that if the Russians didn't believe it, you'd find a way to let them know I had been in Nguyen's store that morning and make sure the Russians thought it was me who shot Nguyen. For some reason, she doesn't trust you, and I'm wondering why?"

"That doesn't concern you. What happened between Eddie and me happened a long time ago. It's none of your business."

"Alright, then, let's talk about what is my business. Let's talk about you setting a meeting for me with Eric."

"Look, I like Eric. He's probably the only reason you're still alive. And I'm sorry about what happened. I'm sorry he got himself shot down and never came home. It sucks. That's war. Grow up and face the facts. He doesn't want to see you. What you had back then? It's over. It's been over for years. He wants you out of here—"

"I don't believe you!" Crockett started to walk away, and I grabbed his elbow. "Stop! Listen to me. I'm not leaving until I see him. If Eric wants me to go home, he's going to have to tell me himself."

Crockett pulled away and tossed his beer bottle into a trash can. "Trust me, you're not going to like what he has to say to you."

"I'll be the one to decide that. You get me time with Eric, and I'll find out where the kids are."

"And just how is it you think you're going to find that out?"

"Because I'm going to do the very thing you would have done if the Russians didn't believe Ahn shot Nguyen."

Crockett scoffed. "And what's that?"

"I'm going to tell them I shot Nguyen?"

"What?"

"I plan to tell them I was in the shop that morning, and why."

"You want to tell them you were there to drop off a payment and passports and ended up shooting Nguyen?"

"Why not? It's the truth. I'll tell them Nguyen was on the take. That months ago, my client, whose name I can't reveal, had visited Nguyen's Jewelry store and, while speaking with Nguyen, learned that the jeweler had more to sell than what sparkled beneath his glass counters. Long story short, my client, who needs to keep his private affairs, particularly his appetite for young boys and girls, out of the news, agreed to provide forged passports and safe passage for Nguyen and his family to America. I was here to arrange for delivery. But Nguyen reneged, said he wanted more money, and when I couldn't reason with him, I shot him."

Crockett shook his head. "You know you're damn lucky Eric didn't have anyone following him last night, and the Russians didn't see you in the shipyard. Just what makes you think this story of yours is going to work?"

"What I think, and what should make you very happy, is that my story not only saves Buddy but explains if the Russians did see me leaving Nguyen's store the morning of his murder, why I was there. In short, your cover's intact. You're still the randy drunk at the bar who tried to put the moves on me, and I'm exactly who I say I am. I'm a journalist on assignment representing a client with unusual tastes, and I need to see the kids before I approve the deal."

Crocket rubbed the back of his head. "Look, Legs, you're not going to like what I have to say. But if the Russians find out who you are, they'll kill you. And if they find out who Eric is and I lose an asset, *I'll* kill you."

"Don't threaten me. Nobody's going to kill anybody. There's already been too much of that. Let me do this. I find out where the kids are, you can take the Russians down, and your mission will be complete."

"This isn't exactly by the books."

"I'm not by the books. And in case you hadn't noticed, I'm not an agent. I'm a desperate American journalist who just learned the husband she thought was dead for the last twenty-five years is alive. And I want answers. I find out where the kids are, you get me a meeting with Eric, and we call it even. After that, I give you my word: whatever happens with Eric, I'll never mention anything about this operation or what happened here. Ever."

Crockett looked at his watch. "Okay. You're on. But don't say I didn't warn you. The Russians don't play fair, they're ruthless, and they play for keeps."

Chapter Twenty-Four

One place I had yet to visit in Ho Chi Minh City was the Russian Market. Crockett told me he had seen our *Russian friends* inside the Central Garden Building, a new shopping center for Russian food and clothing made in Vietnam. For the Russians, it was becoming a kind of mini-Moscow in the center of the city.

"There's a café on the third floor that just opened. The Russians like to frequent it. They're usually there this time of day."

"Good. If they're there, I'll find them." I sounded more confident than I felt and swallowed hard. Part of me figured Crockett had bought into my idea of going to the Russians because he knew I wasn't about to go home, and I'd be one less problem he would have to deal with if I failed and he let the Russians get rid of me.

"Make sure you go alone. And be careful, if Boris gets at all suspicious of you, there's no telling what he might do."

"You don't need to tell me. I'm well aware of what the Russians can do."

"All the same, I'll send Tomy and Sam in behind you. They'll be discreet, but I can't assure your safety. Things go sideways, you could end up being sent to a Russian prison or worse."

"So, now you're worried about me? I'm touched." I put my hand to my heart. "Don't worry. I'll be fine."

"Let's hope so."

"Hey, all I have to do is convince the Russians I'm as dirty as they are."

I left Crockett in the park and took a cab to the Russian Market, exactly as he had instructed. It was just past noon when I arrived.

* * *

Like any central market I'd ever been to, there was a rush of activity. Tourists and locals, Russians and Vietnamese, crowded aisles crammed with Russian foods—chocolates, sunflower seeds, salted herring, cured pork, vodka, and caviar on the first floor, clothing made in Vietnam to be sold and exported to Russia on the second floor, and souvenirs, Russian nesting dolls, handiwork, and a café on the third.

I wandered through aisle after aisle of merchandise piled high on tables and hung from racks that draped the ceiling from one side of the building to the other. Bumping shoulders with the crowd, I took my camera from my backpack and snapped pictures, bought a few souvenirs, and stopped to chat with various merchants, then worked my way up to the third floor.

I could have followed my ears and nose to the café. The musical sounds of a balalaika, the crowd outside the café's large sliding doors, and the strong smell of herring made me feel as though I had been transported to the motherland. The café, its walls lined with racks of Russian Nesting Dolls and Fabergé eggs, was more of a cafeteria with a long serving counter behind which three matronly-looking women stood in white aprons, dishing out various Russian favorites. I grabbed a tray and joined the line behind a group of Russian diners, eyeing the blinis, dumplings, and borscht soups as I moved forward. As I approached the end of the line, I noticed a short, stocky man standing by the kitchen doors. *Boris Mikhailov.* My heart froze as I paused in front of a server who loaded a plate with stuffed cabbage and kielbasa and slid it under the glass and onto my tray. I added a cold drink from a shelf of Russian beverages, then reached into my pocket, pulled out several *dong*—enough to cover the cost of my meal, and walked over to Boris.

"Excuse me. My name is Kat Lawson. I've been following you, and I believe I have something you want."

Boris jerked his head back and looked me up and down. "I think you have me confused with someone else."

"No, I don't think so. Your name is Boris Mikhailov. You knew the jeweler, Nguyen Tuan. He gave me your name." I nodded to an empty table in the corner of the café. "We should talk."

I could feel Boris's eyes following me to the table. He waited until I had sat down and put my backpack on the empty chair beside me, then approached.

"You're welcome to sit if you like." I nodded to the empty chair across from me. "I'm sure you'll find what I have to say interesting."

Boris smiled, tight-lipped. "And just what is it you think I might find interesting?"

"This." I took the manila envelope I had planned to give to Nguyen from inside my backpack and placed it on the edge of the table closest to him.

Boris glanced down at the envelope and shoved it back in my direction. "Sorry. I don't know what you're up to, but I'm not interested."

"Oh, but I think you will be. Take a look inside." I pushed the envelope back in his direction. "There's fifty thousand US dollars in there, and four American passports. Passports, your friend Nguyen requested that my client have me bring to him."

Boris's eyes swept the room. Satisfied no one was watching, he picked up the envelope and looked inside. A crooked smile spread across his face as he partially pulled out the pack of bills before slipping them back into the envelope. "Where did you get this?"

"Like I said, I have a client. And there's lots more from where that came from. But what I think you'll find even more interesting than the money is the passports. They backed up my story that Nguyen had a plan to defect. Take a look."

Boris removed the passports from his bag and arranged them on the table. Then picked them up one by one, leafing through each before placing it down after he finished. He was about to stuff them back in the envelope when I put my hand on top of his.

"I think you can see from the passports just how serious Nguyen was about leaving."

Boris pulled the chair out across from me, sat down, crossed his arms, and rested his elbows on the table. "Why don't you start by telling me who you are?"

"You don't know?" I picked up the passports and glanced through them.

This was the first time I had seen the doctored photos of Nguyen and his family. Nguyen had a mustache and glasses in the photo and looked very different from the man I had met in the store. Duc had slicked his hair back and wore thicker glasses than I remembered, but his wife, Nguyen's daughter, looked exactly like the sweet, round-faced woman I had met on Duc's boat. The fourth passport was for Duc's small son. "I'm surprised. But then, I suppose you had no reason to suspect me. Like I said, my name's Kat Lawson, and I'm a reporter. I work for a travel publication. I'm doing a feature on tourism in Vietnam."

"Don't bore me with some cover story. Why are you here? What's this all about?"

"I'm here to make you an offer." I slipped the passports back across the table. "I'm sure you know most reporters don't make a lot of money, and sometimes we find ways to subsidize our income. Most, I have to admit, aren't as lucky as I've been or as creative. You see, my work has given me access to some of Hollywood's more *enterprising* clientele, some of whom require the company of younger, more international talent for various household chores, live-in maids, nannies, and some personal services. Services that my client has come to understand that you could provide. I don't think I need to spell it out for you. I'm sure you know what I'm talking about. You have a shipment you're about to make, and my client would like to make you an offer."

Boris's eyes narrowed. I had hit a nerve. He leaned across the table, grabbed the neck of my t-shirt, and fisted it in his meaty hand. "You wearing a wire?"

"No! And if you don't let go of me this minute, I'll scream." I cuffed my hand on top of his and dug my nails into the back of his hand.

Boris let go of my shirt and sat back. "What do you know about any shipment?"

I dipped my napkin into my water glass and dabbed the side of my neck. The water felt cool against my skin, and I forced myself to take a deep breath. I wasn't about to rush into any explanation. The longer Boris sat, the more uncomfortable he looked, and the more I noticed people looking in our direction and then away.

I exhaled. "Let's start at the beginning, shall we? Your Mr. Nguyen wanted to defect. A bit of a surprise, considering you brought him in from the countryside and set him up in a nice business. Of course, we both know the jewelry store was a front for child trafficking. But I'm not here to judge." I shrugged and reached for my drink, cradling it in both my hands to keep from shaking. "But once Nguyen got to the city, it seems he started to see the world differently. Suddenly, he had opportunities he didn't have before."

Boris grunted. I wasn't sure if it was in agreement or if he was surprised.

"Several months ago, my client traveled to Vietnam. He had heard about Nguyen's export business from a friend in Hollywood who said he had used the old jeweler to bring in a nanny for his family and later brought in some household help for some of his friends. He was quite pleased with the relationship. Funny, you wouldn't think it would be all that hard to hire household help in the States. But then again, we're not just talking about household help, are we? We're talking about slaves. Kids are brought in to work in homes without any chance of ever going free. There's quite a business you've got there. Not to mention the *extra child services* that you and your friends specialize in."

Boris leaned back in his chair and hugged the envelope to his chest. "Get to the point, Ms. Lawson."

"As I was saying…" I paused and glanced over my shoulder at the entrance. Tomy had entered the restaurant and was standing just inside the large sliding door. He made eye contact, then turned around and busied himself in front of the curio counter. I felt an immediate sense of relief. "After hearing how happy my client's friend was, he made a special trip to Vietnam to visit with Nguyen. In Nguyen's defense, I must say that he was initially resistant and stated he couldn't help my client. The people he worked with would make life very difficult for him if he tried to put a deal together on his own. But my client, well…he's never been one to hear the word no. So, he sweetened the deal and offered to get the old jeweler and his family passports along with safe passage to the U.S. if he would notify him when the next shipment was ready. Nguyen agreed, and my client was thrilled. And just to show how happy he was, my client threw in a fifty-thousand-dollar bonus. That's the money you saw in the envelope there. So, when I showed up with the cash and the passports, and Nguyen wanted to back out, you can imagine my surprise. I had come too far and had too much on the line to let it go. I tried to convince Nguyen he couldn't back out, but it was a waste of time. I'm afraid things got out of hand, and I shot him."

"You? You shot Nguyen?" Boris sat back, a look of shock on his face. He grabbed the envelope to his chest and tapped it with his left hand.

"I did. But not before Nguyen fessed up and told me all about who he worked for and where I could find you. That's why I'm here." I reached for my drink and took a sip, a cloudy fermented Kavoss in a mason jar with a sweet and sour taste.

"You're a very interesting woman, Ms. Lawson."

"Oh, I'm more than interesting. You don't know it yet, but I've done you a very big favor. By shooting Nguyen, I've cleared the way for you to do business with a much bigger fish. And by now, if your previous buyer hasn't heard about Nguyen's murder, I'm sure he will. I can't imagine he'd want to continue doing business. Not with all the press I'm prepared to leak the story to. By this time tomorrow, it'll be front-page news in *The LA Times* and every other major paper here and in the U.S. But I wouldn't worry. You work with me, there's no story to leak, and my client is more than willing to accept your shipment and more after that."

"And why should I trust you, Ms. Lawson? If I wanted another buyer, I could have one lined up tomorrow."

"You could, except I have something else I think you might like."

"And what might that be?"

"That morning, when I went to deliver the package to Nguyen, he didn't come into the showroom right away. While I waited, his assistant showed me a very unusual necklace. I'm sure you've heard of it. The Saudi Blue Diamond?"

Boris' eyes widened. "You have it?"

"I wouldn't bother to mention it if I didn't. I grabbed it off the counter after I shot Nguyen. I should have shot his assistant, Ahn, too, but I was in a rush and took the necklace instead."

Boris grabbed my wrist. "Prove it. Give it to me."

I pulled my hand away. "What do you think I am, stupid? You think I would walk in here with the diamond hidden on me?"

"I assume you've hidden it in a safe place?"

"Safe enough that neither you nor the Saudis will ever find it. However, I might be persuaded to give it to you in exchange for a business opportunity."

"So, you want in. That's what this is all about."

"Why not? The people I work with have a lot of money and unusual appetites. Certainly, it would be easier for me to make contact with those in need of your services than to risk their coming here. And, now with all the attention on Nguyen's shop, I wouldn't think the store would be much of a draw anymore."

"This client of yours, he's ready to buy?"

"I wouldn't be here if he weren't. But I'll need to inspect the goods before we move forward."

Boris snorted. "That can be arranged. But once you've seen the kids, I'll need full payment, five hundred thousand, before I agree to a shipment."

"Not a problem. But I need to see the kids before there's any money transferred." I reached into my backpack and handed him my business card. "Give me a call when you're ready. I'm at the Majestic."

Boris stood up, and one of the other Russian thugs I had seen with him that night at the puppet theater came through the kitchen's double doors, carrying several plastic bags loaded with food and drinks. Enough food, I thought, for the kids themselves and whoever else might be guarding them.

"We'll be in touch. *Da svidania.* Goodbye, Ms. Lawson. And bring the Saudi diamond with you when you come. I intend to take that as well."

Chapter Twenty-Five

B oris and the bald Russian thug bumped shoulders with Tomy as they pushed their way through the crowd and out of the café's big sliding glass doors. I waited until the two men were out of sight, then got up, walked over to the gift stand where Tomy was checking out the souvenir rack of Russian nesting dolls, and picked one up.

Tomy returned the doll to the shelf and nodded to the door. "Start walking back to the hotel. I'll get the rickshaw and pick you up in fifteen minutes."

I left the Russian Market feeling like I was on a rollercoaster ride that had started long before I came to Vietnam, full of ups and downs, from my past to the present. I didn't realize when Sophie offered me the assignment how much of Vietnam's history was interwoven with my own. For years following the war, I held on to the hope that, since the Department of Defense had reported they had never recovered Eric's body, he might still be alive. But when the government eventually reclassified Eric's status from MIA to KIA, I was forced to move forward. The situation was hopeless. There was nothing I could do. Then, in 1992, as I was driving to work one morning— eighteen years of trying to rebuild my life—I heard a news report on the radio that pulled me backwards. Boris Yeltsin, the then-president of the Russian Federation, announced that there *may have* been a transfer of American POWs from Hanoi to the Soviet Union and that some prisoners might still be alive today.

I couldn't believe what I was listening to, and I nearly drove off the road. As soon as I arrived at the newspaper, I went immediately to my cubicle and picked up my phone. I called every number I could find connected to the DOD and the office for the League of POW/MIA families. No one had answers. They all maintained they had no evidence, no proof, just rumors that any of America's MIA had been transferred from Vietnam to Russia in exchange for weapons. After that, I wrote letters to the DOD. If there was a grain of truth to what I had heard on the radio, someone had to know something. Always, I got the same answer. The Air Force, the Department of Defense, the League? No one knew anything about a trade. If there had been a story, it had been hushed up. The war was over. The world had moved on. But now, years later, as I thought back on all I heard, read, and saw, I had proof. I had seen Eric. He was alive. I felt as though my world was spiraling backward, and I had one chance to grab it and set it straight.

"Hey, Lady, you like ride?" Just like he had done the first day we met, Tomy hollered to me as I walked back to the hotel. But this time he was on his motorbike and he nodded for me to get on. I swung my backpack over my shoulder and straddled the seat behind him.

"I thought you were going to bring the rickshaw."

"There's no time for the rickshaw, we need to get out of here." Tomy gunned the bike's engine and we took off. "How did it go?"

"As good as we could expect. Boris agreed to meet me later and show me the kids."

"When?"

"I don't know. A couple of hours, maybe? He said he'd call."

"Good. That gives us time. Davy called a few minutes ago. He wants me to keep you busy while he puts a few plans in place."

"What does he know?"

"He knows Boris and the Russian thug you saw with him in the café, left the market, and went to Ben Doc Temple. Sam followed them on his bike and called Davy and told him he saw them there."

"Why there?"

"Because the Viet Cong tunnels run beneath the temple, Kat. Sam's pretty sure the kids are hidden there."

I couldn't imagine a worse place to hide than inside the dark, snake and scorpion-infested tunnels like those I had seen outside of Ben Dinh. "So what do we do now?"

"I'll take you to the Jade Temple. It's close, a fifteen-minute ride. We can wait there for Davy to call."

I swept the hair from my eyes and exhaled. After meeting with Boris, I welcomed the warm sun on my face and the relief I felt as we left the market. I leaned forward so Tomy could hear me.

"Thanks for looking out for me, Tomy."

"We're not done yet. There's only so much we can do. From here on, to be safe, you need to take Buddy's gun. You may need it."

I didn't argue. I had no idea what lay ahead, but if Tomy thought I needed a gun, I wasn't about to refuse it. When we got to the Jade Temple, Tomy took Buddy's gun from inside the motorcycle's saddlebag and slipped it into my backpack.

* * *

It felt strange to be sitting in the peaceful sanctity of the Jade Temple with a gun in my backpack.

The peaceful serenity of the grounds surrounding the temple would have ordinarily quieted my mind were I not so aware that, within the next few hours, my life and that of the kids I hoped to find, and Eric's future, all depended on how convincing I could be with Boris. I leaned back against the Temple's warm, pink walls, closed my eyes, and wrapped my arms around my backpack as I played out in my mind the different scenarios of how my meeting with Boris might go down.

Tomy tapped me on the shoulder. "Davy called. It's time to go."

"Where to?"

"Book Street." Tomy walked swiftly ahead of me back to his bike. My heart started to race. This was really happening. When we got to the bike, Tomy stopped. "He wants me to leave you there."

"Leave?" I felt a sinking feeling in my stomach. "You can't just leave me. How will you know when Boris calls?"

"Trust me, we'll know. We'll have eyes on you the whole time. When you leave, Davy will get a call. If Sam's right and the kids are hidden in the tunnels beneath Ben Doc Temple, it's a ten-minute cab ride from Book Street. But you'll need to be careful. Whatever you do, Kat, don't go with the Russians into the tunnel. Insist they bring the kids out to you. We can take it from there. But if you go inside, we can't guarantee anything. You'll be on your own."

* * *

Tomy dropped me off in front of Notre Dame Cathedral, right across from Book Street. My strength faltered as I watched him vanish into traffic. I had no assurance that my plan to meet with Boris would work. What if, when Boris called, whoever was supposed to follow me messed up and lost track of me? In a city of nearly four million people, that would be easy enough to do. I could be walking into a trap. I cringed at the thought. Boris and his buddies would overpower me, go through my belongings, find the Saudi Diamond and the gun, and shoot me. I tugged on the straps of my backpack. *Too late now.* I thought of the little girl in the red sequined dress at the theater, the lost look I had seen in her dark eyes. What kind of life would she have? What kind of life would I have if I didn't try? And Eric? He was alive. War and politics had taken him from me, but I could change that. I looked up at the bell tower, the late afternoon sun in my eyes. I could do this.

Paradise for Bookworms was the first sign I saw as I crossed the street. It hung above a tiny bookshop, halfway down a treelined arcade, peppered with café tables, and stylishly dressed young Vietnamese who sat sipping coffee. A shopkeeper, an elderly woman, was standing outside the store next to a postcard stand. Spotting me, she took a card from the rack and approached.

"You like nice souvenir? A photo of our Notre Dame, maybe?" The woman shoved the postcard in my face. I stopped, looked at the card, shook my head, and was about to move on when she whispered, "Come. I have something for you."

"Me?"

"Your name is Katarina, right?"

Aside from my parents, who had named me, and Eric, who had insisted I write my full christened name on our wedding license, no one knew my first name. I had changed it as a child, and after Eric died, I refused to answer to anything but Kat. Katarina was too fancy a name for a tomboy who grew up in the Arizona desert and liked to climb trees and ride horses. It never felt right to me. And now this woman, this small, elderly Asian woman that I would have passed by had she not approached me, knew my name.

"Follow me." The old woman placed her knotted hand on my arm and led me inside the store, then quickly locked the door behind us. The store was small, dark, and smelled of incense, and was barely big enough to accommodate two aisles with floor-to-ceiling bookshelves crammed with books.

"What's this all about?"

"No worry. I have something for you. Come. I show you."

The old woman toddled down the aisle toward an old brass cash register in the back of the room. Reaching behind the counter, she took something in her hand, fisted it, and held it securely to her chest. With her free hand, she waved for me to come forward.

"You give me Saudi Diamond. I give you this. We make trade."

I glanced back over my shoulder at the door behind me. It was bolted shut.

"Who are you? How do you know about the Saudi Diamond?"

"My name is Kieu." She shuffled toward me. "A friend of yours, he asks me to give this to you." Keiu closed the space between us until she came to stand directly in front of me, then dangled an exact copy of the Saudi Diamond necklace in my face. "You give me Saudi diamond. I keep it safe."

"What friend?"

"Davy Crockett. He wants you to have this."

I placed the palm of my hand behind the dangling diamond and studied it. Aside from the elongated chain, the heart-shaped blue diamond, surrounded by a dozen sapphire stones, was a perfect match for the Saudi Blue Diamond.

"Where did you get this?"

"Your friend arranges for me to have it. He says it's important." Kieu held out the palm of her other hand, as though she were waiting for me to fork over the real diamond. "You give me Saudi Diamond. I give you this."

"That's not going to happen." I shook my head. "I'm not trading anything. You tell Crockett I'm keeping the diamond. I'm not giving it up."

"Davy won't be happy."

"Well, I'm not happy either. And believe me, he knows why." I snatched the necklace from Kieu's hand and put it around my neck. If I needed to, I could use the fake diamond to negotiate with Boris.

"But—"

"But nothing. Tell Crockett I took the necklace as a down payment on a promise he made me."

"What promise?"

"That's not your problem, it's mine. But he'll understand." As far as I was concerned, Crockett could damn well wait to get his hands on the Saudi Diamond. It was Crockett who stood between Eric and me, and I wasn't about to give in to any of Crockett's demands until I had seen and spoken to Eric. I stepped back and put my hand on the doorknob.

"Wait. I have more."

Kieu took a book from the bookshelf next to us. From behind it, she withdrew a small, folded piece of paper, no bigger than a matchbox. She pressed it into my hand. "I was told to give this to you."

"What is this?" I started to open it.

"No. Not here." Kieu put her hand on top of mine. "It's a map of the Cu Chi Tunnels beneath Ben Duoc Temple."

From behind us, a customer tried the door and then knocked.

Kieu looked at me anxiously, then took several magazines from the floor of the bookshelf and shoved them into my hands. "Please, go now, and be careful."

I slipped the map into my pocket, then hugged the magazines to my chest. Kieu opened the door, and I nodded goodbye. Outside, a group of school children, all dressed alike in white shirts and red ties, were headed in the direction of the cathedral. I quickened my pace and hurried past them, down the sidewalk. When I found an empty café table, I dropped my backpack at the foot of a chair and settled myself beneath the shadow of a Bodhi tree.

181

Chapter Twenty-Six

I ordered a cup of sweet Vietnamese coffee, a strong-roasted brew sweetened with condensed milk, and put the magazines on the table. I glanced at the covers. Fashion magazines with pictures of beautiful young Vietnamese models stared back at me. Some were dressed in traditional costume, while others wore smart Western-style clothes, a testament to a country that had opened up to more cosmopolitan, global influences. I waited until the waiter had brought my coffee, took the map from my pocket, and unfolded it in my lap. If anyone were watching, it would have appeared that my eyes were fixed on the magazines.

The map was a grey Xeroxed copy of a tourist map showing the tunnel beneath the Ben Duoc Temple, a network of wormholes outlining the Viet Cong's subterranean living quarters. A thick black line had been hand-drawn onto the map showing an unmarked passageway leading to a large underground chamber with the words *Kids' Dormitory* written above it. The dormitory looked to be about the size of the Viet Cong sleeping areas I had seen on the diorama in Ben Dinh. From the dormitory, several other small tunnels lead to the surface. One was marked *Escape Route*, and another included a warning, *Do Not Use; Booby-trapped!* I traced the thick black line with the fingertips of my right hand, then turned the map over. On the back was a brief note.

I recognized the handwriting immediately. It had been years, but it was as familiar to me as my own.

Katy,

If you're reading this, it means you're alive, and Crockett has found a way to get a map to you. The kids are hidden in the tunnel beneath Ben Douc Temple. I'm sorry. I never expected to see you again. There is so much to say and so little I can tell you. But know this, I'm not a traitor. It was always country first and still is. Whatever you may hear, remember that. If I could tell you to go home, I would. But we both know you're too damn stubborn. Follow my instructions, and God willing, if we come through this alive, I'll explain what I can.

Eric

The remainder of Eric's note was written in another hand and read like a warning label or some type of extremist survival guide. Printed in all caps and underlined were the words, <u>AVOID ENTERING THE TUNNEL</u>. Beneath was penned a series of short paragraphs suggesting that if I couldn't avoid entering the tunnel, what I would need to do if I hoped to get out alive.

CAUTION: Boris will likely choose to enter the tunnel from the tourist entrance behind the Ben Duoc Tower. The crawlspace inside is dark and dusty, but it's been widened for tourist access and cleared of booby traps and snakes. This part of the tunnel should not be a problem. But be aware. Further into the tunnel, beyond the area visited by tourists, there is an unmarked passageway on the left-hand side, approximately sixty feet in. This section of the tunnel will lead to where the children are hidden. But it's much narrower and won't be easy for you to navigate. Be careful. Boris is desperate. If he thinks you might expose him or he's not sure about you, he may lead you inside the tunnel and bury you there.

I stopped reading and folded the note over. If there were any other way…if I hadn't seen Eric and was so desperate to know what had happened…if I hadn't seen the little girl in the red dress and the terror in her eyes, I would have left right then, but I couldn't. I opened the note and continued.

If you reach the dormitory, position yourself between Boris and the children and move away from the tunnel entrance as far as possible. You won't be able to leave through the tunnel you came through. Tomy and Sam will be inside the tunnels, and if possible, they will set off a diversion.

You will need to move quickly. There are several quick exits to the surface marked on the map. Study them. They are the only way out.

I folded the map and put it back in my pocket. Tomy and Sam knew the tunnels better than the streets of Ho Chi Minh City, along with the horror stories of boobie traps, hidden spikes, grenades, poison gases, trap doors, and snakes hidden inside. They had worked with American GIs as tunnel rats during the war, helping to flush out the Viet Cong. It was a dangerous job, best suited for small, slightly built men who went into the tunnel with nothing more to protect themselves than a flashlight, a knife, and a rope. If I couldn't convince Boris to bring the kids out of the tunnel, at least I knew Tomy and Sam would be inside.

I reached into my backpack for the guidebook Sophie had given me and looked up Ben Duoc Temple. Built in 1993, to commemorate Ho Chi Minh's 103rd birthday and as a memorial to the soldiers and those killed in the Saigon-Gia Dinh region during the war with the French and later the Americans. The temple sits atop the Ben Duoc tunnels, or what marks the end of the Cu Chi Tunnels.

My cell phone rang before I could finish what I was reading. I put the guidebook down and answered.

"Hello?"

I wasn't sure as I pressed the phone to my ear, if what I heard was the sound of Boris' heavy breathing or my heart pounding in my ears. My palms felt clammy. I braced myself against the back of my chair.

"Ms. Lawson?"

"You were expecting someone else?" I adopted a sarcastic tone. It helped to cover my nerves. I figured if I sounded confident, I could keep Boris guessing. Make him think I had nothing to fear. That I was backed by big bucks and even bigger deals down the road. Deals I was confident he wouldn't want to pass up.

"Cut the crap, Ms. Lawson. We've checked you out."

My voice caught in my throat. If this deal fell apart now, everything—the kids, Eric, all of it disappeared.

"And?"

"You're a washed-up, middle-aged newspaper reporter. You were fired from your last job, and then you went to Hollywood, where you worked for a PR agency, handling "catch-and-kill" stories for a few movie stars who wanted to keep their names out of any negative press. The money was good, but after a while, you must have started to realize all the money you were missing out on. Killing a story to protect someone's reputation wasn't nearly as good as getting in on the action."

I pressed my lips together. My real backstory, and the one the FBI had fabricated, held up. Not exactly a stellar reputation, but shady enough that Boris would believe my connections to the seedier side of Hollywood would benefit his business plan, and that I was nothing more than a woman on the take.

"What am I supposed to be, impressed? Couldn't have been too difficult for you to figure me out. When I checked into the hotel, they asked for my life history."

"Don't try to get smart with me. With a name and ID, we can access tax and employment records, as well as any other information we need, anywhere in the world. Do you think we don't have spies in your country? A quick call to your last employer, the PR agency, the newspaper where you used to work, and we know everything about you."

"Well, goodie, goodie for you. So now you know who I am. But it's not me you want. It's my contacts, and they've got plenty of money. So, what are we going to do here? Are we going to cut a deal or not?"

"Not so fast. I want your source. I want to know who's buying and how you found out about us.

"I told you. My buyer heard about you through a friend who used your services. He was interested in cutting a deal for himself, so he traveled to Vietnam, met with Nguyen, and saw an opportunity. The rest you know."

"I want a name, Ms. Lawson."

"Sorry, you don't use names, and I don't either. Besides, I already gave you fifty thousand dollars. I'd say that's good-faith money. You show me the kids, and I'll give you the Saudi Blue Diamond. Then, perhaps we can discuss setting up a nice, friendly little meet-and-greet while I arrange for the rest of your money. What did you say you wanted? Half a million. Not a problem, but not before I see the kids."

Boris was silent, and for a moment I thought I had blown it.

"We have a deal or not?"

"You're lucky, Ms. Lawson, that I have a shipment I need to unload, or I wouldn't bother with you. You bring the Saudi Blue Diamond with you, and we'll make a deal. Meet me in front of Ben Duoc Temple. It's an hour and a half from the city. Get a cab and come alone. We see you with anyone, the deal is off."

Boris hung up, and I sat back and closed my eyes. My hands were shaking.

Chapter Twenty-Seven

I took a cab to Ben Duoc Temple and instructed the cab driver to drop me off in front of the Tam Quán gateway. If Boris was watching, I wanted him to see I had come alone. But I saw no sign of the Russian; only several Buddhist monks in their long, orange robes passed me, their heads bowed in mindful meditation. The temple had just closed. It was after six p.m., and a blanket of twilight covered the temple's six-thousand-square-meter garden campus.

I walked beneath the temple's entry archways, a series of ornately designed red-tile-roofed porticos, trimmed with gold, that led to the temple courtyard. Directly ahead of me was the main temple, a quiet but imposing structure with a wide set of stairs, guarded by four stone dragons. At the top of the steps was a long, open porch with thick, round pillars that resembled Roman columns. These supported the temple's red, two-tiered pagoda roof, adorned with gold and red eaves that looked like wings and featured large, decorative dragons.

"You come alone?"

Boris walked out from beneath the temple's shadows and stood at the top of the steps. Dressed in black and his face white and pasty, he looked like a vulture, waiting to swoop down from his stoop.

I steeled my nerves.

"I did. Did you?"

"You ask a lot of questions, Ms. Lawson. Or shall I call you Kat? After all, it's just the two of us. We're here alone."

Boris moved slowly down the steps until he came to the center of the courtyard and stood directly in front of me. So close I could smell the stench of his foul breath. I stiffened, my backpack heavy with the weight of the gun against my back. I steadied my eyes on his.

"Ms. Lawson would be just fine," I said.

"Did you bring the diamond?"

"It's what you asked for. But if you think I'm going to give it to you before I've seen the kids, you'd be wro—"

"Wrong? Ms. Lawson, let me assure you. I'm never wrong." Boris put his right hand behind my neck and pulled my face to his. "But you might be."

Then, tracing the side of my face with the back of his index finger, Boris slid his hand down my neck and curled his fingers around the gold chain Kieu had given me.

"Well, what do we have here?" Borris pulled the fake Saudi pendant from beneath my shirt.

I grabbed the necklace. "What are you doing?"

Boris's hand seized my wrist, and I screamed in pain.

"What do you think I'm doing? I'm taking what's mine." Boris yanked the chain from my neck. "I think it's time you and I take a little walk. You wanted to see the kids, right?"

I twisted my arm free and massaged my wrist. *What a fool. Did he think I'd be stupid enough to wear the diamond?*

"You don't need to get rough about it. I'm here, aren't I? You already have the fifty thousand I gave you, and now you've got the diamond. So, yes. I think it's time I see what my client's paying for. You show me the kids, I'll arrange to get the rest of the money to you."

Boris stuffed the diamond in his pocket. "All right, let's go."

Taking my elbow, Borris led me from the courtyard to a garden area behind the temple. The smell of jasmine was heavy in the air, and the quiet between us was so thick that the only sound I heard was the crunch of gravel beneath our feet. We walked, maybe a thousand feet beyond the temple, when Boris broke the silence.

"Nice, isn't it?" Boris moved his hand from my elbow to my upper arm and squeezed it tightly. "My Vietnamese friends are very accommodating.

They allow me to come here at night so I can be alone. The security guards won't bother us. And the gardeners have all gone home. It's just the two of us now, Ms. Lawson. We don't need to worry about being interrupted."

"Good to know. I feel safer already knowing you run such a secure operation." I ran my free hand through my hair, slyly pulled the three-inch stiletto hairclip from my head, and slipped it into my pocket. My stomach knotted. If Boris threatened me, I planned to open the stiletto's steel blade and fight him off. Or at least buy enough time that I might be able to get the gun from my backpack.

"No reason for you not to feel secure. As long as you're telling the truth, neither of us needs to worry." Boris stopped and nodded to an area beyond the flower garden. "I hope you like close quarters, Ms. Lawson. If you want to see the kids, they're hidden inside the tunnel that runs beneath our feet. You'll need to crawl inside."

I tried to jerk my arm from Boris's grip, but he held tight. "No way. I'm not crawling inside any damn tunnel. You want me to see the kids, bring them out in the open where they can get some fresh air."

"I'm afraid that's not possible." Boris yanked me, pulling me behind him, until we reached a staging area beyond the gardens, where several canopied tents and kiosks with information about the tunnels had been set up for tourists. Directly in front of me was the entrance to the tunnel. Nothing more than a dark hole in the ground, two and a half feet wide and surrounded by leaves and grass still wet from the rain.

"I'm not going inside. That wasn't part of the deal."

"What, are you frightened?" Boris mocked me. "Don't be. The tunnel has been hollowed out so even fat Americans can fit in.

"Really? And what about fat Russians?" I elbowed Boris in the side. A big mistake. He grabbed the back of my neck again and pushed me down on my hands and knees.

"This fat Russian does just fine. But you never know. There are snakes or scorpions inside, but I'm not worried, I'll be right behind you."

Boris let go, and I brushed my hands off and sat back on my knees. I was stalling for time. I had been warned not to go inside the tunnel, but I had no choice. I didn't see any out, not if I wanted to find the kids, and without the kids, I'd never convince Crockett to let me see Eric. I stood up. If Tomy and Sam were somewhere in the garden, I was hopeful they might make a move before Boris forced me inside the tunnel, but I knew better. With Crockett calling the shots, he would wait until he had the kids in sight before coming to my aid.

"This the only way in?"

"What, you want an elevator? Americans. You're all so soft. There are other tunnel entrances, but at night, here in the garden, this one is best. The entrance to the kids' dorm is hidden just beyond the tourist tunnel. It's a snug crawl, but we've swept the tunnel for booby traps and mines. You'll be fine."

I shook my head. "You need to give me some proof. I'm not climbing inside some dark dungeon without knowing the kids are there."

"You want proof. Fine, I give you proof." Boris put his hand beneath my shoulder and dragged me over the mouth of the tunnel. Then he took a small square flashlight from his belt and directed the light into the hole. "Take a look!"

I stared down into the tunnel entrance, a dark, deep, narrow space, like a well, had been hollowed out ten to twelve feet beneath me. A small ladder, the rungs not quite reaching the surface, had been fastened to the side of the hole. Tourists who chose to crawl down into the tunnel would reach the bottom, then crouch down on all fours and enter a small wormhole leading to an underground passageway for curious sightseers. They would then return the same way they had entered.

"Dimitry!" Boris hollered into the hole.

From the bottom of the hole, Dimitry crawled into the light, shading his eyes as he stood up. Even standing, he was at least five feet from the surface.

"Ms. Lawson wants to see one of the children. Bring out our little butterfly."

Like a good soldier, Dimitry crouched back down in the hole and disappeared into the tunnel, out of the light.

"How many kids are inside?" I asked.

"A dozen. Six boys. Six girls. You want more? We'll see how this goes."

I glanced over my shoulder, and a shiver ran down my spine. The garden was dark, and the only sounds were a few crickets and the ghostly hooting of a lone owl, adding to my sense of unease.

"Ahh, here she is. Our little butterfly. Come, look for yourself. This is Diep."

I looked over Boris's shoulder. Beneath us was the little girl I had seen in the red sequined dress at the puppet theater. She couldn't have been more than forty pounds and three feet tall. Her face was dirty, and her long, dark hair was tangled. She was dressed in a cotton rag that hung on her tiny body like a dirty washcloth. Dimitry pulled her awkwardly into the light, holding her upper arm tightly. She looked frightened, her eyes pleading.

"You want to see the rest? We go now." Boris clapped me on the back and pushed me ahead of him toward the ladder.

I stepped onto the ladder and crawled down into the open pit that had been hollowed out as an entry point for tourists. I wanted to pull Diep away from Dimitry and comfort her, but before I could, the Russian pushed the little girl down onto her knees, and with a flashlight in one hand, crouched on top of her and forced her to crawl into the tunnel.

Boris ordered me to follow. There was no escape. No one had come to rescue me. I was on my own. The kids were in the tunnel. My future, if I had one, and that of the kids, depended upon my rescue. I had to move forward.

With my backpack in front of me, I dropped to my hands and knees and followed Dimitry into the tunnel. The first sixty feet were an easy crawl, dark but not suffocating. This section matched Eric's note exactly, designed to give tourists the Cu Chi Tunnel experience. But unlike curious tourists who would enter, crawl a hundred feet, then turn around and get a photo op while climbing back to the surface, we weren't heading back to the entrance. Instead, Dimitry pushed aside a dry wooden door-like shield. If there had been a sign above it, it would have read: Do Not Enter. From this point on, the dirt walls narrowed, and conditions changed. My body brushed against the walls. I felt as if the earth was closing in on me. It was hot and stuffy. The air was thin, and I struggled to breathe. Sweat dripped from my brow, and the palms of my hands were sticky. When I thought I couldn't go any further, Dimitry stopped and pushed a second wooden plank aside. A rush of fresh air flowed into the tunnel. Dimitry shoved the little girl ahead of him, then dropped onto his elbows and dragged his legs behind him.

"How much further?" I asked.

"Not far."

I knelt on my elbows and squeezed through the narrow opening as best I could. Behind me, I could hear Boris's heavy breathing as his body scraped loose rock and dirt from along the sides of the tunnel. Ahead, I heard children's voices.

The little girl screamed as we reached the end of the tunnel, then scampered ahead and jumped from our wormhole into a large, open area. Dimitry followed and leaped to the floor behind her.

When I reached the end of the tunnel, I stopped to catch my breath. The air inside the dormitory, though thin, was fresher than inside the tunnel. Tomy had told me the Viet Cong had designed these rooms with multiple air shafts that tunneled to the surface and had been disguised to hide their locations. For all the misery of the narrow tunnel leading into the room, the air shafts appeared to be working. The room, the size of a basketball court, was lit with portable lanterns that cast dark shadows on the walls. Pushed against the far side of the room were broken pieces of bamboo that had made the frames for bunk beds once used by the Viet Cong. In front of them were piled several small suitcases and plastic bags of food I recognized as being from the Russian market.

I jumped down from the wormhole. Diep hurried across the room to join an older girl sitting on a dirty blanket with four other children. In front of them, Luka, the third Russian I had seen at the Puppet Theater, stood guard. The children stared vacantly ahead, as though too afraid to move. Boris crawled out from behind me, brushed himself off, and then approached one of the young boys on the blanket. He pulled the boy to his feet, took his chin in his hand, and turned the boy's head toward me.

"Is this what your client wants?"

I reached into my pocket and curled my fingers around the stiletto hairclip I had brought with me. Every fiber in my being wanted to take the hairclip from my pocket, release the blade, and sink it into his chest before he could say another word. But I didn't get the chance. Boris moved further away, his gaze shifting to a second child—a girl who shied away as he grabbed her.

"Or maybe this one?"

Suddenly, from inside the hole we had just climbed out of, an explosion erupted. A blast that sent a cloud of dust and dirt flying into the room. The sides of the hole began to collapse. The children screamed. Boris, Luka, and Dimitry watched as the wall crumbled, blocking their escape.

I ran toward the children. Something was going on, but I didn't know what it was.

Boris lunged at me, grabbed my arm, twisted it behind my back, and dragged me away from the kids. Then, with my head in a choke hold, he screamed at me. "What have you done? Who followed you here?"

"No one followed me." I dug my nails into his arm. "I came alone. Just like you asked."

I could only hope that the explosion had been one Tomy and Sam had deliberately set off and not because they had accidentally tripped a wire and were trapped inside.

"Bitch! You're never going to get out of here."

Then, in Russian, Boris yelled at Luka and Dimitry. I knew, despite the language difference, we were in trouble. Luka stepped back from Boris, while Dimitry reached into his cargo pants, took out a palm-sized round canister, and waved it in my face. *A grenade!*

"You know what this is?" Boris snarled in my ear.

"You wouldn't. You'd never get out fast enough. It'd blow us all up."

"Trust me. We've no intention of dying down here. There's a timer on it. You'll never be able to stop it, and we'll be gone by the time it goes off."

"You wouldn't. These kids are innocents."

"Yes, but you're not. And I can't afford to leave any witnesses. We douse the lights here, and this place becomes as dark as a tomb. You'll never find your way out. Meanwhile, my friends and I take another tunnel to the surface. There's more than one way in and out of this ant hill." Boris nodded toward a second tunnel on the wall behind him. The same tunnel Eric had marked on the map as booby-trapped. Boris must have believed that with all the work he and his team had done to secure the children's hiding place, the tunnel had been cleared. Either that, or he was so desperate that he was willing to take the risk. "Once we reach the surface, this room and every wormhole leading to it will have collapsed."

"You'll never get away with it," I said.

"You don't think so? This room's not on any tourist map. The tunnels leading here aren't marked. Nobody's going to miss kids they never knew existed. As for you, journalists go missing all the time."

"Not this one!"

I bit down hard on Boris's forearm, grabbed the hairclip from my pocket, and released the safety. Boris fought back, his arm tightened around my neck, pulling me off my feet. Then, catching the glint of the blade in my hand, his eyes went wide with surprise. Too late! I jammed the stiletto into his leg. Boris screamed. Blood spurted from the wound as he let go of my arm.

Dimitry stuffed the grenade back into his pocket without pulling the pin, then hurried to help Boris. Luka ran toward me, and I dodged him, dove for my backpack, and grabbed the forty-five from inside. Out of breath, shaking, and with both hands on the handle, I aimed the gun at the Russians.

"Take one step and I fire! And believe me, this close, I can't miss."

Luka raised his hands and slowly moved toward Boris. Dimitry froze. He had taken his kerchief from around his neck and tied a tourniquet around Boris's leg to try to stop the bleeding. Boris shouted something in Russian, then draped his arm over Luka's shoulder. Together, they limped toward the second tunnel that had been boarded up behind them. Boris and Dimitry yanked at the boards until the tunnel entrance was open, then Luka helped Dimitry lift Boris into the crawl space. With Luka and Boris inside the tunnel, Dimitry reached into his pocket for the grenade.

I raised the gun. "Don't even think about it."

Dimetry took his empty hand out of his pocket. "Goodbye, Ms. Lawson."

I watched with the kids behind me as Dimetry turned and climbed into the tunnel. At any moment, I expected Boris or one of his thugs to toss the grenade back into the room.

And then—

Kaboom! A loud explosion! Much louder than before. The room shook, and a sudden rush of air from within the tunnel doused the canteen lights. I thought this was the end. Diep ran to me and threw her arms around my legs. I picked her up and hugged the small girl to my chest. Dust and smoke filled the air. But we were alive.

Diep started to cry.

"It's okay, Butterfly. I have a light."

I stuffed the gun into the back of my waistband, then took my lipstick penlight from my pocket and flashed the light on the tunnel entry where the Russians had escaped. The tunnel had fallen in on itself. Dust and dirt clouded the opening, blocking any chance of the Russians' return or escape to the surface. The grenade in Dimitry's pocket had either gone off, or one of them had tripped a wire to an old explosive hidden deep inside the tunnel. Whatever happened, the Russians weren't coming back.

Chapter Twenty-Eight

"Hey, Lady. You need help?"

"Tomy?" From the air vent somewhere above my head, I could hear Tomy's voice.

"Are you okay? We heard an explosion."

"We're fine!" I flashed my penlight to the vent above my head and exhaled. "Boris got spooked by the blast from inside the tunnel we crawled through. He thought I had set him up, and he and Dimitry and Luka escaped through a second tunnel."

"Sounds like they chose the wrong tunnel. Too bad. It was booby-trapped. One of them must have tripped a wire, and everything caved in on top of them."

I patted Diep on the back and tried to comfort her. She was shaking in my arms. Wet tears rolled down her cheeks. "Can you get us out of here?"

"That's the plan. There's a third tunnel leading from where you are to what was once an infirmary. It's marked on the map Kieu gave you."

"You knew Kieu gave me a map?" I put Diep down and took the map from my pocket.

"I told you we had eyes on you the entire time. It was all part of the plan. But right now, we need to get you and the kids out of there. Do you see the tunnel?"

With my penlight, I focused on the map, then flashed my light across the room to the stack of bamboo bunk beds that had been torn down and piled up against the wall like junk. I moved closer to get a better look.

"I think I know where it is. It looks like the Russians moved a bunch of bunk beds against the wall. If I'm right, the tunnel is hidden behind them."

I flashed my light back at the kids. Their eyes were all fixed on mine. Even without speaking the same language, the kids seemed to understand.

I motioned for them to follow. "There's a tunnel hidden behind that stack of bunk beds. We need to move them. It's our only way out. Help me."

Together, we attacked the pile of bamboo frames, pulling them away from the wall until we could create enough space for me to walk behind the pile and see where a tunnel hole had been patched with rotted wood and barbed wire. One of the boys pushed me aside, took one of the blankets the kids had been sitting on, covered his hands, and pulled at the wire and the wooden frame until they gave way. Behind it, a nest of mattresses blocked the entrance.

Several of the children ran forward and started to pull at the mattresses.

"Wait!" I raised my hands and stepped in front of the kids and the tunnel entrance. The children looked at me, and I could see the anxious look in their eyes. I moved back to the center of the room and yelled up at the air vent, "We found the tunnel."

Tomy yelled back. "Good. Do you have a rope?"

"I do." I took the macrame rope belt from around my waist, pulled the slip knot, and with my hands shaking, began to unravel it.

"How many kids are there?"

"Twelve."

"Tether them together. It'll give them something to hang on to. It's a long tunnel, and it'll be dark."

"The entrance is blocked. It looks like there's a bunch of old mattresses stuffed inside."

"You'll need to be careful. There's no telling what's nesting behind what's stuffed in the tunnel. Use one of the bamboo poles to loosen the mattress from the tunnel walls. Then stand back."

"Why?" I had a creepy feeling I knew the answer.

"If there are any snakes inside, they'll slither out."

I felt a chill run down my back. "Great! Then what?"

"Stand back and leave them alone. Once you clear the hole, secure the tethers and get yourself and the kids inside the tunnel. But be aware. This was a hospital. There's no telling what you'll find. Could be some skeletons down there. Keep the kids tethered to you, and Sam will meet you there and lead you out."

None of this sounded good, but I was out of options. I looked back at the pile of bed frames, grabbed my backpack, found the longest bamboo pole I could find, then did exactly as Tomy told me. Holding the pole at one end, I pushed and prodded until the mattress piling fell loose from the tunnel walls, then stepped back and waited. Nothing.

I gave it another try, this time rattling the pole as far as I could inside the hole. Still nothing. I stepped back, and then, silently, a fifteen-foot-long cobra slithered out from the hole.

I froze, and the kids didn't move. Nobody did so much as breathe as the snake slid silently across the dirt floor and coiled beneath the bamboo bed frames.

Convinced the snake was far enough away, I motioned for the kids to come close. "Come. We need to go."

After untangling the rope, I loosely wrapped a section around each child's wrist until we were all tethered together. Then, with the flashlight in one hand, a thin section of rope tied around my wrist, and a sharp bamboo stick in my hand for protection, I got down on my hands and knees. With one final deep breath, I pushed my backpack into the tunnel, told the kids to follow me, and crawled inside.

Inside, my flashlight was useless, casting little more than a thin grey light into the black abyss. The air was thin, dry, and dusty, and all I could hear were the sounds of us scraping against the sides of the tunnel as we inched forward. I jabbed ahead with the bamboo stick. This tunnel was even narrower than the one I had crawled through before. Diep started to cry.

"Don't worry. We're going to be fine." I don't know why I said it. The kids couldn't understand, but I said it anyway. Maybe because it made me feel better to hear my voice resonating inside the tunnel. I kept repeating myself as I moved slowly. One hand, then one knee. Then the other. Finally, a light ahead. "We're almost there. Keep moving."

"Kat!"

"Sam?" My heart raced. "Is that you?"

"I'm here, Kat. Keep coming."

My hands dug into the dirt. *Just a few more feet.* I gave a firm shove to my backpack, pushed it ahead, then hunched my shoulders to my ears, and, on my elbows, pulled my body to the tunnel opening. Then, shining the small penlight ahead, I saw Sam's face.

"The kids with you?"

"They're behind me."

I reached out my hand, and Sam took my arm, lifting me from the hole and into yet another dark, dusty dungeon. As I brushed the dirt from my clothes, I watched as the kids crawled out from inside the tunnel and then untied the thin piece of rope from their wrists.

Sam moved ahead. "Follow me. Tomy and I figured out a way to get you out."

In the center of the room, several of the infirmary's bamboo bunk beds had been pushed together, forming a makeshift fortress; they were stacked three and four high, one on top of the other until they almost reached the ceiling. Sam walked ahead of me, stood in front of one of the ladders, and nodded for me to climb up.

"Climb up to the top bunk. From the center of the bed, if you look up, you'll see there's another tunnel entrance directly above your head. Tomy's outside waiting, and once he sees you there, he'll lower a rope to help you with the kids. Tie the rope around them, give it a tug, and he'll pull them out. Once we get all twelve kids out, I'll help you, and we're home free."

I picked Diep up. She put her small arms around my neck, and I climbed with one arm around her and one hand on the ladder's rail to the top bunk. The first person I saw was Tomy. He had climbed halfway down the rope and reached for the little girl.

"Hand her to me, Kat."

"Take his hand, Butterfly. It's okay." I kissed Diep's forehead, then lifted her as high as I could until Tomy had hold of her. Carefully, he wrapped the bottom of the rope firmly around her small body, then strapped it to his chest and climbed up the rope like an Olympic champion.

I waited until I knew Diep was safe, then helped each of the kids as they climbed up onto the top bunk, assisting them in grabbing hold of the rope and securing it around their waists. When the last kid had gone, Sam joined me on the bunk.

"After you, Kat." Sam took hold of the rope and handed it to me.

I grabbed the rope and threw my arms around him. "Thank you."

"You can thank me later. You need to go now. Hurry." Sam tied the loose end of the rope around my waist and gave it a tug. I clung to the rope, engulfed in blackness all around me, until finally, I saw a glimmer of light and Tomy's face leaning into the hole.

Tomy reached down, grabbed my hand, and pulled me up the last few feet. Sam followed me out of the hole. I walked away to catch my breath, then looked back at Tomy and Sam, the men who had risked their lives to save me and the kids. I bent over, my hands on my knees, and exhaled. I felt as though I had run a marathon. My heart was pounding so hard that my chest hurt. I took a deep breath, and I stood up. The worst was over. We had survived.

Tomy put his hand out to me, and I took it. We hugged, and then he brushed the dirt from my clothes. "You have the gun?"

I reached behind me to my waistband, where I had tucked the gun before climbing into the tunnel, but it was gone. I shook my head and looked back into the hole.

"It must have fallen—"

"Leave it. It's better if it stays where it will never be found again."

I looked around.

"Where are the kids?"

Tomy answered, "You don't need to worry about that right now. They're safe. That's all you need to know. It's better that way."

"What about the Russians?"

"The Russians didn't make it out. The tunnel collapsed. They're dead. And believe me, nobody's gonna miss them."

"And Crockett? Where is he? I need to talk to him."

"I don't know. But I do know he wants you to go back to the hotel. He said he'll talk to you in the morning."

Chapter Twenty-Nine

Eddie was sitting at the bar when I got back to the hotel. She had a half-empty glass in her hand, and when she saw me, she patted the seat beside her and smiled politely.

I dropped my backpack in front of the empty stool. "I assume this isn't a social visit. You're here to make sure I don't leave the hotel unexpectedly?"

"Davy thought it would be a good idea. I don't know where you think you would go, but I have a pretty good idea who you might be looking for. Trust me. If you think you can find Eric on your own, you won't. The only way you'll find him is if Davy agrees."

Eddie signaled the bartender to bring two more of whatever she was having. I sat down. I didn't care what she was drinking as long as it was strong. I needed something to settle my nerves.

"And what about Eric? He doesn't get a say in this? Does Davy get to decide everything?"

"There are a lot of things Davy gets to decide. I don't agree with them all, but when it comes to Eric, let's just say, you need to be careful."

"I've been careful. I've done exactly what you needed me to do and more. The kids are free. The Russians are dead. And now I want to see Eric. Crockett owes me that much."

Look, Kat. I understand what you want. You want to take Eric home with you. You think you can fix him, and everything will be alright with the world. But it won't. Eric knows too much, and there are people—Russian spies he trained when he taught at the American school—living deep undercover in the US right now. They're part of what we in the US call the

Illegals Program. Spies, working as ordinary citizens, planted by the Russian Foreign Intelligence Service, the SVR. If Eric were to go home and word got out that a former MIA had been lost and was now found, his picture would be on the front page of every newspaper in America. Do you think he wouldn't be recognized? The ripple effects would jeopardize the entire operation we've put together here. You can't keep a story like that secret. The war may have ended in seventy-five, but there's a cold war going on, and the country needs Eric right where he is."

"What are you trying to tell me? That Eric's a pawn? Some kind of secret double agent, you can't ever let go of?"

"I'll leave that for Davy to explain. But don't be so quick to judge. You've no idea what Eric's been through, or what he wants."

"I know he loves me, or that he did. And that he's going to want to come home, and that's what he's going to do. What else could he want?"

Eddie finished her drink and pushed the empty glass across the counter.

"No, Kat. You're wrong."

"You don't know that. You don't know Eric."

The bartender returned with two scotch sodas. Eddie picked up her glass, swirled it, and took a drink.

"What I know is that if the Soviet Union hadn't fallen apart in eighty-nine, my grandson would be living in America as a Russian spy right now, and I never would have found him. But because he did come home and he found me, we found Eric."

"We?"

"I think you know who we're talking about. I won't name names, but I'm sure you can figure it out. Call it the Agency, whatever you like. Because of the work Eric did in Russia and continues to do today, we've gained insight into the network of Russian spies operating within the US. We've been observing them for years."

I took a sip of the scotch and soda and put it down. "Tell me something, after you met Eric, and realized he had been MIA and traded to the Russians, where he spent sixteen years of his life as a teacher in some spy school, did you ever think to ask him if he wanted to come home?"

"I didn't need to. It wasn't a choice."

"How could it not be a choice? He paid the price. He—"

"He couldn't come home, Kat. Not ever. Too much had happened. Eric's not the same man you knew. He knew that. We all knew it. It was too late. Too much had happened. But he could start over. He could have a better life here. We could help him, and he could help his country."

"So, you turned Eric over to Crockett, a man you told me you don't trust?"

"It's not a matter of trust, Kat. I knew Crockett. And I knew he'd do the right thing."

"You're going to have to explain that to me. Because I don't see how keeping Eric here was the right thing."

Look, I hated Crockett when I first met him. I hated everything about him. He's brash. He can be vulgar. Misogynistic. It took me a long time to understand that with men like Crockett, it's country first. Always was. Always will be. Right or wrong. They have one mindset. They have a job to do, and they do it."

"So why work with him now? If you hated him so much, what changed?"

"Time. Distance, maybe. As I mentioned before, I was a reporter for Rolling Stone when I first arrived in Vietnam. My husband had died the year before, and my only child, my son, had just been drafted. I wasn't a fan of the war, and I wasn't about to stay home and watch it on TV. I wanted to be part of the action and report on it. I convinced an editor at Rolling Stone to hire me as a stringer, and I bought myself a one-way ticket to Tan Son Nhut International. Crockett was my son's field commander. I remember Mark telling me he was excited about Captain Crockett. He was young, just a couple of years older than Mark, and he had a good reputation with his men. He didn't have a good reputation with me, though. Crockett was the reason Mark was killed. I found out about it in the worst possible way. I was at the Rexford for the Five O'clock Follies when I got the news. Crockett had come in from the field and reported on a massacre. One of the units he had sent into the jungle the night before to protect a village of innocent civilians had been ambushed. The VC had crawled out from the tunnels beneath the village and slaughtered them. They never had a chance."

CHAPTER TWENTY-NINE

"I'm sorry. That had to be awful."

"When I realized Crockett was talking about Mark's unit, I lost it. I went after Crockett, hit him, and screamed at him. I told him I thought he was a coward. He, of course, had no idea who I was, and once he learned I was Mark's mother, he wanted to send me home. He said he didn't understand how I could be allowed in the country when my son was fighting. I told him I wasn't under his command, and I'd damned do what I wanted. And I did. I made sure I was there for every briefing he gave, and that he knew I wasn't going home. How could I? I had a grandkid and a daughter-in-law in Vietnam, and I wasn't about to leave them."

"So, you stayed."

"Until the war ended in seventy-five, and I had to leave, yes. It was a nightmare. Things came unglued quickly. I couldn't get my grandson or my daughter-in-law out. I was forced onto a plane, and when I got to the States, I spent the next fourteen years trying to find any way to return to Vietnam and look for them. Then, in the late eighties, Vietnam opened to foreign investment, and a couple of years later, Nike offered me a job. As far as Nike was concerned, I was a retired war correspondent who spoke the language and wanted to return to Vietnam. That's when I met Crockett again. We ran into each other at a Red Poets Society meeting. By then, I had found Buddy, and life looked pretty good. However, it turned out that Buddy hadn't only been trying to find me but also his uncle. Only Nguyen wanted nothing to do with him, and Buddy began to worry that Nguyen might try to get the Russians to take him out. I figured Crockett was more than just a fellow expat, hanging out at the bar and selling insurance. It didn't take much. Those of us who have been around for a while know each other. That doesn't necessarily mean we know all the details, but you start to figure it out. So I told Crockett about Eric, hoping that he might do me a favor and get the Russians off Buddy's back."

"Did it work?"

"It did. Or maybe the Russians just didn't care. For all I knew, they thought Buddy was some half-breed Asian American kid trying to get by and got lucky working for Nike. Davy didn't think the Russians here knew that Buddy had escaped from some underground Russian spy school. They weren't interested in him. Those who took Buddy back to Mother Russia after the war were long gone, and those who came back after the fall of the Soviet Union? They had all escaped a collapsing country and economic chaos and weren't looking back. Things were in turmoil back home. Once I turned Crockett onto Eric, he and Buddy distanced themselves. I'm sure it was for appearances, but I wasn't going to ask."

I stirred my drink with my finger. "So, you made peace with Crockett after all."

"I had to. It wasn't Crockett who murdered Mark; it was the VC. If I wanted my grandson to be safe, I'd have to put Crockett's decision to send my son into a losing battle behind me. Realistically, I knew that no matter how hard the decision was, Crockett had followed orders. I had to live with that. It's easier to deal with people when you know who they are than with people you don't. That's why I told you to leave that night at the theater. When it comes to doing the right thing, Crockett will do it, no matter whose life is at stake. You need to remember that. You're an expendable commodity, no matter what. If Crockett needs to get a job done and you're in the way, don't think he'll save you."

Chapter Thirty

The phone rang in my room at 8:45 the next morning. After a sleepless night, I rushed out of the shower to answer it just before voicemail picked up.

"Gooooooood mornin', Vietnam!" Crockett was doing his Robin Williams impersonation from the movie with the same name. "Get yourself downstairs, Twinkle toes, and bring your bags. I'm parked outside. We're not coming back."

"Where're we going?"

"You'll see. Curbside, oh-nine-hundred." Crockett hung up.

I slammed the phone down. I needed Crockett to reach Eric, and Crockett wanted the Saudi Blue Diamond. Seemed like a fair enough exchange. I gathered my belongings from the room, including cosmetics from the bathroom, my notebook and cell phone from the nightstand, and tossed my clothes from the dresser and closet into my rolling bag. Then I threw my backpack over my shoulder. Fifteen minutes later, I was downstairs.

Crockett was parked in front of the hotel. Judging from the bags under his eyes, he had been up all night.

Seeing me, he opened his arms. "Ahh, just what I like. A woman who knows how to follow orders."

Crockett took my rollie bag from me and threw it in the back of his Jeep.

"I hope you're not planning on taking me to the airport. I'm not leaving, not until I've—"

"Had breakfast!" Crockett pulled me close and whispered in my ear. "Just shut up and get in the Jeep." Then, as quickly as he had grabbed me, he let go, leaving me on the curb, and climbed into the driver's seat. "You coming or not?"

I tossed my backpack ahead of me and climbed into the passenger seat.

"You want to tell me where we're going?"

"Anyone ever tell you that you ask a lot of questions?" Crockett slapped his cowboy hat on his head and pulled away from the curb.

I clutched the grab bar to steady myself.

"Yeah, you. And I think after all we've been through, you can answer a few."

Save it, Legs. I already know what you're going to ask. The kids are in an orphanage. They're fine. And no, you can't see them. As for where we're going? We're taking a little drive, and you're going to be a real lady and act like you're enjoying it.

"You are such a—"

"Terrific host. Yeah, I know, I hear that all the time."

"Give me a break."

"Actually? That's exactly what I am going to do. And let me tell you, if I didn't like Alexi so much, I wouldn't be doing this."

"His name's not Alexi. It's Eric."

"His name *was* Eric, Kat. But whoever he was back then, he's not the same man. Not now." Crockett shook his head.

"I'll be the judge of that."

"Alright. But you need to understand, this never happened. And you and I…" Crockett waved his finger between us. "I never took you to meet him. No matter how this turns out, you can never talk about it. Ever. Too many lives are at stake."

"You act like you think he won't come home."

"He won't, Kat."

"You're wrong. You'll see." I sat back and buckled myself in. I couldn't imagine Eric wouldn't want to come home. It was a long time ago, but we had something special. We always did. The idea of being together again, a second chance. I needed that. I wanted it. More than anything, I wanted to believe we could turn the clock back and start over. I understood we could never say anything about what had happened or where Eric had been. But I didn't care. What I cared about was that Eric and I would leave here, together. I closed my eyes and fantasized about moving to a new city, or maybe a new country. Being together. We didn't need to tell anyone what had happened; we had each other and a lifetime ahead to share everything that mattered.

Thirty minutes outside the city, Crockett slowed the Jeep, turned off onto a dirt road, and followed a finger of the Mekong River through a thick forest of mangrove trees.

"You recognize any of this?"

"Are you taking me back to the safe house?"

"You got the diamond?"

"It's in my backpack. I'll give it to you when I see Eric."

Crockett found a spot to stop beneath a canopy of trees. "I won't go any further. Leave your backpack here. The safe house is one hundred and eighty feet up ahead on the right. You'll see it as you approach the river. Eric's inside. He's waiting for you."

* * *

I remember walking down the narrow jungle path to the safe house. The heat pressed against my skin. The sounds of birds and monkeys in the trees overhead. The mud beneath my sandals, and the knot in my stomach as I stood at the bottom of the stairs and gripped the rough wooden banister.

When I reached the top of the stairs and looked inside, I had to squint. The morning sun spilled into the room, and Eric was standing in front of the window with the light behind him. All I could see was his shadow as he stood in the center of the room. Fighter pilots aren't tall. A height limit mandated that F4 pilots be no taller than six feet. Eric was only slightly taller than I was, just shy of five-eleven. Used to be, we met eye to eye, but the man in front of me was shorter, and his shoulders weren't as square as I remembered.

I moved closer. How had I pictured this moment? Would I run to him, throw my arms around him, and let all the years fade away as if they had never been? Or would we stand like strangers, face to face, politely trying to recognize each other and remember who we once were and who we've become? I looked into the face of the man I fell in love with and married in college. A wave of longing and resentment churned inside me. The man I knew so well was a stranger. Eric's hair, once sandy blonde, was now longer and graying. His face was drawn and thin, and his blue eyes had dulled, shadowed by a long history that had robbed us both of our youth.

Eric was the first to speak. "Katy. I'm so sorry. You shouldn't be here."

"But I am." I reached out; my right hand trembled as I touched his arm. He smiled faintly and stepped back. "What's wrong?" Eric looked at me blankly, his eyes void of recognition. "Eric, it's me. It's Katy. Don't you remember?"

Eric shook his head and looked away. "This was never supposed to happen. You were never meant to be here."

"But I am! Don't you see," I took Eric's hand. Somewhere inside this stranger standing in front of me was the man I had married. "We have a second chance. Why else would this happen?" The words flowed from me. I didn't need to think about what to say. The words escaped my lips before I even knew what I was saying. I was overjoyed, choking with emotion. We were together again.

"No, Katy. That's not what this is." Eric shook his hand free. "This isn't a second chance. This is a mistake."

"What do you mean, a mistake?" I shoved the heel of my hand into his shoulder. I was angry. How could he be so cold? "What's wrong with you?"

Eric turned his back and walked slowly to the window overlooking the river, then looked back at me.

"It's been a long time. I was shot down more than twenty-five years ago. Things happened. Terrible things. Things I did to survive that I don't want to remember. I don't even know who I was back then or how I lived through it. All I know is that after the VC captured me, I was traded to the Russians, and for a while, things got better. I ended up teaching in a school and—"

"I know. I know all about it—"

"No, you don't, Katy. I wasn't just a teacher. I was a traitor. I instructed kids and Russians how to walk, talk, and act like Americans. I taught them everything I knew. And for a time, I even thought I was doing something good. I was convinced I had been part of an evil empire, and I never wanted to return. I forgot about my life. I forgot about who I was and who I had been before the war. I forgot about you. I'm sorry, but I did. And then ten years ago…the Soviet Union fell apart, and I escaped with one of my students. We came back to Vietnam. I could have come home then, but when I thought about what had happened to me, and what I had done. Katy, I trained spies against my own country. How could I ever go home?"

"You were shot down. You were a prisoner. You did what you did to survive. It's behind you now. You can come home. No one ever needs to know. We could go—"

"No. It's not behind me. It's part of me. When I first came back, the Vietnamese didn't care who I was. To them, I was Alexi Petrova, just another Russian exile."

"But you're not a Russian! You're an American. You were a prisoner of war. You did what you needed to do to stay alive." I couldn't believe I needed to come up with reasons why Eric would want to come home. "The war's over. You can come home now. We can start fresh."

"Kat, that's not what I want to do."

"What do you mean, not what you want to do? You were lost. You were confused. Brainwashed. And now it's over. I've found you. No matter what happened, you can come back."

"This is my home now."

"It can't be your home. It was never your home. I was your home—"

"You *were* my home."

"What's that supposed to mean?" I yelled. This wasn't at all the reunion I had hoped for.

"It means I have a job to do. I didn't know it at first. Once I left the Soviet Union, I didn't know what I was going to do. But I knew I could never return to the United States. Not after what I had been through. I didn't want to go back. Even for you, Kat."

"But—"

I stepped forward. I wanted to grab Eric and shake some sense into him. But he raised his hands and went on,

"No, Katy. Too much time had passed. I knew you'd go on. You've always been strong. Remember how I made you promise if anything ever happened, that you wouldn't wait for me?"

"Yes, but that was different. How can I go on now knowing what I know?"

"I'm sorry, I—"

"Damnit, Eric. The war's over."

"The war's not over. We may not be dropping bombs on each other, but we're still doing what we can to destroy each other, and I'm a part of that."

"What part? If you're going to tell me you're a spy, I already know that. Eddie and Crockett recruited you. You've done what they needed you to do. And the Russians you spied on, the sex traffickers—they're dead. They blew themselves up inside the tunnel last night. Your job is done here. The war's over. You can come home now."

Eric dropped his head. "Katy, it wasn't just those three Russians I spied on. I know too much to ever come home. Crockett and people like him need me."

"I need you."

"No, you don't. I don't think you ever did. You've always been able to figure things out on your own. You don't need me, Kat."

I squeezed my eyes shut. I didn't want to believe I couldn't convince Eric to come home, but I could hear it in his voice. "You're not coming with me, are you?"

"Katy, my life is here now. As difficult as it was for me, I found life again. I started over."

"Over? What do you mean you started over?" It hadn't occurred to me that Eric's life might have gone on. That he might have put a life together and maybe had a family. "Are you...are you married?"

Eric nodded. "I have a wife."

"And children?"

"Two," Eric said. "And I'd like you to meet them."

"They're here?"

"In the next room." Eric opened the door to the sleeping area, and two small children, who had been waiting behind the door, peeked out. "Come, I want you to meet someone."

The first child, a little boy about four years old, ran to Eric, grabbed his leg, and looked up at me. He had dark, curly brown hair, big brown eyes, and a wide smile.

"This is Trung. He's four. And this," Eric looked back to the bedroom door, where the second child stood holding hands with a young woman, "is my wife, Lan, and my daughter, Kieu. She's named after my mother-in-law, who you met at the bookstore."

Lan picked up her daughter and, holding the child on her hip, walked to Eric. As they passed me, Kieu reached out her small hand, and I took hold of her fingers. Lan stopped, and I touched Kieu's hair and swept it from her eyes. They were soft and blue, like Eric's.

"She's beautiful."

I could feel the tears start to swell from behind my eyes, and I wiped the back of my hand against my face. I couldn't believe I was on the verge of tears. Eric and I had never had kids. We hadn't even talked about it. We were married young and for such a short time. Eric was right. We were both very different people. And now, here we were, where I never expected to be with a husband who I thought was dead but was very much alive, and with a family I never had any idea existed. I couldn't be angry. This woman hadn't stolen my husband. A cruel war had stolen him. All Lan had done was give Eric a life that I wasn't able to.

I put my arms around Kieu and Lan. The tears flowed, and Eric came and put his arm around us all.

"It's okay, Katy."

"Does Lan know who I am?"

"No. Her English is not all that good. I told her you were an American friend of Davy Crockett."

"Crockett?" I rolled my eyes.

"He's not as bad as you may think."

"I'm not so sure about that." I look at Lan. "Does she know you're an

American?"

Eric shook his head. "All she knows is that my name is Alexi Petrova, that I lived in Russia, and that I teach school here now."

The baby pulled my hair. I took her small hand in mine and kissed it. "Don't ever tell her differently. It's safer that way."

Trung tugged at his father's pant leg. Eric leaned down and picked up his son. They looked so natural together. Healthy and happy.

"Are you going to be okay?" Eric raised a brow, a once familiar expression I used to love.

"I'm going to be fine," I said. There was so much I wanted to tell him. But it didn't matter. Not anymore. We weren't the same people. "But I do think I'd better be going before I start bawling. If I get any more attached to these kids, I'll want to take them with me." I kissed Trung and Kieu on the forehead, and Lan hugged me as if I were a sister. I hugged her back. She was soft, beautiful, and gentle. She was exactly what Eric needed.

"I'll walk you out." Eric put his arm around my shoulder and walked me to the balcony.

I looked back at Lan and the children. I wanted to take a picture, but I couldn't. This was a memory I could never share with anyone.

"Thank you."

"For what? Getting shot out of the sky? Ruining your life?"

"You didn't ruin my life. A war interrupted both our lives and the lives of thousands of people, oceans apart. We didn't have any control over that. But I think I understand now why it's so important that you do what you do."

"I'm sorry, Kat."

"Don't be. Just continue to be good at what you do. And don't get caught. Those kids are going to need a dad growing up."

Chapter Thirty-One

Crockett was snoozing when I got back to the Jeep. His arms were crossed over his chest, feet on the dash, and his cowboy hat low on his brow, covering his eyes.

"Hey! Wake up. Time to go." I hit the Jeep's hood with the palm of my hand, then swung into the passenger seat.

"You're alone." Crockett sat up and straightened his hat.

"You knew I would be." I looked away. I didn't want to meet Crockett's eyes and let him see the disappointment or the tears I was fighting.

Thankfully, Crockett didn't say anything. He turned the key in the ignition and backed out, down the muddy trail away from the safe house. It wasn't until we got closer to the city, and I started to notice signs for Tan Son Nhat Airport, that Crockett spoke again.

"Going to be a long flight home. You going to be okay?"

I looked away and wiped a tear that had escaped my eye. "Yeah. Hopefully, I can get some sleep." Although I knew it wouldn't come easily.

"I'm sorry, Kat. I know this wasn't what you wanted. This was never supposed to happen. None of us had any idea when you attempted to make a delivery to Nguyen's Jewelry store that morning that you'd get drawn into this. Sophie didn't know you had any connection to Vietnam. Nor did any of the rest of my team. And me? When Eddie introduced me to Eric, all I knew was that he was a downed American pilot who had been MIA for years and then reclassified by the DOD as KIA. His records indicated his folks were his emergency contact, and they were both dead. End of story. He never mentioned a wife. As far as we were concerned, Eric was what we needed when we needed him. It never occurred to any of us that someone like you might show up."

I exhaled. "Yeah, me neither.

"You need to know I never would have agreed to let you see Eric. It was Eric who convinced me you could be trusted. If he hadn't, I'll be honest, I wouldn't be driving you to the airport right now. Much as I hate to say it, you know too much, and you never would have made it home."

"You would have killed me?" I slipped my hairclip from my hair and palmed it in my hand.

"Not that I would want to—"

"But Eric convinced you?"

"You're here, aren't you? But know this, if the Russians were to ever learn that Eric was working with us, his life and that of his family would be in danger. Not only would they be murdered, but we'd lose a valuable source. You can't breathe a word of this. And put that damn hairclip away. If I wanted to kill you, I would have done it by now."

I slipped the hairclip back into my pocket. "Satisfied?"

Crockett glanced over at me. "Yeah, your hair looks better in your eyes anyway."

I shook my head. "You know what? You can be a real jack—"

"You don't have to like me. Just know I'll do my job."

"I suppose that means you're going to ask me for the diamond?"

"I've delivered what you wanted. Now you need to give me what I need." With one hand still on the wheel, Crockett extended his hand. "Hand it over."

I reached over the seat into my backpack, pulled out the necklace, and dropped it into his open hand. "What are you going to do with it?"

"Keep it. Not for myself, of course. The Saudis don't know where it is, but when the time's right, and believe somewhere down the road, the time will be right, we'll use it to negotiate for something we want."

"It never ends, does it?"

"Nope. It never does. But for you, right now. Your job is done."

We had pulled into the airport departure area, and Crockett stopped the Jeep. "You can get out of here. I don't think you need me from here on out.

You'll be fine. But, Kat, remember, this never happened."

About the Author

After 25 years in news and talk radio, Nancy Cole Silverman retired to write fiction. Her crime-focused novels have attracted readers throughout America, and her short stories have appeared in numerous anthologies. Silverman writes the Carol Childs and Misty Dawn Mysteries (Henry Press) and the Kat Lawson Mysteries (Level Best Books). For more detailed information visit www.nancycolesilverman.com

AUTHOR WEBSITE:
   www.nancycolesilverman.com

Also by Nancy Cole Silverman

The Carol Childs Mysteries (Henry Press)

The Misty Dawn Trilogy (Henry Press)

Numerous short stories